CAUGHT

BY RHONDA SHAW

CAUGHT

ISBN-13: 978-0-9962538-1-9

Copyright © 2015 by Rhonda Shaw

Edited by Deborah Nemeth

Cover design by Lily Smith / coversbylily.com

Acknowledgements

Many thanks to Mr. Greg Hoelscher and Dr. Steven Korotkin for their patience and tolerance as I hounded them with incessant questions about the law and medical fields. Their willingness to explain and clarify helped ensure my accuracy.

CHAPTER 1

Matt Buck strolled up to home plate and dug in, trying to look as though he didn't have a care in the world. The crowd was going wild. The game was down to the wire and the Detroit Rockets' fans knew he was the last chance to save the season. Failure would mean the end, which was unacceptable. They refused to give up hope. If anyone could provide the much-needed lift, it was the All-Star catcher.

He'd been in this position before, was used to the pressure, but the sheer volume of the people yelling from the stands never failed to astound him. He ignored the frenzy, however. If he didn't, he'd be a hot mess at the plate.

Behind by two runs in the bottom of the ninth inning against the Cleveland Buffaloes, a loss today meant the Rockets would miss their chances of continuing into the playoffs and instead would be heading home for the winter. Matt couldn't think about what was at stake, though. He needed to stick to the basics and let natural instinct take over. He had to focus on seeing the ball leave the pitcher's hand, and once that occurred, everything else was routine, a deep-rooted reaction he'd honed over the years. He hadn't won four Silver Slugger awards for nothing. As one of the best hitters in the game, he'd led the league in home runs multiple times and was clutch in situations such as this. He lived for these moments and thrived on the pressure.

Settling in his stance, he held the bat quietly over his right shoulder and waited patiently as the crowd noise faded away into the background. He had an inkling they were going to pitch him down and away, and he had to make certain not to chase. Sure enough, the throw came in outside the far left corner of the plate and the umpire called ball one.

He placed one foot outside the batter's box, adjusted his bright red batting helmet with a white block *R* in the middle, and tugged on his white jersey with lettering in the same shade as his helmet, trying to keep the fit loose on his shoulders. Taking a deep breath through his nose, he stepped back into the small box next to home plate outlined in powdery chalk, awaiting the next pitch. The fastball caught the left corner of the plate for a strike, but patience was the name of the game. If he waited, he would get the perfect pitch.

Down the third-base line, the coach signaled to Matt he still had the green light to swing away and put the ball in play any way possible. Matt kicked at the dirt with his cleats and tapped his helmet in acknowledgement before stepping back in. He eyed the pitcher, and as the ball came hurtling toward home plate, it broke again and Matt laid off. No matter how hard they tried, he wasn't going to swing at a bad pitch. He was determined and they could keep pitching him low and outside as much as they wanted.

The crowd grew louder with the count now two balls and one strike. At this point, they'd be happy with anything, even a walk. Anything other than an out.

The Cleveland pitcher wouldn't purposefully dig himself into a hole any more than he needed to, however, so one of the next pitches was going to be the one. Even with first base open, the Buffaloes didn't want to chance loading them up, especially since they only needed one more out. They could have gone with the pitch out on four straight pitches, walking Matt on purpose, but since the Rockets were an offensive threat throughout their entire lineup, they were taking a gamble with him.

Matt cleared his throat and returned to his stance. Again, all noise and commotion faded into the background, and his tunnel vision included only the pitcher and the ball. The pitcher went through his motion and Matt swore the ball was the size of a grapefruit as it came racing toward him.

This is it. Instinct took over and he reacted, swinging with everything he had.

The ball soared through the air as everyone in the stadium stood up to will it out of the park. It had the height, but the distance was questionable. Matt made the turn at first base and continued to track the ball. The Cleveland center fielder gave chase and almost had the fence at his back. He put out his left hand to feel for the wall while he held up his glove.

"Damn it," Matt muttered. The ball wasn't going to make it. The center field at Rockets stadium was extremely deep at over four hundred and twenty feet, and he'd missed by mere inches.

With his back against the wall, the outfielder reached up and snagged the ball, closing the door on the Detroit Rockets' season. The Buffaloes all ran out onto the field to celebrate as Matt, struggling to ignore them, stopped when he reached second base and took off his helmet. He hung his head and kicked the bag. A chorus of boos rang out from the crowd, and he tried not to notice, but it was hard. The ball should have been out of here.

Walking slowly toward the dugout, he shrugged off the pats on his back and ignored his teammates' encouraging words. Instead, all he heard was the berating voice in his head lecturing that his approach should have been different. What or how, he had no idea, but surely he could have done something to ensure the ball left the stadium, cementing the win for the Rockets. But it hadn't, and now it didn't matter.

The season was over and he was heading home for the winter. Like it or not, he'd failed.

* * *

Returning home that night, Matt tossed his gym bag on the floor in the laundry room and stepped into the kitchen, hitting the light switch as he walked over to the fridge. As he poked through his slim options for dinner, a noise sounded from the other room like someone was opening the front door.

He straightened and frowned, listening. He was grouchy and this person was entering at his or her own risk, as far as he was concerned. Tough losses were part of the game, that was how it rolled, but for whatever reason, this time nagged at him. His teammate and good friend, Ace pitcher, Jerry Smutton, tried to remind him that their season hadn't ended with his at-bat, but Matt was tired of this "close enough" bullshit. He wanted them to win the pennant and he was willing to give all he had in order to make it happen.

When the deadbolt clicked, he ground his teeth and hissed in a breath, so not in the mood to deal with whatever was going on. He should be worried someone was entering his home, or at the very least uneasy, but anger consumed him instead and he threw the refrigerator door shut, his long legs quickly eating up the space between the kitchen and the front of the house. Matt entered the entryway at the same time the door opened revealing Natalie, his ex-girlfriend. He stopped in shock, a few choice words on the tip of his tongue, but unable to articulate any of them, when she glanced up.

"Oh, you poor thing," she said with a pout. "I came as soon as I saw what happened."

She walked over and wrapped her arms around his waist, giving him a squeeze.

He was so stunned that he had no idea what to do, what to say. It was as if nothing had changed and she was here playing the comforting role of the supportive girlfriend. Unbelievable.

A few months back, he'd ended things with her, tired of her possessiveness and incessant accusations of him cheating on her while he was on the road. According to her, he kept a different woman in each city, a ludicrous statement because he was nothing but loyal and he never, ever considered straying. The breakup hadn't been amicable and it had taken some work to get her to stop contacting him, but he'd believed she'd finally gotten the hint. Apparently not.

She hugged him a little tighter, which kicked him into gear. Grabbing her shoulders, he wrenched her away and stepped back, putting some distance between them.

"What are you doing?" he asked. "Why are you here?"

"I'm here for you," she said with earnest big brown eyes. "I knew you'd be upset after the game and I wanted to be here to support you."

"No, no." He shook his head, not understanding how she was not getting this. "No. This is not how this works. We are done. Over. Through. As in, you don't come here anymore. We don't see each other anymore." He glanced at the front door. "How the fuck did you get another key?"

"Seriously, Matt, come on," she said with a smile as she started to walk past him to the kitchen. "I'll fix you something to eat and we can talk—"

He grabbed her arm, stopping her in her tracks. "You need to leave."

She tugged, but he wouldn't loosen his grip. "Knock it off. This isn't funny."

Matt gave her a cold stare, letting her know he was serious. He refused to go through this again. He'd already changed his cell phone and home numbers twice. "No, this isn't funny. Not at all."

He pulled her back to the front door, paying no attention to her struggles as she dragged her feet and attempted to twist out of his tight hold. "Don't come here again, Natalie. I'm serious. We're through."

Ignoring the look of shock on her face, he pushed her outside and slammed the door shut, engaged the lock, and took a deep breath as he leaned against the hard wood, running his fingers through his short hair. He couldn't believe she actually showed up…at his house. He'd demanded she hand over her copy of his house key before, but apparently, she'd had additional ones made.

What wasn't she getting? Why was she continuing to act as if everything was the same? She drove him mad and he had no clue what else to do to get it through her head. If she refused to believe him or hoped she could convince him otherwise, he wasn't sure there *was* anything else he could say. He didn't love her, he didn't want to be with her, and he didn't know any other way to tell her things were over.

Nothing from the get-go with her had triggered any alarms. Everything had been fun in the beginning and they'd really enjoyed each other. They liked the same things, never finding it difficult to talk about anything, which led to him wanting to progress to the next level. Natalie was ecstatic when he asked her to move in with him. And not long afterward, the problems started.

Eventually, Matt reached his breaking point, pretty much around the time he started acting like a hermit simply in order to avoid the drama, and threw her out, thankful that was the end of it. Little did he know he'd still be dealing with her all this time later. He wasn't comfortable with the control being out of his hands, but he'd deal with it somehow.

Peeking out the side window by the front door, Matt saw her car no longer sat in the driveway. He sighed, relieved that perhaps the drama was over, and returned to the kitchen. Natalie had pretty much killed what little appetite he'd had after the loss, but he had to eat something. Otherwise, his stomach would wake him up in the middle of the night starving and he hated that. He wanted nothing more than to pack up and head home to Arizona and be away from everything—Natalie, Detroit, the Rockets, baseball, women. He wanted to get away from it all and forget, but leaving wasn't an option. He had a lot to do before then and one of them included standing up in Jerry's wedding.

And now, a new addition to his list. He had to change his locks.

CHAPTER 2

Resting her forehead against the steering wheel of her rental car, Shannon Morrison turned off the engine and let out a deep breath, more than happy to be off the road. The usual forty-five minute drive from the airport to her sister Karen's house had taken close to two hours because of a fresh snowfall, and her eyes were beginning to cross. And after barely making her flight out of Chicago because she'd been convinced she could squeeze in a last-minute consultation before taking off for a long weekend, her tank was empty.

The front door opened as she trudged up the steps in her heels, trying not to slip and twist an ankle. She smiled at her soon-to-be brother-in-law, Jerry Smutton.

"You made it," Jerry said with a big grin as his brown eyes twinkled at her. He reached forward to grab her bag out of her hand.

"Ugh! What a horrible drive."

"I could have picked you up. You didn't need to rent a car." He pulled her into a hug.

"I know, I know. My parents offered as well, but it'll be easier for everyone if I have my own ride."

He took her jacket from her. "Well, thank God you're finally here. She's been going back and forth all day between being happy you're coming and bitching that you're not here yet. Now she'll shut up."

Despite the timing of the wedding not being the best for her schedule, Shannon was excited to return home for Detroit's version of the Wedding of the Century. The ceremonies were still a few days away but Karen had declared, in her own dramatic fashion, she needed Shannon home early and, if not, then she should prepare for World War III. It wasn't as if Shannon wasn't planning to get there as soon as she could, but Karen was already slightly irritated at her due to her lack of participation in any of the planning. Shannon really had wanted to help, had had every intention to, but work had always gotten in the way. Even Shannon had to admit her involvement was appalling if she didn't even know which groomsman she was walking down the aisle with (which she didn't) and she'd only seen her dress in a picture online. She'd failed as a little sister and co-Maid of Honor, and guilt would eat at her for a long time, but Karen understood, as she always did. She recognized the pressure put on Shannon from her job and, while she bitched about it, she respected it.

Shannon laughed and headed toward the kitchen. "Where is the lovely bride-to-be anyway?"

Walking through the archway, she found Karen exactly where she always was—behind the stove. She had her Because I Said So apron on and her blond hair shoved into a messy bun. She was chopping a variety of vegetables on a cutting board, but she stopped and put the knife down, her blue gaze hard as she took her in from head to toe.

Shannon rolled her eyes. "Yes, I'm here, in the flesh, and in one piece."

Karen's mouth twisted as she fought a smile before stepping around the island to pull her into her arms. "It's about friggin' time."

"Sorry. I got here as soon as I could get away from work."

As an Associate Attorney in the law offices of Bickles, Bickles and Barnes, Shannon was at the bottom of the totem pole and therefore, requesting time off was not encouraged, but this was for Karen, her only sibling, and so of course, Shannon had asked for the personal time. Consequently, however, no doubt her schedule was going to be a bitch when she returned, and new grunge tasks would show up on her to-do list. But she'd suck it up and pay her dues.

Karen squeezed her tighter before going back to her chopping. "You work too damn much, it's unhealthy, but I'm so glad you're here. Everything finally feels real now."

Shannon peeked in the simmering pots, enjoying the hearty and spicy scents tickling her nose. There was no arguing her sister was an excellent cook. "What are you cooking?"

"Some soup." She nudged Shannon out of the way to dump the vegetables in. "I figured it would help de-stress you after all of your travels."

"It smells amazing. Thank you," Shannon smiled at her sister before leaning down and kissing her on the check, which was rosy from the heat of the stove. "You look great. I'm so excited that you're getting married."

Karen flashed a big smile. "I know! I am too, but don't tell Mr. Ego that. It will just inflate his head even more."

"Don't tell me what?" Jerry asked as he stepped into the kitchen. "I put your bag in the guest room at the end of the hall," he told Shannon.

Shannon laughed. "I'm not even going to ask how you knew Mr. Ego was you or why you're okay with it."

He shrugged and grinned, which popped his dimple. "It's only one of her many endearing names for me."

"And you deserve them all," Karen said with a sly smile at her fiancé, whose eyes visibly warmed in return.

Shannon smiled at their exchange. They were crazy about each other, even though they had both acted like fools the year before. Neither had wanted to admit their true feelings, insisting things between them were strictly casual, but eventually a hit to the head—literally in Jerry's case—knocked some sense into them. Now they were inseparable when Jerry was in town, and Karen was on cloud nine, exactly where she deserved to be. Shannon was ecstatic that Karen finally found her "one," even if it made her a teensy bit jealous. Who wouldn't be?

Shannon cleared her throat loudly as she sat on one of the stools lining the island, toed off her heels and removed her black blazer, hanging it over the back of the chair. "Now, now. You have a guest. No getting hot and heavy, you lovebirds."

"You heard her." Karen shooed him away. "Let us girls chat. Go in the other room and stop distracting me."

He leaned over and planted a loud kiss on her lips before heading toward the basement where he was the lord of his domain. "Let me know when dinner is ready. I'm starved."

"When aren't you?" Karen asked his departing back. She turned to Shannon with one hand on her hip and sighed. "I swear. I love to cook and all, but that man is going to wear me out with how much he eats. Where does he put it?"

"He must burn it off with all of the sex you guys have," Shannon teased.

"Okay, but then why doesn't that work for me? I'm an active participant too."

"Who knows." Shannon eyed her sister and, while she couldn't put her finger on it, something stood out as changed. "What's going on? You look different."

Karen scowled as she stirred the soup. "Different? What are you talking about?"

"I don't know," she said with a shrug. "You just look...different. Maybe it's your new bridal glow or something."

"Yeah, maybe," Karen muttered before she turned with a smile. "Tomorrow you try on your dress. They said they should be able to make any changes, if needed, in time, so we need to get there early."

After the dash through the busy O'Hare airport followed by the stressful drive on the slick roads, Shannon needed some liquid assistance in order to relax before they dove into wedding planning. She stood and opened the fridge, pulling out a bottle of wine. She held it up to Karen with an arched brow in question.

"No, thank you," Karen said. "I'm good."

"You're good? You're turning down wine?" Shannon asked in disbelief.

"Yeah, I had some before you got here," she replied as she kept her back to her, busying herself with wiping down the counter.

"Hmmm." Shannon pulled down a crystal stemware from behind the plate glass cabinet. "Never stopped you before."

"I'll have some with dinner, probably," Karen replied in a noncommittal tone as she turned her focus back to the soup.

Shannon took a sip and pondered this anomaly—her sister *never* refused a glass of wine—when it clicked. Karen had told her she and Jerry wanted to start a family, but Shannon hadn't realized she meant so soon. Since Shannon didn't want to ruin the surprise, she wouldn't prod further. She'd let Karen spill the news in her own time, even though she was thrilled with the prospect of being an aunt.

"So, who am I walking down the aisle with exactly?" Shannon asked instead. "You mentioned it before, but I forgot. Jerry's little brother? What's his name? Nate?"

"Nick. His name is Nick." Karen spun around and leaned against the counter. "See? This is why I say you work too damn much. You can't even remember what his name is and you've met him at least a couple of times." She gave Shannon a good big-sister stern stare, which made her shrink in shame. Karen didn't let her say anything in her defense, however, as she pressed on. "But there's been a change. You're walking with Matt."

Shannon's heart tripped in her chest. If it was the Matt she was thinking of, things were about to get interesting. "And Matt is?" she asked hesitantly, almost afraid to hear it was Jerry's thirteen-year-old cousin or something, rather than a gigantic step up from Jerry's younger brother.

"You know Matt." Karen frowned. "At least I thought you did. You've met him before, haven't you? The catcher? Hot, Chris Evans lookalike?"

Shannon stopped herself before she threw up a thank-you to the heavens. "Um, yeah. I met him once a long time ago. He does sort of look like Chris Evans. Bigger though," she said casually as if they weren't talking about the same man who'd played a starring role in all of her fantasies since meeting him.

"Oh, yeah. The guys are always teasing him, especially when people who don't know Rockets' baseball ask him if he's Captain America. I think they're just jealous," Karen said with a chuckle. "Anyway, when he finally let Jerry know he'd be his Best Man along with Chase, we switched things around. So, we put you and Matt together, because obviously we're going to keep Maddie and Chase together," Karen said of her best friend and her new husband, Jerry's teammate and former roommate. "It should be good since Matt's tall. You won't have to worry about having heels on and towering over the guy, like I know you always do."

Shannon tried to play cool even though internally she was doing handstands and back flips. "Okay, sounds good."

"He's a nice guy, too," Karen went on, apparently still believing she needed to justify things. "I don't know him that well, but from what I do know, he seems real sweet. He and Jerry are pretty close, so that should give some indication as to what his personality is like. You'll meet him at the rehearsal dinner Friday night."

She clapped her hands. "We have so much to talk about and we even have tomorrow night, since Jerry will be gone for his bachelor party."

"Sounds good." Shannon took another drink of her wine, tuning out her sister as she visualized Matt and his crystal blue eyes. She shivered, recalling how they had trapped her, as if seeing right through her, causing her skin to tingle and flush. Perhaps the festivities were not going to be as bad as she originally feared. She'd pretty much planned to have to endure one well-meaning family member after another asking when she was next. When she would settle down and have some kids, particularly since everyone had believed only she would ever get married, considering Karen's aversion to the possibility for the longest time. But Shannon's life was work, no more, no less. She didn't have room in her life for anything else. She didn't question her decisions, but she did get tired of defending them constantly. No one understood, except for her father. She envisioned the look of pride on his face as she filled him in on everything related to her work, and a glow of pleasure washed over her foreseeing his approval. She enjoyed that they shared a common interest and that he was proud of her.

She was going to have to find some way to ignore the comments and not let them get to her. Her life was the way she wanted; she had no reason to be ashamed.

And if she could manage to hang around a hot guy for the night, then perhaps some good could come out of the Wedding of the Century for her after all.

CHAPTER 3

Heavy bass throbbed throughout the dark room while strobe lights flickered and pulsed, casting scantily clad women in and out of darkness as they gyrated on a pole and ground against the raised floor. An upscale club with trendy and sleek décor, Pink's boasted having the sexiest, most desirable women in the metro-Detroit area and for a hefty price, exclusive party rooms were available for private groups, giving the occupants a bird's eye view of the dancers while separating them from the rest of the crowd. It was in one of these rooms that Jerry and his best buds gathered for his bachelor party.

A petite woman with long blond hair—and boobs so big he wondered how she could remain upright—strutted by with a tray of shots, and Matt reached out to grab one. She stopped short when she spotted him and her mouth dropped open.

"Omigod! Are you—?"

He interrupted her before she could finish. "No, I'm not."

She flipped her hair, giving him a slow, promising smile as her tongue darted out to wet her pouty red gloss-drenched lips. "You could totally be him. He's so *fucking* hot as Captain America," she purred as she sidled closer to him.

"Thanks, I think." Matt slammed the shot before turning his back to her. He hadn't missed her invitation; he simply wasn't interested. He grew weary of the girls who offered themselves up because he played ball or because he supposedly resembled some actor.

His blue eyes watered and he cringed at the burn of Jäger racing down his throat, but he smiled when Jerry let out a hoot from across the room where he stood joking around with a group of guys. Jerry Smutton was getting married. Matt couldn't believe it. Jerry was the last person Matt would have believed to be hitched before him, but here they were. A few days before the wedding and it was really happening.

He was happy for his friend—really happy. He liked Karen. She was perfect for Jerry, but it still amazed him that all his buddies were settling down before him—the one who actually *wanted* to be married. Even though everyone always teased him for being the romantic of the group, Matt couldn't seem to shake off his single status.

He wasn't going to deny it. Right behind baseball as the absolute love of his life, was love and he loved being in love. He wanted what his parents had—a loving relationship, a wonderful marriage and a perfect-sized family. Whenever the "she" part of the equation decided to show up, he was more than ready.

And sometimes because he wanted to settle down, he progressed relationships quicker than he should, but he couldn't fault himself for trying. How did he know for sure if he didn't try? But the situation with Natalie had rocked him and now his interest in meeting anyone had waned.

He sighed, eyeing the empty shot glass in his hand before tossing it onto the table and dropping his big frame down in a chair. Things with her had exploded from being mildly uncomfortable to right out bat-shit crazy, and he still didn't know what to do, resulting in his downer attitude despite the occasion. The night was Jerry's, however, and being one of his best friends, Matt wouldn't be anywhere else.

The chair next to him pulled out and Chase Patton, one of the pitchers on the team, sat next to him.

"You're quiet over here tonight, Bucky. You not liking the scenery?" he asked, his dark eyes sparkling in amusement.

"Yeah," Matt said with a shrug. "Just not feeling it I guess."

Chase's expression turned serious. "Everything all right?"

Matt caught the glint of a spotlight bouncing off the platinum wedding band on Chase's left ring finger and tried not to let the reminder of his own unmarried status bother him along with everything else. "Yeah, no, everything's fine. Just tired or something."

"What the fuck are you two boring asses doing sitting down over here?" Jerry lumbered toward them, the numerous shots that he'd taken obviously already taking effect. "Get up and enjoy the party, man! I'm not going to be single for much longer!"

Matt laughed as Jerry hooked his arms under his armpits, attempting to haul him up. Jerry wasn't small himself, but Matt had some pounds on him and, adding alcohol to the mix, it was proving difficult for Jerry.

"Stand up, you fat ass," Jerry grimaced.

"And do what?" Matt asked calmly, ignoring Jerry's huffing and puffing. "You're going to end up hurting your arm and Coach will kill me."

"My arm is fine, don't you worry about that. Get up so you don't look like a boring old man, even though you are."

"Fine." Matt stood right as Jerry tried another mighty heave, which sent Jerry sprawling back, landing on his ass in the middle of the group. He glared up at Matt for a second before they all started roaring with laughter. Matt leaned down and grabbed Jerry's shoulders, hauling him back up.

"Get off the floor, you idiot."

A big, goofy smile spread on Jerry's face as he threw his arm around his catcher. "I'm so glad you're here, man."

"I know you are."

"No, really. You're more to me than just my catcher. I mean that," he said as his words started to slur, but his grin never fell.

Matt chuckled as he listened to his drunken friend ramble. "You're drunk and you're an asshole."

Jerry just laughed. "Yes, I am." He straightened up suddenly, looking over Matt's shoulder. "Wait a minute! Wait a minute! Who ordered a private dance? I can't have any of that, boys. My baby will kill me if there's any touching or sitting on Mr. Happy…"

Matt turned to see what had caught Jerry's attention and his heart thudded with dread.

No, no, no! Not now. He shot away from Jerry and rushed to her side, pulling her out the door she'd just come through.

"What the fuck are you doing here?" he hissed with his teeth clenched together.

"Ow! You're hurting me," Natalie whined as she tried to tug free from his grasp, but he wouldn't loosen his grip.

Ignoring her protests, Matt dragged her out of the private room and across the club until they emerged outside, where he let go with a little shove. So much anger pulsed through him that he didn't even notice the cold as the snow fell around them. He spotted her car in the parking lot, not far from the door, and stalked over to the small compact, waiting for her to follow. When her soft footsteps fell in behind him, he spun around.

"What the fuck are you doing here?" he repeated.

She let out a huff, which showed as a puff of white in the air. "I had to talk to you, Matt."

He rolled his eyes. He'd heard it all before. "There is nothing to talk about. We're done. We're over. Please get that through your thick skull."

Natalie shook her head, her dark wavy hair bouncing around her face as her eyes quickly filled. "Please, no. Don't say that. We can fix this."

Matt hated to be so mean and cold to her, but she'd pushed him to this. He'd tried to be patient and understanding, and even talk to her when she'd asked, but everything had gone on for too long and he was done. "There is nothing to fix, Natalie. I don't love you. I don't want to be with you. That's it."

"No, don't say that," she pleaded.

"You need to move on."

"I don't understand what happened, what changed." Big, fat tears fell down her cheeks.

"Nothing happened, nothing changed. We just grew apart. That's it. End of story. There is no more *us*. You seriously need to get past this."

"There's someone else, isn't there?" she hissed as her tears quickly dried and a hard edge replaced them. "There's some other slut."

Matt rubbed a hand over his hair in frustration, tired of going through the same thing over and over again. "No, there is no one else."

"One of the girls in there." Natalie jerked her head in the direction of the club.

"Jesus Christ." He closed his eyes. "You need to go, okay? I have a party I need to be at and you just need to go."

"You can't make me go! This is a public place."

"Natalie, please. You're making this worse than it needs to be. Please go before you cause a bigger scene than you already have."

Her small rosebud mouth pursed as she glared at him. "Fine," she sniffed as she moved over to her car door. Before climbing in, she rested a mitten on the top of the frame and a beautiful smile broke out on her face. "I'll see you later and we'll talk, okay? Miss you and love you. Bye!"

Matt stared in disbelief as she climbed in and drove out, and he remained frozen in place even after she'd driven down the street. The girl was insane. No other explanation worked. He put his head back toward the dark winter sky, took in a deep breath and let it out, watching the white cloud of air dissipate. He let the soft snowfall lightly kiss his skin, making no move to wipe the moisture off.

He had to do something. He couldn't keep going on like this, looking over his shoulder all the time, wondering when she would show up with her crazy. He didn't want to have to take drastic legal measures, but if he wanted her to stop, it had to be done.

His phone rang in his pocket and his blood froze, thinking it was her calling him, even though she shouldn't have the new number—at least he hoped. He pulled his phone out, trepidation coursing through him, but let out a sigh in relief that it was his best bud, Jason.

"Hey, man. What's up?" Matt said as he answered.

"You hear the news?" Jason said without preamble. "You're talking to your newest shortstop."

"No, shit. That's fucking awesome!"

It was no secret the Rockets were in talks with Jason and his agent since his contract with the Seattle Sea Dogs ended, but Matt had no idea things had progressed that far so quickly. One of the best shortstops in the league, Jason Kirby played the position better than anyone Matt had ever seen, and he was Matt's longest and oldest childhood friend. He couldn't believe they'd be playing on the same team again as they hadn't played together since college.

"Yep. We're finally back on the same team."

"I can't wait to tell everyone."

"When are you coming to Arizona?" Jason asked. "I thought you'd be home by now."

"Smutton's getting married, so I'm stuck here in cold-ass Michigan until the wedding is over. I need to see the sun, though. It seems like I haven't seen it since the beginning of October. Does it still exist?"

Jason chuckled. "Get your ass home and you'd see it. Where are you? You sound like you're near a freeway or something."

"Yeah, I'm outside this strip joint right by the freeway."

"Why the hell are you outside? Last time I checked, all the action is inside."

"I know, I know. I had to take care of something, that's all."

Jason sighed loudly. "She showed up there, didn't she?"

"Yep, she sure did. Just walked right into the private room. Jerry thought she was there to give him a lap dance or something."

"What are you going to do about it? You can't keep going on like this. You need to file a restraining order."

"That seems so...I don't know, extreme." He kicked at the snow by his boot. "There's got to be some other way to handle this without involving the law."

"Bucky, what she's doing is breaking the law. She's fucking stalking you, not to mention she essentially broke into your house."

"Yeah, yeah, you're right. I know I have to go that route, but I don't want to."

"You've got to before she goes even further," Jason said. "Stop being so god-damn nice to her since she doesn't deserve it. She's obviously sick and maybe this will get her the help she needs."

Matt glanced at the neon pink lips above the door. He needed to get back inside before Jerry came out looking for him, even though he wanted nothing more than to go home since Natalie had killed whatever buzz he'd been working up. But the guys would be pissed if he left, especially Jerry—if he was still conscious.

He turned and trudged toward the entrance to the club. "Look, man. I have to go back in there. I'm going to take care of it."

"Matt," Jason warned. "You've got to do this. Don't make me involve your dad."

"I know and I will, I promise. Don't go there with Dad, all right? I'll kick your ass if you do. I'll talk you later."

Matt hung up, ignoring Jason's grumbling, and stretched his neck, trying to work out the tension taking up residence in his shoulders, as he walked back into the dark club and headed toward the private room. He knew what he had to do, he just didn't want to because doing so would be admitting he'd lost control. It *was* out of control, however, and Jason was right. But he didn't want to drag his father into this mess, so he'd hire someone else to file the restraining order. Because, as much as he hated to admit it, he had no idea what she was going to do next.

CHAPTER 4

When the pounding started on the bathroom door, Shannon cursed. Her reflection told the entire story—her long blond hair hung flat and lifeless around her face, and her makeup did nothing to help her blue eyes pop or remove the paleness from her skin—but, she'd pushed the limits of time and Karen was done waiting.

"What in the hell are you doing in there?" her sister asked. "You never take this long."

Rolling her eyes, Shannon threw down the blush and opened the door. "I look blah and I'm trying to improve things." She studied herself in the mirror and frowned. "It isn't working though."

Karen stepped in and eyed her in the mirror over the sink. "What are you talking about? You look awesome!"

"You're just saying that because you're my sister."

Karen scowled at her. "Me? Lie? When have you known me to soften the blow for anyone?"

Shannon chuckled. "No, you're right. You'd tell me how it is."

"Exactly. Now let's go. We can't be late."

Karen walked out of the bathroom, and Shannon gave her reflection one last glance and stuck out her tongue before following her sister. Ever since learning Matt and her were walking together, she'd been obsessed with looking amazing. She didn't know if he would remember her or not, but she hoped to make things interesting, and if she could do that in the company of a sinfully sexy man, then game on. First, however, she had to get his attention.

She sat in the backset of Karen's SUV as Jerry drove them to the church.

"So, how was the bachelor party, Jer?" Shannon asked.

He shrugged. "The usual. Lots of tits, ass and booze."

Karen shook her head at him in mock disgust, ignoring her sister's laugher from the backseat. "You're a piece of work, you know that? Real classy."

He grinned and reached for her hand. "And you love the hell out of me because of it."

"Right, you wish."

He laughed before glancing at Shannon through the rearview mirror. "It was fun. Although, Matt was acting weird all night. I never did get the details from him about whatever his issue was."

Shannon's interest piqued, but she didn't say anything. Luckily, her sister pressed for her.

"Why? What did he do?"

"Nothing, that's just it. He kind of sat like a bump on a log the whole night." He shrugged. "I don't know. That's not like him, I guess."

"Maybe he's more mature than you and doesn't need to gawk at naked boobs," Karen suggested.

"Naw, that's not it. Matt loves a great set of boobs just as much as the rest of us," Jerry said with a lopsided grin. "This chick showed up and next thing I knew Matt and her were gone. He came back a little bit later, but he was definitely a downer."

Shannon wanted to hear more, but Karen started questioning him about possible violations of their no-touching policy, leaving Shannon to her musings in the backseat.

What kind of girl would show up at a strip club? A jealous, needy, and insecure one. If this was his date to all the wedding festivities, then it was in her best interest to steer clear from Matt as much as possible. She didn't need or want any kind of drama in her life.

Jerry pulled into the church parking lot, and Maddie met them at the door. "There you guys are! I was worried about you since you're never late to your wedding stuff," she said to Karen.

Karen gave her a quick embrace before hitching her head in Shannon's direction. "That one took forever to get ready. It's like she thinks she's the bride or something."

Maddie smiled at Shannon and reached up for a hug. "Well, it paid off. You look beautiful."

Shannon leaned down into the embrace. She always felt like an Amazon around most women, but especially when it came to the small brunette. "Thanks." She admired Maddie's deep sapphire-blue dress, which perfectly complemented her porcelain skin and dark brown hair. "You look gorgeous. I love that color on you."

Karen cleared her throat as she handed her jacket to Jerry. "Uh, excuse me? The bride is over here, if you guys are done ooohhhing and aaahhhing over each other."

Maddie gave Shannon a knowing look before she linked her arm with Karen's and led her into the chapel. Jerry smiled at Shannon as he bent an elbow and held it out. "Mind second best?"

"Prefer it, actually," Shannon said with a laugh.

Entering into the church, she barely noticed the deep mahogany pews gleaming under the lights or the charcoal stone, which rose into dramatic arches from the floor up to meet dark wood trusses. She hardly glanced at the large, beautiful stained-glass windows depicting different stories from the Bible, which not only stood above the pulpit but also lined the high ceilings, filtering the sunlight through multicolored glass. Or the expansive white marble dais with sermon desks constructed of the same dark mahogany wood as the pews. Her undivided attention was on the tall man who stood at the end of one of the long benches, laughing and smiling, with his perfect movie-star good looks, as he talked with Chase.

Matt was exactly as she remembered him. Tall with light brown hair, which now had some blond highlights, cut short on the sides, spiky and styled to the left with a few pieces grazing his forehead. He had the bluest eyes ever—mesmerizing as well as potent. His mouth was perfect—not too wide nor too small—with the most kissable full lips. His face had sharp lines with chiseled cheekbones and a strong, squared chin. His gray suit accentuated his broad shoulders and athletic physique perfectly.

Her heart threw itself hard against her chest and her hands grew damp. Nervous energy riddled her, which was ridiculous since she didn't experience this amount of nerves when standing in front of a courtroom. With this hot, sexy man, however, she was full of jitters. He probably wouldn't even remember her and would only see her as a stranger, drooling like a fool for no reason.

Shannon couldn't hear what Jerry said to Matt and Chase or what they said in greeting, over the roaring in her ears from the spike of adrenaline rushing through her. She kept her eyes trained on Matt, though, and when he spotted her over Jerry's shoulder and stood straighter, she felt almost giddy.

Recognition lit his eyes and one corner of his mouth lifted, and she barely restrained herself from doing a fist pump in celebration. She smiled as Matt's eyes met hers and he broke into a wide grin. They smiled stupidly at each other for the longest time before Jerry finally cleared his throat.

"Uh, Matt, this is Shannon, Karen's sister."

"Yeah, I know…I mean, I remember. We met before," Matt said, his attention never leaving her.

"Yeah, we met before."

"You did?" Jerry asked, obviously confused and not remembering.

Shannon tore her gaze away from Matt and nodded. "After one of the games. You…uh…came over, giving Karen a hard time. He was with you."

Jerry still wore a blank expression before shrugging. "I always give Karen a hard time, don't remember a specific one. Well, whatever, you two are walking together. My job is done."

He walked away with Chase, who was immediately ambushed by Maddie's eleven-year-old daughter Bree, one of the flower girls, as they headed over to Karen and Maddie, where they chatted with the wedding planner.

She turned back to Matt. "So, how are you?"

"I'm good, thanks. You?"

"Good." They laughed with the awkward silence that followed neither quite knowing what to say.

"So," he finally said. "Jerry's getting married. Crazy."

"Same with Karen. I never thought I'd see the day."

"What have you been up to?" Matt asked, quickly changing the subject.

"I moved to Chicago."

"Chicago?" he repeated with what sounded like a hint of disappointment in his voice, which made no sense. "What's in Chicago?"

"My job. I'm an attorney," she added when he looked like he was going to ask.

"Oh, one of those," Matt teased.

Shannon smiled, used to the snide remarks about her chosen profession. Standing up straighter on her heels, she was happy to see he was still taller than she was. "I can't tell you how happy I was to hear that you and I will be walking down the aisle together. I was afraid I was going to tower over whoever it was."

He chuckled as he checked out her shoes. "Yeah, I don't think you need to worry about that. To be honest, I haven't been paying much attention to the details. I've just been doing whatever Jerry tells me to, but I'm very glad to learn I'll be spending most of my time with you so we can be tortured together," he added with a small smile. He crooked his arm. "Shall we?"

She took in the warmth of his eyes before she linked her arm through his. Maybe things would be interesting after all.

"Absolutely," she said, hoping for much, much more.

* * *

Holding a cold bottle of beer, Matt stood alone in the corner of the banquet room at the Italian restaurant Jerry and Karen had reserved after the dress rehearsal. The gathering was in full swing and he'd enjoyed visiting with everyone until prickles had started to crawl up the nape of his neck. He'd been experiencing unease more and more lately and whenever the sensation fell over him, he needed to put his back to a wall, which is how he found himself in his current position.

What a fucking mess. Resentment coursed through him as he took a swig of his beer. He should be enjoying himself, not hiding in a corner. He should be getting back out there and playing the field, not taking a hiatus. He loved women, he didn't want to separate himself from them, but this last one had thrown him for a loop and he couldn't help but be gun-shy. His eyes passed over the room and stopped when he spotted the tall blonde talking to her sister, laughing at something Karen had said.

Shannon. He'd been looking forward to seeing her again after agreeing to stand up for Jerry. Matt would have said yes to being his Best Man anyway, but he couldn't deny having an ulterior motive for accepting when Jerry told him whom he'd be standing up with.

He'd never forgotten how beautiful she was. Her face so fresh and alive, her blue eyes full of laughter and intelligence, and a bright smile, quick and dazzling, that lit up everything. Matt had wanted to get to know her more after meeting her previously, but then he'd met Natalie and the rest was history. And now, here they were again, opportunity presenting itself, and he was hesitant thanks to the healthy dish of craziness being served by his ex.

Matt let his eyes travel down her lean figure showcased in the black scoop-neck cocktail dress ending mid-thigh and displaying miles of legs capped by sling-back shoes with a silver toe and heel. Shannon was tall to begin with, but her height didn't stop her from adding a few additional inches with heels. He liked that. He hadn't dated any tall girls in his past and now he wondered why. He didn't miss having to slouch down all the time.

Shannon glanced up and her gaze caught his, giving him a shy smile in return. She excused herself from the group and headed his way with a flirty look on her face.

"What are you doing tucked in the corner all by yourself?" she asked as she approached him.

Matt shrugged. "Just chillin'. Taking in the scene."

"And? See anything interesting?" she teased.

He smiled back. "You could say that, yeah."

Her face flushed a pretty pink, making his mouth go dry as he imagined her skin holding the same blush in the heat of passion, before she cleared her throat. "It was too bad the season ended the way it did. I thought for sure you guys were going to go all the way."

Great. He didn't want to talk about one of the biggest failures of his career, but he put on his game face.

"We all did, but we just couldn't pull it out at the end. It sucks, but now there's next year," he said, striving for nonchalance even though his stomach tightened with disappointment as the final catch replayed in his mind—again.

Shannon tilted her head as she studied him, concern in her eyes. "It still bothers you."

It wasn't a question, but he nodded, being honest. "Somewhat. Did you see it?"

She shook her head. "No, but Jerry told me everything. You did what you could," she insisted. "It wasn't just you."

He let out a huff of frustrated laughter. "I got out. It was pretty much all me, but there's next year," he repeated again, wanting to move on.

"You like your chances?"

"Of course I do. With the likes of Smutty and Chase, plus we're adding my buddy Kirby at short. He's got a good bat and speed, not to mention a hell of an arm."

"And your...bat," Shannon added, keeping her expression neutral.

Matt studied her before a slow grin grew. "And what do you know about my bat?"

Her lips twitched. "You swing a big one."

He laughed and shook his head as his face heated. "Now you're embarrassing me because I'm not sure what we're talking about."

Shannon raised a brow as she reached for a glass of wine from the tray of a passing waiter. "Of course I'm talking about your almost three hundred batting average including your forty home runs last year. What are you talking about?"

"Of course that," he replied dryly. She managed to stay serious for a couple of seconds before starting to laugh and he joined in.

"Do you play any sports?" he asked.

Her eyes traveled down the length of herself and back up again, making him take another sip of his beer when his throat suddenly parched. "Are you seriously asking that?"

"Well, I didn't want to make any assumptions," he said with a chuckle. "Besides, it could be volleyball."

"Basketball would be the correct assumption. Played until college."

"You didn't want to play there?"

Shannon shrugged. "I didn't love it enough to put the dedication into it. You play basketball or only baseball?"

"Yep, and football until I settled on baseball later in high school." He eyed her shoes. "Too bad we can't have a pickup game now. I'd like to see your game."

She gave him a smirk. "I bet you would."

Matt hid his wide smile behind a drink of beer. Yeah, it was definitely too bad she lived in Chicago and he was in a fucked-up situation with his ex-girlfriend. Otherwise, he'd be stupid to let this opportunity pass by again. But, for the second time, that's exactly what he had to do.

CHAPTER 5

The day of the wedding was a blur and had Shannon running in a million different directions without accomplishing anything. Even though Karen had planned
every single detail, scheduled everything down to the exact minute, they still were
constantly late. Finally tucked away in the dressing room at the church, Shannon took the first opportunity to get off her feet for more than two minutes. She
lounged on one of the chaises, resisting the urge to rest her head back, already
hearing Karen's bitch if she should loosen even one strand of hair styled in a low,
messy bun with a diamond flower clip securing bangs that swept across her forehead.

"You better not mess your hair up."

Shannon caught her sister's eye in the mirror of the vanity table at which she
sat touching up her makeup, clad only in her white lace corset. "I won't. Just let
me relax for a few minutes, my God," she groaned.

"Relax all you want, just don't mess anything up."

The door opened and Maddie rushed in. She held up a bottle of champagne
and three flutes. "I snagged this for our little pre-celebration."

Karen turned and glared at her. "Did you go out there where everyone could
see your dress?"

Maddie rolled her eyes. "No, my dear, as you can see, I put a robe on. Don't
worry. Nobody saw anything," she assured Karen as she poured.

"You better be right," Karen murmured, warily eyeing the glass of bubbly
liquid in her hand.

Shannon was more than ready to start the celebration, and anything to help her relax she was taking. She took the flute from Maddie and had to restrain from downing it immediately.

Maddie held her drink in the air. "To the most beautiful bride on the planet on your wedding day. I'm so happy for you and Jerry. He's one lucky man."

"Damn right he is," Karen said.

"Even though I still can't believe you're getting married, I'm so happy for you! To the best big sister a girl could have," Shannon added, fighting back the tears.

"Don't you make me cry," Karen warned.

They clinked their glasses and giggled at the emotional mess they were. Shannon and Maddie each took a healthy drink of their champagne and just as Karen's was practically to her lips, she put her flute down.

"Oh! I almost forgot. I need you to go get Nancy," she said to Maddie of the wedding planner. "I forgot to tell her that I want to switch up one of the table arrangements."

"Oh, okay." Maddie took another sip and headed out.

Shannon waited until Maddie was out of the room before she turned back to Karen, noticing the champagne still sat ignored.

"I can't pretend not to notice anymore. Spill it, please," she pleaded.

"What are you talking about?" Karen adjusted some of the pins in her hair to ensure they were not showing.

"You and not drinking. When are you going to tell me you're pregnant?" Karen's eyes bugged and a slight blush stole her cheeks, and even though Shannon had been sure, Karen's confirmation gave her a jolt. Shannon gasped. "Oh my God! You are! You're pregnant?"

Karen stood and grabbed her hands. "Don't tell anyone! I've been trying to keep it a secret and pretend to be drinking and stuff, only taking little sips here and there, and I've been going crazy thinking I'm not going to fit in my dress, but luckily I'm still kind of small."

"How far along are you?"

"Going on four months. Jerry and I wanted to wait to tell everyone until after the wedding and all the craziness."

Shannon pulled her sister into a tight, bouncy hug, and they were giggling with laughter when Maddie walked back in.

"She'll be up in a minute. What's going on?"

Karen smiled at Shannon before turning to her best friend. "Shannon figured out my big secret, so I'll tell you, but you cannot tell anyone else."

Maddie sat on the chaise. "Tell anyone what? That you're pregnant? I knew that."

The smile fell comically from Karen's face. "How the fuck did you know?"

"Please, girl. I know you like the back of my hand. You think I haven't noticed you don't drink wine anymore, always ready with some excuse, or that you're practically glowing from head to toe? I know wedding glow and I know baby glow, and you've definitely got baby glow." She stood and walked over to her with her arms outstretched. "I'm so glad you finally told me! It was almost impossible for me to keep my mouth shut."

The three of them were hugging each other with teary eyes when Nancy walked in.

"Why aren't you in your dress yet, Karen? We've got to get moving!"

"Oh!" Karen extracted herself and rushed over to the portable rack. "Let's get this bitch on and get this thing over with. There's a hunky man out there waiting for me to put a ring on it."

* * *

The ceremony went off without a hitch. Everything was beautiful. Red and white roses filled the chapel, skillfully arranged around a multitude of candles, creating a warm, intimate environment even though almost two hundred people packed the church. Karen and Jerry made a heartwarming sight standing on the altar reciting their vows to each other, the love between them apparent in their eyes and the big grins on their faces. Karen had been worried she would break down into sobs, insisting Shannon hide a wad of tissues in her bouquet, but she was strong and smiled at Jerry the whole time.

Matt was incredibly handsome in his tuxedo and Shannon felt beautiful on his arm. She wasn't wild about the ruby-colored strapless floor-length dress she wore, but next to Matt, she could be wearing a black garbage bag and still be presentable.

He smiled warmly at her when she walked to his side before they headed down the aisle. For a moment, everything else fell away and it was just the two of them. Matt tucked her arm into the crook of his and said, "You look beautiful," and Shannon believed him as she gazed into his warm eyes, her heart beating faster, but Nancy quickly broke the moment when she shooed them forward. She hoped that after the ceremony they could resume the harmless flirting started the night before, but she was now alone and Matt hadn't paid her one iota of attention after dinner.

They'd enjoyed conversation while they ate, but when Shannon played the exchange back in her head, however, she could pinpoint exactly where he'd lost interest. What had started out as a nice and playful discussion quickly turned when her job came up, and that was all she'd talked about—how much time she had to put in, how she had no life and how all of her focus was on her career. That was the exact point he'd quieted down, and as soon as he'd finished eating, he'd excused himself.

She sighed and took another drink of her wine. Alone at the head table while everyone else mingled—even her nosey relatives were avoiding her—and she was trying hard not to, but she was starting to feel sorry for herself.

Happy people surrounded her, her sister was married and pregnant, and the one guy Shannon hoped to engage in some mindless flirting with had ditched her. She didn't know why the melancholy, but it'd hit her suddenly as Karen and Jerry danced together, their first time as a married couple.

Shannon was happy with her life and loved her job, as demanding as it was, but there was a small worry that perhaps she was missing a great deal more and that panicked her. Was she truly okay with sacrificing so much now—the boyfriend, the wedding, and the kids—for a career that left no room for anything else? Was she really going to put *everything* off until sometime down the road? What if "sometime" never came? What if she missed her one chance because her focus was solely on her work?

Shannon scanned the room and her eyes kept coming back to Matt. He stood by the bar talking with some of his teammates. He'd removed his jacket, exposing his white shirt and charcoal vest and tie, looking like he should be on the cover of a magazine. She let herself daydream and imagine being with someone like him. It would be nice to have someone to talk to, to come home to and eat dinner with as they discussed their day; someone to get into bed with each night and have his strong arms wrapped around her. It would be nice, but she'd made her choices. She barely had time for herself, so she definitely did not have any for anyone else. If she wanted success, then this is what she had to do. There was no other choice.

The sound of throat-clearing boomed out loudly from the microphone on the stage where the band had cleared. She turned to find Jerry standing with Karen at his side.

"Can I get everyone's attention for a second?" When the room quieted down, he smiled. "Thank you.

"Karen and I wanted to say we are so thankful all of you were able to share in our special day with us. I know I repeat some other opinions when I say I am shocked I managed to convince this beautiful, wonderful woman to marry me. I don't know what I did to deserve her, but what I do know is I will spend the rest of my life paying her back the favor."

Their guests cheered and clapped as Karen beamed at him, nodding.

Jerry cleared his throat and the room quieted again. "I don't want to make all of you listen to me drone on and on with annoying lovey-dovey stuff, but I did want to say one thing." He turned to Karen and took her hands in his. "I love you so much and I can't wait for our lives to start together. Thank you for doing me the honor of being my wife. You make me so incredibly happy."

Karen's eyes filled and Shannon knew if she glanced around there wouldn't be a dry eye in the house. Her tears had started the second he'd climbed on the stage.

Jerry reached behind him where a table stood. "And since I have your attention, Karen is allowing me to do this even though she didn't want to yet, but I couldn't wait a second longer. I'm excited as hell." He pulled out his hands and held up a tiny Rockets jersey made for a small baby with the name Smutton on the back. "Sometime in the spring, the Rockets are going to have another Smutton on their roster!"

The room erupted in cheers and everyone rushed toward them to extend their congratulations. As happy as Shannon was for them, it all became a bit too much and she needed fresh air. She stood, but hesitated when she spotted her father's tall frame heading in her direction.

Richard Morrison looked quite debonair in his black tuxedo and his silver hair combed back neat and slick, always perfect. A sophisticated and handsome man, and when Shannon stood next to him, it was clear where she'd inherited her height.

"Your mom is beside herself with this news," he said, clasping his hands behind his back and facing the stage to watch the commotion around Karen and Jerry. As Karen's stepfather, there was no love lost between them, as they were both opinionated and didn't shy away from expressing it, especially with each other. But Shannon suspected he was at least a little excited at the possibility of a grandchild in his future, even if his demeanor said otherwise. "She's been dying for a baby in the family. She was certain she was going to have to wait for you to have one, even though I told her no chance in that, since we never believed Karen would settle down."

Shannon frowned. "What do you mean, no chance with me?"

His cool blue eyes assessed her. "Your career is your priority, not settling down and starting a family. You're not interested in all that."

"Well, I don't know about not interested…" she started to say, but broke off when his eyes narrowed at her.

"Of course you're not interested in that *now*," her father clarified. "You need to focus and you can't be distracted. We've talked about all of this. The sacrifices you need to make in order to follow your dreams."

"Oh, yes. Of course."

This was her dream, the one she'd had ever since she was a young girl and trailed her father to his office and even into the courtroom to watch him. She'd always admired him and was proud of the respect he received. He was so powerful and so confident that people looked up to him. Shannon wanted that and so he'd groomed her for success.

"Did you ever feel like you gave up too much?" she asked him suddenly.

"Hmm? What do you mean?" He turned toward her with an arched brow.

Shannon shrugged. "I don't know. Like maybe you had to sacrifice too much?"

"Absolutely not," he said. "It takes dedication, drive and hard work to be successful. You can't achieve that if you only give part of yourself to it. If you want it all, you have to commit it all."

"Makes sense," she murmured.

He turned fully to her. "Is there a problem?"

"No." She shook her head and gave him a small smile. "I was only wondering…if…I don't know…if perhaps I shouldn't give up too much."

"Shannon, you are a driven, intelligent and exceptionally bright young woman. I have no doubt you're going to be very successful. You're young and have all the time in the world for whatever you want. Don't worry about that," he said with a smile and a pat on her arm before he turned and walked away.

Shannon eyed his departing back, and even though he'd been trying to cheer her up, she felt worse.

* * *

Matt was only half listening to his teammate as he watched Shannon talk with her father. He had no idea what they were discussing, but she appeared upset, and for some reason it bothered him more than it should that her always-present bright smile was absent.

He'd been looking forward to getting to know her over dinner, but then she'd starting talking about her job, the center of her life, and he'd understood that was all she had time for, all she wanted now. The revelation had been a mood-dampening dose of reality, even though he'd already known there was no point in asking her out, but a deep sense of disappointment settled over him anyway. He tried to ignore her, tell himself it wasn't his business—*she* wasn't his business—but when her father left her side and when he'd completely tuned out his buddy, he accepted he wasn't going to be able to do just that.

Excusing himself, he strode across the room to her. "May I have this dance?"

Shannon turned and her eyes widened in surprise at the sight of him before a smile broke out on her beautiful face. "Sure," she said letting him take her hand in his to lead them to the dance floor.

Matt settled one of her hands on his shoulder as he held her close to him while trying to retain a respectable distance between them. The light citrusy scent of her perfume made his mouth water, and he had to restrain from pulling her closer.

"So," Matt said, striving to make casual conversation but coming up empty.

"So," she repeated and they both chuckled. Shannon cleared her throat and said, "I thought I'd run you off."

"Why is that?"

"All the talk about my work. When I get on a roll, I don't stop sometimes. Sorry."

He turned them to avoid crashing into another couple who appeared at their side as he gave a small shrug. "There's nothing wrong with being passionate about something. For you, it's your job."

"You too, but you're not spouting off about it all the time."

Matt smiled. "I get tired talking about my job. People are always asking me questions and sharing their opinions, whether I want them or not. It's nice not to talk about it every once in a while."

"I guess I feel the need to justify things," Shannon told him.

He frowned. "Why's that?"

It was her turn to shrug. "People don't understand the sacrifices and commitment I need to make in order to be successful...to make partner. They feel sorry for me or think I use my job as an excuse as to why I don't have a boyfriend or am not getting married and having kids, or whatever."

"Who cares what other people think?" Matt asked. "As long as you're happy with your decisions, then that's all that matters. Are you happy with your decision?"

"Yes." Her reply seemed rushed and forced, as if she was trying to convince not only him, but herself as well.

He didn't point it out, however. "Then that's all there is to it."

"I know it sounds stupid. You think I'm stupid that I'm letting this bother me."

"I don't think you're stupid. You should do what you want. If that's being a lawyer, then go for it. If not, then find what you really want."

"Yeah," Shannon agreed as she stared off over his shoulder, but there was no mistaking the doubt in her voice. "I know. I only wish…never mind," she said as she shook her head.

"What? You wish what?"

She gave him an embarrassed smile before looking down at their feet. "I just wish there was a way to know for sure, you know? Before it's too late…"

"I think everyone wishes that. A quick peek into the future," Matt said with a grin as she glanced up at him. "Definitely would make life easier."

Shannon studied him. "Do you ever wonder?"

"Me?" Matt shook his head. "No, but that's because baseball is all I ever wanted. There was no question for me. Without baseball, there's nothing."

"Nothing?" she asked with a raised brow.

"Nothing," he repeated. "It's who I am. I can't even imagine not playing the game. I don't want to, so don't make me," he joked.

Shannon laughed. "Okay, I won't make you."

They smiled at each other and heat passed between them, making him slightly dizzy. It was killing him not having her completely against him. Unable to resist anymore, he tightened his grip on her waist and pulled her closer. She felt wonderful in his arms. He loved being able to gaze directly into her eyes as they danced and that her lips were at the perfect height for his should he want to take them, and he realized that he did, very badly.

He cleared his throat. "Can I tell you something?"

"Sure," she said with a questioning look.

"Remember when we met the first time? After that game?"

"Yes," Shannon answered, sounding a little breathless.

"I really wanted to ask you out," he admitted.

Her face flushed and filled with surprise. "You did?"

"Oh, yeah. Big time."

"Why didn't you?"

Matt turned the question back on her. "What would you have said?"

The corners of her mouth tipped up as she eyed him, probably wondering if she should be completely honest or not. She finally said, "Yes. I remember hoping you would."

Matt tugged her closer still and, with the front of her flush against him, Shannon moved her arms around his neck, but her gaze stayed on his. The blacks of her pupils expanded as her lips parted slightly. "That would have been fun," he said, his voice sounding rough and gravelly to his ears.

"It would have," she agreed in almost a whisper.

"Too bad we can't do anything about it now," he said, keeping his focus on her to judge her reaction. "I mean, given everything…"

Shannon gave a slow nod as she swallowed, her attention fixated on his mouth. Her eyes flitted up to his before she closed the remaining gap separating them. Matt leaned the side of his head against hers as they moved in slow, tight circles. His hands traveled slowly up and down her back before lightly tracing a line across her narrow shoulders, and her arms tensed around his neck as her breasts rubbed against his chest. The clothes between them dulled the sensation, driving him mad, and he wanted nothing more than to remove all the layers separating them.

The song ended and the band started a club beat, but they still didn't separate. As everyone danced around them, Matt stopped and turned so his lips brushed against her ear, and a shiver passed through her. "Do you want to get some air?"

She nodded and he took her hand in his, leading them out the doors at the back of the room and into a quiet hallway of the hotel. It was empty and the lighting dimmed, offering them a secluded area away from the crowd.

Matt turned and Shannon was right there, her mouth immediately seeking his. Their lips touched softly at first, but soon the kisses became drugging in their intensity. His mouth moved hungrily over hers and Matt pulled her to him, walking them back until she hit the nearest wall. Her arms slid from around his neck, down his chest and she started to unbutton his vest. His hands skimmed up her sides, grazing the sides of her breasts, before he cupped her nape, angling her head in order to deepen the kiss. Deserting the buttons, Shannon's fingers threaded themselves through his hair, pulling him toward her as she arched against him, causing a flood of desire to surge within him.

He should slow them down—at any point someone could walk in on them—but he was lost in her. For so long Matt had wondered about her and now that he had her where he wanted, he wasn't eager to let her go, and she wasn't exactly an unwilling participant. Flattening one palm on the wall next to her head, Matt settled his other hand onto the small of her back. He slowly trailed his fingers down her arm before circling around to find the zipper of her dress. He'd started to tug down when she jerked away from him.

Her eyes were unfocused, dazed and confused, and a high flush covered her face, but she quickly snapped out of it. "What are we doing?" Shannon asked as she tried to straighten up.

"Um," Matt said, unsure how to answer since what they were doing was fairly obvious. At least to him.

"No, I mean, we can't do this." She shimmied her dress back into place.

"Okay," he said, disappointed and not bothering to hide it.

Shannon gave him a sideways glance. "Not that I don't want to, but I just… I'm not…I can't *do* this."

"No, I get it. Don't worry about it. It's probably for the best anyway. It's not like we can go anywhere from here."

"Right," she agreed, but her eyes searched his as if trying to determine what his true opinion was on the matter. "I mean, me with my job, and you with yours…it would be impossible."

"Right." He stepped away from her, needing to put some space between them. "I'm sorry."

"Don't be sorry, Shannon." Matt buttoned his vest. "No harm done."

"None?" she asked, with a teasing hint to her voice.

Matt smiled. "Okay, well, maybe a little bit of discomfort, but I'll be all right. No worries."

She ducked in and gently kissed his cheek. "I really wish things were different, Matt. Really."

He squeezed her hand with his. "Me too."

Shannon gave him one last smile before walking away down the hallway, most likely in search of a bathroom in order to check herself before making a reappearance. He closed his eyes and took a deep, shaky breath. It had taken a lot to step back from her and not try to convince her otherwise, but he respected her and her wishes. He also didn't beg. He was above that…for the most part.

Maybe another time, another place they might have worked, but it wasn't now and might not be ever. And as much as Matt hated regrets, the fact that he hadn't acted on things when he'd first met her would be one he'd have for a long time.

CHAPTER 6

Shannon blinked hard at the computer screen as the letters started to swim together. She closed her eyes for a longer pause and reopened them, trying to force them into focus, but it didn't help. She leaned back and blew out a breath. She needed to step away for a second and rest before restarting. She'd been going for God knows how many hours straight, trying to catch up from the time lost while she was in Michigan, and the strain was finally catching up to her.

She stared out the tiny sliver of a window in her office, watching the city move below her. Regardless of time of day or the season, the city constantly breathed with movement and life, drawing her in and mesmerizing her when she allowed herself a few moments away from work, a rare occurrence. The view wasn't much, but she considered herself lucky to have one since many of the other associates' offices were windowless. The favoritism was most likely because of her father's friendship with one of the founding partners, inciting her co-workers to grouse and comment on the obvious partiality behind her back. Usually it bothered her, but about this, she didn't care.

At the buzz of her intercom, she turned from the window.

"Who is tall and utterly yummy?" her assistant's voice whispered.

"I'm sorry, what was that, Megan?" Shannon asked, certain she'd misheard her.

"Since when do you know Chris Evans?" Megan murmured in a low voice.

Shannon froze. Chris Evans? That could only mean one thing since there was no way the real Chris Evans stood outside her door. It had to be the next best possibility, and that was Matt. What on earth was he doing here?

She'd done her best not to think about what happened between them at the wedding, since all she had to do was conjure up his crystal-blue eyes and his pulse-raising smile and she melted. Asking him to stop had been the hardest thing she'd ever had to do, and then he'd had to make it that much harder when he hadn't even tried to make her feel guilty, increasing her respect for him. For such a good-looking guy and a star in his chosen profession, he certainly didn't walk around with a sense of entitlement. But she didn't do casual, not even with a guy as gorgeous as him.

"Uh, one second," she stammered as she rushed back to her desk.

She yanked open her bottom drawer and pulled out her purse. Digging into the deep pockets, she unearthed her mirror and grimaced at her tired reflection. She tugged a brush through her lifeless hair, cringing with a curse when static lifted the strands around her face and on top of her head. She tried to tame it before wiping at the black smudges of mascara under her eyes. Pinching her cheeks to bring some color back to them, she quickly dabbed on lip gloss and called it good enough on such short notice.

Shannon brushed a hand down her tweed skirt and took a breath, trying to still the butterflies suddenly fluttering around in her stomach. She lifted her chin, striving for an air of confidence she hoped she pulled off, and opened the door.

Matt, who was chatting animatedly with Megan, glanced up. He smiled when he spotted her, his blue eyes brightening and his perfect white teeth on display. With his loose fitting jeans, dark chocolate boots and a hunter-green winter jacket, he could have stepped straight out of a winter spread of a fashion magazine. Faint ruddiness remained on his cheeks from the cold air outside.

"Matt! This is a surprise. What are you doing here?" she finally said as her brain reengaged, forcing herself to ignore how gorgeous he was.

He stepped forward. "I'm sorry. Did I come at a bad time? I didn't mean to interrupt."

Shannon shook her head as if trying to clear out the massive amounts of confusion thrashing around, while Megan watched their exchange with interest. "No, no interruptions. I'm sorry. You caught me off guard. Please, come in."

She held out her hand toward her office and followed him in. She closed the door behind them, but not before quickly turning and mouthing "Oh my God!" to Megan, who gave her two thumbs up.

Shannon smiled at him as she sat behind her large mahogany desk. "Please, have a seat," she offered before her mind winced, hating the formality in her tone. She tried not to stare as Matt unzipped his jacket, revealing a navy V-neck sweater coupled with a gray T-shirt, which outlined his broad shoulders and strong chest, before he sat down. He glanced around, taking in everything.

"This is a nice office. Nice view," he said as he craned his neck to see out the small window.

"Thanks. I try not to get distracted by it too much."

"I can see that. Although a bit too high to do any good people watching."

"Yeah. So, what are you doing here?" She sat back in her chair, trying to appear calm and relaxed even though excited jitters skipped inside her. She didn't mean to sound rude or impatient, but she had to know why he'd shown up at her office out of the blue.

"Oh." Matt turned back and slouched down in the chair comfortably, propping one ankle on his knee. "I'm in town to work out with a buddy of mine, Dusty Reynolds—he's the catcher for Chicago—and so I thought I'd stop by..." He broke off and gave her another big smile. "I remembered you mentioning that you worked here." At her continued silence, he cleared his throat. "Anyway, I wanted to see if maybe one night we could do dinner or something while I'm in town. Nothing big or anything…just…hang out."

"I see," Shannon murmured, struggling to ignore the disappointment coursing through her that she couldn't be anything more than a friend to this fine specimen of a man. "Yeah, that'd be fun."

"Great!" he said with another big smile. "It's cool to know someone else here in the city to hang with."

"Just let me know when and where and we'll go from there. With my schedule, the more advance notice, the better. Where are you staying, by the way?"

"The Waldorf."

She smiled. "You don't skimp, huh?"

Matt shrugged. "I like it. It's nice."

"Nice? I guess that's one way to describe it. Expensive is another."

He lifted his big shoulders again, his gaze lingering on her and her skin prickled in anticipation of something—what, she didn't know—but soon his eyes broke away and he stood. "I won't keep you. I'll call you to schedule something."

She rose as he walked over to the door. "Sure, sounds good."

Shannon waited until he disappeared from sight before sinking back down into her chair. She couldn't believe he'd showed up. In Chicago. At her office. She hadn't expected to have contact with him again anytime soon, if ever, but now here he was and he wanted to get together with her for dinner. As a friend.

"That's all you want, Shannon," she muttered aloud. "All you can have at the moment. A friendly, gorgeous, ridiculously sexy *friend*."

But, as she turned to her computer to force herself back to work, she struggled to ignore the voice calling her a liar.

* * *

Matt walked out of the office building and shoved his hands into his coat pockets feeling somewhat successful. His and Shannon's interaction right off the bat had been stiff and formal, not as smooth as he would have liked, but he could fix that, no problem. Next step, calling her and scheduling dinner.

He'd found his mind wandering back to Shannon as he packed for his trip home to Arizona, unable to forget the taste of her on his lips and the feel of her in his arms, and he'd pondered whether to try something before bolting the door completely on any possibility between them. He hated playing the what-if game, so he decided to at least try, and if she turned him down, then at least he'd made an effort and his mind would be free of second guesses, which he hated.

He'd had to make a call home, informing his mother of his decision not to be home for Thanksgiving, which had upset her as he expected, but he'd promised to be there for Christmas. Then he'd had to come up with a reasonable excuse to be in Chicago since he didn't think Shannon would react well to learning he'd come to town just to see her. She'd already made it abundantly clear she didn't have time for anything else in her life outside of her job. Plus, he wanted to gauge her reaction. If she responded positively, happy and interested, and agreed to go out with him a few times as a "friend," then he'd make a move. If she acted put out and annoyed, turning him down…well, then they'd all save face, he'd have his answer, and could head out to Arizona on the next flight.

Pleased with things so far, despite the slow progression, Matt headed down the sidewalk in the direction of his hotel. A quick blare of a car horn caused him to glance across the street. His eye caught someone standing on the opposite side of the busy road watching him. When recognition clicked, his heart froze and a flash of cold panic washed through him. He stopped, ignoring the grumblings of everyone around him as they bumped into him on the crowded sidewalk, and stared at Natalie. She gave him a small smile as a crowd swallowed her up. After the mob dissipated, an empty space faced him.

Matt's head swiveled back and forth, but he didn't spot her again, and he wondered if he'd imagined everything, if the girl only strongly resembled her. Another person collided with him and swore, spurring him into motion, and he made his feet move.

He'd been a little worried about the situation with Natalie, not really sure if he should pursue anything with anyone else until he was confident she would adhere to the restraining order, but he couldn't put his life on hold because she wouldn't accept they were no longer together. Things had been so quiet that he'd believed she'd finally gotten the message. He hoped she'd moved on, realizing there was no going back, which meant he could move on himself. But now he questioned his decision. If she was following him, in direct violation of the order, the last thing he wanted was to involve anyone else in his messed-up state of affairs.

Matt spotted his hotel up ahead. He needed to call his lawyer and discuss whether he should notify the authorities, especially since he lacked proof other than a vision he questioned the validity of. He didn't believe the situation was volatile, only an annoyance, but he'd lay low for a couple of days before calling Shannon in order to make sure the coast was clear. His eyes were playing tricks on him, however. Natalie was back in Michigan and would have no knowledge of him traveling to Chicago. As far as she knew, he was home in Arizona where he normally was this time of year. There was no reason for him to believe otherwise.

CHAPTER 7

A few days later, Matt pulled his big body out of the tight confines of the backset of the cab and studied the building in front of him. Shannon lived in a high-rise not horribly far from the water and he had to guess each apartment sported a spectacular view. Rent must cost a pretty penny here—not that Shannon didn't make a healthy salary. Associates at big law firms usually pulled in a solid pay-check in order to compensate for the long hours they put in as they climbed their way up to partner. His father had been one of them until he broke out on his own.

He nodded to the doorman who opened the door for him, and headed across the shiny black marble floors toward the elevators, appreciating the lavish lobby area with its dark wood paneling and strategically placed floral arrangements. Pressing the button for the forty-eighth floor, he rode up while trying to ease the nerves inching into his neck and shoulders. He wanted things to go well, but he was still drawing a blank on how to tell her the training story was lie and that he was actually here for her. Inspiration was not striking, so he was going to have to roll with the punches and see how things went throughout the night.

Stepping out of the elevator and onto the dark gray plush carpeted floor of the short hallway, Matt stopped outside Shannon's door and knocked. He waited a few seconds before hearing the tip-tap of her heels and then the door swung open.

"Hi," Shannon said, friendly enough, but she appeared a little frazzled, still dressed in her work suit.

"Hi," he said and stepped in when she made room.

"I got home a bit later than expected," she explained as she closed the door behind him. "Make yourself at home and I'll be ready in a minute."

He nodded as he walked into the main room. He'd been right about the view; wall-to-wall windows faced the water in the faraway distance behind the surrounding buildings. Soft beige carpet sat underneath a loveseat, which faced a flat-panel television, and a couple of matching chairs, all situated around a glass coffee table whose top was barely visible beneath the scattered books, clutter of flies and a laptop.

Matt unzipped his black overcoat and inspected the tiny kitchen area, which was snug and would barely fit more than one person. The apartment was nice but a little too small for him. Tight corridors made him uncomfortable, his big frame clumsy and in the way. Aside from the mess on the coffee table, the rest of the place looked unused, since she was most likely never home.

Hearing her footsteps on the tile in the hallway, he turned as Shannon entered the room. She'd changed into black leggings and riding boots, highlighting her sexy long legs. A rose cowl-neck sweater accented her fresh skin nicely, making her cheeks glow a soft pink. She wore her hair down and she'd refreshed her makeup as her eyes appeared darker and smokier than when he'd arrived.

"Sorry again. Are you ready?"

"Yep." Matt held out his hand. "Your coat?" he said when a puzzled expression crossed her face.

* * *

Shannon gave him a shy smile as she handed her wool peacoat over to him and put her arms through the sleeves. She couldn't remember the last time any guy had helped her into her jacket, if ever. His mother had trained him well. If he had manners like this and they were simply friends, she could only imagine how he would treat anyone he was romantically involved with.

Once her coat was on, he held out his elbow and said, "Shall we?"

She grinned, recalling he'd said the same thing to her at the wedding. "Absolutely."

They walked over to the elevator and waited for the lift to arrive. "I like your place," he said. "Nice views."

"Thank you." She gave him a sideways glance. "You really notice the views, don't you?" she teased.

Matt shrugged with a crooked grin. "I'm all about the views. You should see the amazing mountain views I have in Arizona."

The elevator dinged, and they stepped in. "They are nice when you have the time to appreciate them," she agreed. "Here, it's dark when I leave and dark when I get home for the most part, so I don't get to enjoy them too much."

"You need to make time."

"Stop and smell the roses, huh?"

He chuckled. "Yeah, something like that."

They walked through the lobby and out onto the street, where he took her lightly by the elbow and led her to a taxi waiting for them.

"I paid him to wait," Matt said when she raised her brows in surprise.

They climbed into the backseat and Shannon tried not to notice how close Matt sat next to her. His woodsy cologne tickled her senses, which made her want to bury her nose against his neck, so instead she turned away to watch out the back window.

"May I ask where we are going?"

"Sullivan's. I hope you like steak?" he asked, suddenly looking concerned. "I guess I shouldn't have assumed you ate meat…"

"Oh, it's fine. Totally love a good steak." She gave him a reassuring smile, which turned timid when she caught him studying her.

Matt cleared this throat before leaning away a bit. "So, tough day at the office?"

"Long…like always," she said and they were silent until the cab pulled up to the restaurant.

Shannon waited as Matt paid before following him into the building. He walked over to the host and informed him that he had a reservation, a sign he was a good planner. Which made sense since, as the catcher, he was acting manager on the field. He had to keep the game going, calling plays fed to him from the dugout, and collaborating with the pitcher to work through each hitter strategically and in an organized fashion. He had to have structure and order, which most likely spilled over into his personal life. She appreciated a good sense of organization.

The host walked them to a small corner table not far from the bar where live entertainment was setting up. Shannon started to shrug off her jacket and jerked a little in alarm when Matt's hands landed on her shoulder.

"Your coat?" he said with a hint of a smile.

"Oh, sorry," she said with an embarrassed laugh, still not used to a man acting chivalrous.

Matt walked over to the coat check while Shannon sat down at their table and opened her menu. When he returned, his blue eyes were intent on her. "Everything okay?" he asked.

"Yes, this is perfect. Thank you."

A waiter appeared to take their drink order and Shannon ordered a Blueberry Lemon Drop Martini while Matt asked for a Whiskey Sour.

Matt sat back in his chair and raised one brow after the waiter left. "A Blueberry Lemon Drop? That sounds nasty."

Shannon gave a small shrug with a crooked smile. "I think they're pretty tasty, as a matter of fact."

"I'll have to take you word on that." He paused when their server arrived with their drinks. After they put in their orders, Matt leaned in and gave her his perfect smile, making her heart skip a beat. "You look very nice tonight."

She paused for a second thinking perhaps she'd misunderstood the hint of flirtation in his voice, but she spotted the gleam in his eye. She cleared her throat, unsure how to process this new information. Friends who flirt?

"Uh, thank you." She tucked some hair behind her ear with her fingers.

Shannon studied her glass, trying to hide her discomfort since she was having a hard time reading the situation. She had no idea what to do, what to think. She'd totally expected the evening to be on a friends-only level and now he was switching everything up. Did she want him to flirt with her? Hell, yes. Did she want to flirt back with him? That…that she didn't know, afraid of where things might lead.

"So what have you been doing since the wedding?" Matt asked her as he raised his glass to take drink.

Shannon cleared her throat. She could do this…whatever this was.

"Working. That's pretty much all I do."

"Come on, there's got to be something else you do? You don't do anything outside of work?"

"Nope. As I told you before, this is the sad reality of my life. Get up, go to work, come home, go to bed. Repeat."

Hearing herself made her realize how boring and pathetic her life was. It also didn't help she was having a difficult time ignoring the stirrings of uncertainties about whether she was giving up too much after learning her father was telling others she wasn't interested in settling down and having a family.

Matt scowled. "That doesn't sound exciting. You should go out and have some fun. Go to a bar. You'd have a ton of guys hitting on you."

She laughed before she could stop herself. Surprise filled his expression and she held up her hand. "Sorry, it's funny to hear that. I don't ever have a 'ton of guys' hitting on me, even when I did go out."

"What?" he asked, sounding genuinely shocked. "Why wouldn't you? They're idiots then."

Shannon shrugged. "My guess is because I'm almost as tall as a lot of them. Most guys don't like tall women."

Matt shook his head as he sat toward her again. "Your height really bothers you, doesn't it? I didn't think anything of it when you mentioned it at the wedding, but I can tell it is a thing with you."

She gave an awkward lift of one shoulder and averted her eyes down, uncomfortable under his steady gaze.

"Shannon," he said and waited until her head lifted. "You are incredibly sexy. You're probably just intimidating to most of them. Most guys would dream about having your long legs wrapped around them."

Shannon choked on the sip she'd taken and gaped at him in astonishment. He, however, sat back in contemplation, making her wonder if he was envisioning her legs around him right then. Heat flooded her cheeks and she was probably as red as a lobster.

She finally laughed. "Is that your idea of a come-on line?"

He grinned as he shook his head. "No, that wouldn't be my come-on line, if I needed one."

"If you needed one? That sounds pretty self-assured." Shannon crossed her arms as she studied him. "Oh, I get it. You don't need one because the whole Chris Evans thing does the work for you."

Matt laughed out loud, a full, low, rumble, making her tremble at its masculinity. "Oh, man. That's funny." He caught her eye and started chuckling again. "Okay, you got me. I have to admit, it doesn't hurt. But," he continued on when she started to jump in, "I have to say, I really don't understand it. I don't look anything like the guy."

"Come on! You don't look like him? Yes, you do."

"I'm way bigger than that guy!"

Shannon rolled her eyes. "I didn't say you were identical twins or anything, but you do *resemble* him. And yes, you are bigger than him."

"Is that a good or bad thing?" he asked with a crooked smile.

"I'm sorry?"

"We were discussing how you being tall is not a bad thing, and so I'm wondering if the same applies to me."

Shannon laughed as she shook her head. She couldn't believe she was actually sitting here, flirting with Matt. How the world had changed overnight. She wasn't sure, however, if it was for better or worse. She eyed his broad shoulders and chest, which displayed strength and solidness even under his black sweater, and recalled all that muscle flush against her. The hand holding his glass had a wide palm and long, thick fingers, and she shivered, remembering the hot path they'd trailed over her skin. She crossed her legs under the table and squeezed, trying to relieve the pressure building at the memory of his demanding mouth on hers.

"It's a good thing," she finally said with a sly smile.

Matt gave her a big grin and played with the tines on his fork before clearing his throat. "Good, because I was wondering—"

"Shannon?"

Her head shot up at the interruption and she instantly wanted to disappear when she spotted her father's friend, otherwise known as her boss, heading over to their table.

"Mr. Barnes, hi," she said with a bright smile as she stood, almost tripping over the tablecloth in her haste. "What a nice surprise."

"It *is* a nice surprise," he said to her with one white brow raised. "I'm surprised to find you out of the office with all the work going on with the Watkins case."

Shannon tried to ignore the implication behind his statement. His opinion clearly being she should be working, not out on what most likely looked like a date. "Oh, yes. Well, I plan on picking it right back up tomorrow morning, if not later tonight," she added to appease him. She pointed toward Matt as he stood towering over her boss, but Mr. Barnes wasn't easily intimidated. "A friend of mine came in from out of town, and so I wanted to spend some time with him before he left. Can I introduce to you Matt Buck? Matt, this is Marcus Barnes. He's one of the founding partners at Bickles, Bickles and Barnes."

Matt held out his large hand. "Pleasure to meet you, sir."

Her boss took Matt's hand in a firm shake and narrowed his eyes as he studied him. "You look awfully familiar, Mr. Buck. Do I know you?"

Matt gave a small shrug. "I don't know. You a baseball fan?"

"Season tickets to the Gales for the past twenty years."

"Matt's the catcher for the Detroit Rockets," Shannon quickly provided, hoping to help Mr. Barnes forget his earlier irritation at her for not being at work, billing hours for the firm.

"Yes," Mr. Barnes said, his shrewd eyes still focused on Matt. "That's exactly where I know you from. Well, it's nice to meet you, son." He shook Matt's hand again with more enthusiasm and a friendly pat on the back. He glanced at Shannon. "I guess it makes sense, given your sister married Jerry Smutton."

"Yes, sir."

"Well, I'll let you two return to dinner so Shannon can get back to work," he said with a chuckle, but Shannon read between the lines clear enough. "Mr. Buck, I'm afraid the Gales are going to beat the Rockets in the standings this coming season."

Matt gave him a friendly but tight smile. "Oh, well, we'll just have to wait and see, won't we? I have some intel that says the Rockets are going to be a force to reckon with this season."

Both men laughed as her boss gave a slight wave and walked away.

Shannon let out a breath and sank down in her chair, guilt washing over her. She deserved to eat dinner out occasionally, didn't she? But Mr. Barnes was right. It was an important case for the firm, and as soon as she got home, she'd get back to reviewing the depositions.

"Wow," Matt said. "He runs a tight ship, huh? Can't even eat dinner?"

"It's a big case, that's all," Shannon said, trying not to sound defensive.

"Shannon, big case or not, you deserve a life and some you time. He shouldn't make you feel guilty for that."

"I'm not guilt—"

"Don't bother denying it. It's clear as day on your face, and even now I can tell you're thinking about what he said, planning what you'll work on once you get home tonight."

They paused when the waiter returned to their table with their dinner. Shannon didn't like how Matt had been able to read her so easily, but she couldn't deny that what he'd said was true.

"Okay, fine," she said once the server had departed. "I do feel guilty because it *is* a big case. I can't mess it up for the team. I need to hold up my end of things."

"You won't mess anything up. You can't do everything, be on all the time, or else you'll burn out. You need to enjoy life, not spend it sitting at your desk, drowning in work. Trust me, a lot gets missed that way."

"True, but couldn't you be considered to be in the same boat?" Shannon asked him, turning the tables.

"What do you mean? I do other things outside of baseball."

"No, what I mean is essentially you were stating I shouldn't be so career-driven, and I'm saying couldn't the same be said for you?"

Matt frowned. "What do you mean?"

"Okay, let's say you get married and start a family. Your kid is in some big competition or something and it's in May. You're on the road, you have your own games, and so what do you do? Aren't you putting your job ahead of everything else?"

"It's different," he insisted.

"How so?" she questioned, not backing down.

"I don't have a choice."

Her eyebrows raised. "And I do? How is it that you don't have a choice, but I do? Don't you dare pull out the gender card," she warned, reacting to the look on his face that suggested he was going down that road. "This is part of the requirements for my job, just like it's a requirement for you to travel."

"Okay, okay." Matt held up his hands in a sign of peace. "I think we're getting into a touchy area here and I wasn't going to pull out the gender card, for your information." He narrowed his eyes, letting her know she'd insulted him. "I see your point. Yes, I guess it is the same."

"Let's face it, no matter how you look at it, it's tough for anyone to have demanding careers. This is exactly why work is all I have in my life right now. I don't want to be put in a predicament of making others unhappy or forcing difficult choices which only leads to arguments and hard feelings."

Shannon was unable to interpret the expression on Matt's face. It was almost frustration, but she had no idea why he should be disappointed. He sat back in his chair, calmly taking a drink, as his eyes wandered the restaurant before finally landing on her.

"You're right. That's the last thing you'd want to do. You had to make a choice and you did. End of story."

He picked up his silverware and returned his attention to his meal, successfully concluding their conversation. Heavy silence fell across the table, leaving Shannon unsure how to liven it up. She didn't understand why things had quickly taken a downturn. What would he care about the decisions she'd made? They had no impact on him.

They finished their dinners, never regaining the friendly banter between them before her boss had ruined the mood. When they did pick up other safe topics of conversation, there was a discernable difference in Matt's behavior toward her. He was back acting like the friend from out of town, rather than the guy telling her he wanted her legs wrapped around him, and she was back to wondering exactly what was going on in his head.

As she lay in bed later that night, she couldn't deny the euphoria that had flowed through her when Matt had begun flirting with her. And even though getting involved with anyone was out of the question, she wanted him to want her, she wanted him to pursue her, and she wanted to let it all happen. She couldn't ignore the rock of disappointment in her stomach when the night had ended on such a sour note and things had moved back into the boring neutral zone.

She rolled over onto her side and let out an irritated huff. It was just like her. Interested in someone she damn well shouldn't be nor had time for. Her career was number one and she'd even told him as much. If that wasn't a mood killer, then she didn't know what was.

CHAPTER 8

A week later, hurrying out of her office, Shannon flipped the light switch off and struggled with the sleeves of her jacket when she attempted to thread her arm through while juggling her brief case and purse at the same time, but only succeeded in being tangled. Par the course, she was running late to meet Matt. She'd planned to arrive before him in order to freshen up in the restroom, but that wasn't going to happen. Who was she kidding? Work always put her behind. She prayed she hadn't kept him waiting too long since her last conference call of the day had run longer than anticipated thanks to a long-winded in-house attorney for her client.

Megan glanced up from shutting down her computer as Shannon breezed by. "Meeting Mr. Hunk?" she asked with a knowing smile.

Shannon smiled back, but kept moving. "That's the plan, but running late."

"You always are," Megan said good-naturedly. "Have a good time."

Shoving at the down button for the elevator while she continued to try to untangle herself, relief pulsed through her when the doors opened shortly afterward, thankful she didn't have to wait long. She jumped in, ignoring the curious stares by the few occupants wondering at her haste. Urging on the descent, she studied the numbers over the door as they slowly flashed down one-by-painstakingly-one.

Once on the ground floor, she rushed through the lobby and pushed her way outside. The harsh cold hit her, causing her to wince, but she put her head down against the blustery wind as she pounded down the sidewalk, forcing her narrow heels to carry her faster than they normally allowed, and making her thankful for the absence of snow and ice.

When her eyes watered and her skin started to tingle from the brisk air, she found herself questioning why she continued to meet him each time he asked, especially considering the amount effort required by her to do so. Something as simple as a dinner entailed rearranging her schedule, not an easy feat, and certainly a frustrating one. After their first meeting, she hadn't expected to hear from him again, with the way the evening had ended, but sure enough, a day later, he called to set something up. Nothing had changed, however. He was still distanced, but friendly…always friendly. The situation was odd, to say the least, including her inability to say no.

Each time she rushed out to meet him put her further behind at work, but she couldn't seem to stop despite the not-so-quiet grumblings of her coworkers. Sooner rather than later, she'd be sitting down with Carol, their team lead, for a "chat" about being a team player, and each person needing to pull his or her weight. In addition, a not-so-subtle reminder of the minimal billable hours requirement to be met, if not exceeded, by each associate by the end of the year, as if she could forget.

Shannon was getting her work done, but she did more outside of the office—especially recently—rather than in. Whenever Matt called, she couldn't find it within herself to politely decline, holding out hope he would start flirting with her again, even though there was no chance of them going anywhere, which was all sorts of backward. She couldn't get involved with him. End of story. She was her own worst enemy, constantly setting herself up for a letdown each moment she spent with him. Her high stress level clearly served to prove her point.

She needed to stop and she needed her head checked, obviously, but the restaurant was only a block away and she refused to turn back now. She'd might as well get a decent meal from her pains. No more after this evening, however. She promised herself. Tonight was the last time. She'd ask when he planned to leave for Arizona and gently inform him this get-together was the final one. She appreciated the dinners and conversations they'd had, enjoyed spending time with him, but her work was piling up, which she couldn't ignore any longer. Matt would understand. Even if he didn't, the madness ended here.

Shannon entered through the front doors of the busy, trendy restaurant and had to shove her way past the patrons who milled around waiting for a table. She spotted Matt leaning an elbow on the long bar, smiling in conversation with a beautiful strawberry-blonde bartender. Jealousy surged through her when the girl gave her hair a flirty flip and brushing his arm with her fingers as she laughed at whatever he'd said. Shannon had no claim on him, but the resentment stung nonetheless, especially considering her already frazzled and haggard state after a long day.

She took a deep breath and strolled over, putting on her most dazzling smile when he turned his head.

"Hi! Sorry, I'm late."

Matt pushed off the bar as his blue eyes twinkled at her and a big grin broke out. "Hey, no problem. I'm glad you could make it." He pointed at his drink. "What can I get you?"

"Oh, a glass of Chardonnay would be perfect," Shannon said to the bartender. The woman appeared crestfallen by Shannon's appearance, and Shannon took that as a small victory, albeit meaningless and insignificant. The triumph was purely personal.

While she waited for her drink, Shannon let out a breath. "I hiked it from the office. My feet are ice and my face is frozen."

"What? Why didn't you call me? I could have come and picked you up in a cab or something." Matt stepped back and his eyebrows shot up when he spotted the thin, tall heels on her feet. "You hiked it in those? You're lucky you didn't break an ankle."

Shannon waved him off. "Oh, it's fine. I needed to blow off the residual stress from my meeting that went longer than I'd planned. Sorry again." She nodded thanks to the bartender when a full glass appeared in front of her.

"No problem. I was able to pass the time."

"Yes, I see that." She'd meant to sound teasing, but even she recognized the slight edge to her voice and she cringed.

Matt frowned, hearing the sharpness too. "What does that mean?"

"Nothing. It meant nothing. Sorry, still destressing obviously." She smiled, took a healthy sip of her wine and hoped he bought the act.

He studied her before giving her a small grin. "Okay, if you say so."

"I do. So, what did you do today?"

He shrugged and cleared his throat. "Oh, not much." He turned, facing her and the front of the restaurant. "I spent some time…"

Matt paused for a second before dread washed down his face. When he muttered, "Oh, fuck," Shannon spun around to identify what had caught his attention, expecting to find a gorgeous, tiny ex-girlfriend eyeing him with hatred. Instead, all she found was a group of people congregating by the door with no one appearing to notice them, but then a man, standing head and shoulders over everyone, spotted Matt and a big grin broke out over his face as he headed toward them.

Matt swore again under his breath and she frowned, wondering what the problem was. "Matt?" she asked.

He dropped his head with a small smile of resignation, but didn't answer as the guy approached.

"What the fuck are you doing here, my man?" The stranger slapped a huge paw on Matt's shoulder and held out the other.

Matt grinned as he shook the hand he offered. The man stood almost as tall as Matt did, with short buzzed blond hair, and even with the winter jacket he wore, his physique screamed athlete. "Just passing through town," Matt replied.

The stranger's gray eyes flitted over Shannon before returning to Matt. "Why didn't you let me know? We could have trained together at that place I was telling you about."

Training? The word caught Shannon's ear. He *was* here to train with someone, at least that was what he'd told her.

She missed Matt's reply, since he mostly stammered, but she didn't miss when the other man said, "Aren't you going to introduce me to your lovely friend?"

Shannon observed in fascination as an interesting shade of red worked up Matt's face, and wondered just who this guy was and why his appearance had thrown Matt out of sorts. He paused, avoiding eye contact with her, before taking another deep breath. "Uh, yeah. Shannon, this is Dusty Reynolds. Dust, this is Shannon Morrison."

The name made her start, but Shannon quickly recovered and smiled as Dusty's large hand swallowed up hers. "It's nice to meet you, Dusty."

She glanced out of the corner of her eye while Dusty returned the sentiments and saw Matt studying her, most likely trying to read her reaction. She had no idea why he'd lied about coming to town to train with Dusty or why Matt would even be playing a stupid game such as this, but she didn't like it. Her life had enough complications that she didn't need to be wasting her time with a liar, and about something so stupid.

Shannon remained quiet with a pleasant smile plastered in place while Matt and Dusty finished catching up, and gave Dusty's hand another shake as he left. When they were alone again, she eyed Matt coolly.

"So," she started. "He's the one you said you were coming to train with?"

"Yep. That's him," Matt said, unable to stand still and fighting an embarrassed smile.

"He didn't seem to even know you were here, yet you'd told me you'd gone to a couple of sessions with him."

Matt finally caught on to her anger and leaned toward her, his eyes pleading. "Please don't be mad. It isn't what you think."

"I honestly don't know what to think, but what I do know is I've spent a couple of weeks getting further and further behind at work in order to spend time with a guy who lied to me about something that seems pretty ridiculous to lie about. I don't have time for games, even though I have no idea why *we* would even be playing them."

He hung his head and studied the floor, clearly at a loss for words. Since he wasn't quick with a response, most likely formulating another lie, she let out a huff. "I'm out of here. This is stupid and I'm too busy for this BS."

Turning on her heels, Shannon grabbed her jacket off the back of the bar stool and tugged her arms into the sleeves, making her way back out of the restaurant. Hitting the sidewalk, she started to hail a cab when someone caught her arm.

"Shannon, wait! Let me explain, please." Matt turned her around to face him.

She put her hand on her hip as she waited, but said nothing.

"Ask me why I lied," he told her.

"Matt." She closed her eyes willing for patience. She was tired and hungry, and in no mood for this. "We've already established that you have—"

"Ask me," he insisted.

"Fine. Why did you lie?"

"Because I knew if I told you the real reason I came here, you would…I don't know, freak out or tell me it was a waste of time."

Shannon frowned. "Why would I freak out? Are you involved in something shady? God, this is the last thing I need. This is so stupid! I don't have *time* for this," she grounded out as she turned, looking for an available cab again.

"I came here for you, okay?" Matt declared as he pulled her toward him, his eyes insisting and adamant. "I came here with the sole intention of seeing you. I wanted to spend time with you and I didn't want you to freak out if you knew I'd made a trip to Chicago just to see you, which I did. So, I made up the stuff about training."

Her breath caught in her throat. That wasn't what she'd expected him to say. She must have misunderstood. "Wait, what? You came here to see me?"

"Yes."

Her brain struggled to find sense in the whirlwind and put the pieces together. If he'd specifically come for her, then why did he act only as a friend? This had to be the weirdest pursuit ever by a guy. "You came here because of me," she repeated, not really for him to answer but more to help her comprehension. "As in, you're attracted to me?"

The look of concern on his face lifted as he gave a small chuckle. "Well, yeah. I thought that was obvious."

"Obvious?" she exclaimed. "Aside from what happened at the wedding, nothing about this has been obvious. It's been mixed messages left and right," she said as she walked away a couple of steps, trying to rid of the loud buzzing in her ears. "I can't even process this."

Shannon shook her head. The cold air helped to clear the confusion, but her mind was still going a mile a minute trying to put everything together. She whirled back to him. "But you haven't even done or said anything! I don't get it."

He gave her a shy grin. "Yeah, I wasn't quite sure how you felt about me. Plus, there's that whole thing about your work…"

"You seriously don't know?"

He frowned. "Don't know what?"

His blue eyes were so bright and his handsome face so full of worry that she didn't even stop to think, didn't care she was in public with thousands of people walking around them. She did what she'd being telling herself she shouldn't. She launched herself at him...again. She would think about the consequences, figure everything out later. She was going for it. She was doing this...with him.

Matt caught her and held her tight against him as her mouth collided with his. His lips were soft and warm under hers, and, after a few seconds, he moaned and opened to her, his hands sinking into her hair. He tasted like the whiskey he'd been drinking, and she warmed all the way down to her toes when his tongue curled with hers.

They remained locked together, neither wanting to pull away and dampen the fire erupting between them. A few people snickered as they stepped around them, a couple even muttered, "Get a room," but she didn't care.

When Matt broke the kiss, he kept her close in his arms.

"Come back to my hotel?" he asked in a soft voice.

There was no question. She was going to break one of her own rules and enjoy a wonderful night with a sinfully gorgeous man. Since her personal life was on hold for the most part, she deserved this one night, and there'd be no regrets.

She nodded.

CHAPTER 9

Throwing money at the driver, not caring he'd given the man an extremely healthy tip, Matt jumped out of the cab under the porte cochere, grabbing Shannon's hand in his and pulling her toward the lobby.

He couldn't believe how everything had all played out. When he'd seen Dust walk through the restaurant doors, he hadn't known whether to laugh or hide. Even with Shannon's repeated insistence about having no time for anything but work, something refused to let him throw in the towel. He continued to ask her out, and she continued to say yes, which gave him confidence in his decision to persevere, yet the opportunity for full disclosure still eluded him.

It certainly wasn't how he would have scripted it and there were moments when he feared she'd deck him before rushing off into the night, but he'd been able to get her to listen. And her reaction after she'd gotten past her initial anger at him…he still couldn't get the picture out of his mind of her throwing herself at him. Now they were heading up to his room and he was anxious to get them both naked.

They beelined toward the elevator, their rapid footsteps loud against the marble floor, where they waited in impatient silence. The doors opened at last, but they had to pause as another couple emerged. Once the coast was clear, Matt pulled her in and hammered at the button to close the doors before anyone else stepped in. The elevator closed with a hushed thud and he yanked Shannon against him, unable to wait any longer. Her arms went around his neck while his hands grabbed her hips through her jacket and held her tight. His mouth moved hungrily over hers, urging the kiss deeper and deeper. With the wall at her back, he pressed himself against her and groaned in appreciation. She was the perfect height.

"I've wanted to get my hands on you again so badly that now that I can, I don't know where to start," he murmured.

"I don't care," Shannon said as her mouth sought out his. "Just touch me. Anywhere."

He gave a quick grin before his lips found her neck. "Oh, don't worry. I will."

The elevator stopped and the doors opened behind them. Matt walked them out, loving the intense look of desire in her eyes. He was going to enjoy making her scream.

Matt held the door for her and she brushed by, walking down the narrow hallway as she pulled off her jacket, her footsteps muffled by the thick charcoal carpeting. Shannon's gaze darted around, taking in the quiet elegance of the room and the marble fireplace surrounded by black leather chairs. "A fireplace? I didn't know they had those in hotel rooms."

"Then you haven't been staying in the right places." He tugged off his coat and tossed it on the couch. "Be right back." He stepped into the bedroom behind him before returning a second later.

Shannon placed her purse on the loveseat, looking everywhere but at him. He couldn't tell if she was nervous, and told himself to go slow, just in case, but that was probably going to be nearly impossible. When her gaze finally landed on him, the deep blue of her eyes notched up his hunger for her even more and he swore at that point he would do anything for her, give her anything. All she had to do was ask.

Shannon gave him a lazy smile and that was his opening. Matt reached out and cupped the nape of her neck, pulling her lips to his. He tried to take things nice and easy, his tongue teasing and toying with hers. But soon he urged up the pace, stealing breath-taking, drugging kisses from her like he needed them to breathe before backing off and fighting against the hot need pulsing through him, insisting he take her hard and fast. He couldn't have their first time together be a sprint to the finish line, even if his body was demanding just that.

Matt loved it when she had a wall at her back, pressing the entire length of her body against his, so he walked her backward. As he leaned into her, placing his palms flat on either side of her head, Shannon mewled into his mouth, and the sound nearly broke him.

He stopped and broke off the kiss. Taking a deep breath, he grappled to reign himself in, battling against the strong desire coursing through his blood warring at his fight for control. "I…I need a minute…"

"What's wrong?" Shannon asked and the worry was clear in her voice, most likely concerned he was now having second thoughts.

Matt stepped back enough in order to make eye contact with her. "No, no," he said quickly. "It's not that. God, it's not that. Please don't think it."

"Then what is it?"

"I just…I need to catch my breath," he told her. "I've wanted you for so god-damn long that I'm afraid I can't be gentle…or slow."

"I don't need you to be gentle. I just need you to touch me. Now. Please, Matt."

Any control he had snapped at her words. Matt had to touch her and he had to touch her everywhere. As his lips crashed back down on hers, his hands slid down her shoulders and made quick work on the buttons of her cream suit blazer. He jerked the jacket down, but not all the way off, locking Shannon's arms against her body. His fingers returned to tug at the small faux pearl buttons on her blush silk shirt, fighting the urge to rip the fragile fabric away while his mouth never left hers, continuing its almost punishing possession. When her blouse opened, Matt lost himself in the vision of her breasts swaddled in the silky cup of her bra. His mouth watered as he shoved the fabric down and sucked on the tight peak before rolling the bud with his tongue.

Shannon threw her head back and moaned, ratcheting up his need even more. Hot, heady desire surged, demanding he sink himself deep into her and take what he wanted, but he needed to be patient. He had to hear her scream his name before anything else.

She tugged at her jacket, trying to free her arms, but they remained trapped. Matt was inclined to leave her confined for the moment since once her hands fell on him, it was going to be over. Shannon jerked again before giving up with another throaty moan he felt deep in his gut.

His hands moved to her hips before reaching around to unzip her skirt. He let it fall to the floor and stepped back to take in the sight of her. She stood on long, shaky legs in nothing but her soft pink bra and matching bikini bottoms, with her arms locked at her side by her blazer and her back arched, offering her breasts out to him. Her cheeks and lips were the same blush color, her eyes smoldering, and her hair a messy tumble over her shoulders. At the end of her mile-long toned legs, she still had on her beige pumps with a gold toe, and Matt had never seen anything so sexy in his life.

"Jesus Christ, you're beautiful," Matt rasped before diving in again and claiming her mouth. His hands reached around to squeeze her behind as they ground against one another.

"Matt, help me out here," Shannon murmured.

He shook his head, his lips never leaving hers. "Not yet."

They kissed with reckless abandon and soon it was clear that reasoning was slipping away from them both. Shannon squirmed, trying desperately to wrap her legs around him. Needing skin-on-skin contact, Matt grabbed the neck of his sweater, shirt and T-shirt and yanked them all off in one tug over his head, before pulling her back to him.

His hands wound their way down again and yanked her panties aside. He skimmed through her slick folds, causing her to pant and him to clench his jaw at how wet she was. Matt took in a deep breath, the sharp scent of her want filling his nose, as he slid two fingers into her. Her eyes went blind and her mouth opened with a silent plea as she moved against his hand.

"That's it," he urged her. "Come for me."

Matt continued to thrust into her and stayed with her as she sailed up and over, moaning out his name before dropping her head to his shoulder. He couldn't recall ever seeing anything so incredibly arousing. He returned to her nipple and gently nipped, causing Shannon to jerk as he lightly blew on the tight bud.

"God, that was sexy as hell," he said.

She huffed out a laugh. "I'll take your word on that."

* * *

Shannon opened her eyes and almost stilled at the sight of him. He stood in front of her clothed only in jeans, which rode low on his hips revealing the dark blue band of his boxer briefs. She'd admired some nice chests in her life, but they all paled in comparison to Matt's. His shoulders were massive with strength, while his arms bulked and bulged with solid biceps and thick forearms. His chest, chiseled and carved, was model perfect and smooth, without a spec of hair except for a sparse dark trail starting at the bottom of his six-pack and disappearing into his pants. Her eyes widened when she realized the glistening tip of his erection was peeking out of the top of his underwear.

She lost her breath at the sight of him and somehow became even wetter. After the intensity of her orgasm, she was surprised to be so edgy again so soon, but simply looking at him, the massive size of him, had her desperately wanting—needing—him inside her.

Shannon tugged at her jacket harder, determined to release her hands and put them on him. "Matt, help a girl out here."

His lips twitched as he reached behind her. "I thought I already had," he said with a gravelly voice.

Freeing her arms, she wrapped them around his neck and pulled his mouth back to hers. His hands returned to her panties and pushed them down her legs. She stepped out of them and reached for his pants, her fingers brushing the head of his penis, spreading the beaded pearl of liquid, which pulled a groan out of him.

As Shannon unbuttoned his jeans, she murmured against his lips, "Please tell me you have a condom on you."

His hand stopped hers. "Grabbed one when I went into the bedroom." He reached into his pocket and revealed a square package.

"Oh, thank God," she said as she pulled him back to her. "Good thinking."

Shannon couldn't get enough of him. She needed him all over her, everywhere and anywhere. He was thoroughly seducing her with his mouth and hands, but soon their movements were jerky, unsteady, and they both craved more.

Matt shoved down his pants and boxers before ripping open the gold wrapper. A small flutter of panic quivered in her stomach at the sight of him sheathing himself, quietly taken aback by his size. She didn't have much time to wonder if they were going to have a problem fitting things when he grabbed her hips and started to hitch her up, and she suddenly had very different worries.

"Wrap your legs around me," he demanded.

"No!" Shannon tried to stand her ground. The last thing she wanted was an embarrassing reminder of her mammoth size as soon as Matt realized she was too tall for such maneuvers, making everything awkward as he strained to hold her.

"Come on," Matt repeated and, before she could stop him, lifted her as if she weighed as little as a feather. "Wrap them around me."

Shannon did as he said, although amazed he hadn't pulled something. The head of his impressive erection nudged her, and though a smidgen of worry still niggled at her, she didn't even try to hold off, too overwhelmed by her need.

Squeezing her legs against his sides, she shifted her hips downward, taking him within her, and her breath caught in her chest. His hands gripped her waist, trying to slow her.

"Jesus, Shannon," Matt hissed between clenched teeth. He tried to ease her back up, but seemed unable to resist as he pulled her down at the same time he thrust into her. Tremendous pressure filled her and she sucked in a breath, holding it until she loosened around him. He stilled, his chest heaving as he waited her out.

His head came up and the sharp blue of his eyes had darkened with lust. The lines of his face were tight and strained as he continued to hold himself off, giving her whatever time she needed. The recessed lighting from the ceiling cast them in a spotlight and highlighted the thin film of sweat glistening on his chest and shoulders.

Matt broke into a tight smile. "You're killing me, you know that, right?"

Shannon grinned in return, rocking her hips, and his smile dropped, replaced by a look of intense pleasure. "We wouldn't want that to happen now, would we?"

She didn't have time to react before Matt took over. With his fingers digging into her thighs, he plunged in and out of her without pause, the hard wall behind her colliding with her back. She was being thoroughly battered and it was wonderful.

His brows pinched and he held his bottom lip between his teeth as he concentrated on his task. Lifting his head, he trapped her in the power of his gaze, causing her to moan and push even closer to him. Releasing one hand from her hip, he pressed it against the wall as he widened his stance and leaned into her.

"You look so fucking hot," he rasped next to her ear. "You have no idea how much you turn me on."

His warm lips laid a soft kiss on her neck before gently nipping with his teeth. His hand slid down and found its way between them, his fingers teasing and stroking.

"Omigod, Matt. That feels so good," she groaned which startled her. Had she spoken aloud? She'd never been a talker and had no idea when she'd become one.

She must have because he rumbled deep in his chest as he picked up the pace. Shannon rolled her hips, meeting him thrust for thrust, and rocketed into the light rushing at her.

He responded with a low groan before stopping altogether and they both stilled, their chests heaving as they tried to catch their breaths and their racing hearts. Shannon dropped a leg from his hip and it hit the floor with a thud. She shoved her hair out of her face and turned toward him. Matt's throat moved when he swallowed as his gaze passed over her. He shook his head and lowered his lips to hers, giving her a light kiss.

"That was amazing," Matt said.

"I would agree," she replied with a satisfied grin.

He glanced down toward his feet. "I don't think I've ever had sex with my shoes on before."

A gurgle of laughter bubbled out of Shannon at seeing they both still had on their footwear. "I guess it would have taken too much time to take them off."

Matt kissed her again before he dropped her other leg to the floor and yanked up his pants. "Be right back."

She ogled his incredibly toned and muscular back until he disappeared around the corner. Using the wall behind her for support, she tried to stand, and though she wobbled, she remained upright. She leaned down to grab her discarded clothes, adjusted her bra back in place, and staggered to the nearest chair.

Sitting, Shannon removed her heels before pulling up her panties and skirt. Matt returned as she started to button up her blouse. He'd removed his shoes, but had left his jeans on unfastened. They hung loose around his waist, and simply looking at him had her mouth watering.

"Uh, what are you doing?" he asked.

"Putting myself back together," she answered.

"I see that, but why?" Matt stopped her hands and started to unbutton her shirt again.

"Matt," she protested weakly.

He leaned down to place light kisses along her jawline and down her neck. "Hmmm?"

"I need to go," she insisted, but her words lacked fight.

"And why is that? I'm not done with you yet," he said as he stood upright and took her hand with his.

Shannon let him pull her into the moonlit bedroom. He stopped just inside the doorway and cradled her face. His mouth came down softly to hers as he led them into a slow, ravishing kiss, sending shivers of desire racing through her again. Her toes curled into the plush carpet and she was instantly lost.

"Don't leave," Matt whispered against her cheek.

Unable to resist, Shannon shook her head before his mouth reclaimed hers.

She gave a small yelp and threw her arms around his neck when he bent down to pick her up, walking them over to the side of the large bed. "Matt, put me down. I'm too heavy."

He frowned at her. "Too heavy? What are you talking about? You don't weigh anything."

"If you hurt yourself so you can't play baseball, it isn't my fault," she told him. "I warned you."

Matt laughed. "I don't think you need to worry about that. You honestly are not heavy."

His muscles bulged as he walked them deeper into the room, but true to his word, he didn't seem to be straining or ready to burst a vessel, so she relaxed a bit, loving the feeling of being smaller, for once, and cherished. She gave another small squeal when he dropped her, the duvet cushioning her fall. He stood next to the bed, quickly shedding his pants.

Matt sank down next to her, reaching to remove her skirt and underwear again before tossing them onto the floor. Her skin warmed and tingled everywhere he stroked and his gaze fell. She let out a blissful sigh and wrapped her arms around his neck, pulling him down to her. His kisses started out soft and sweet, his movements slow and easy, but soon the flames between them burned high and hot.

Rising up on one elbow, Matt's gaze sought out hers. If her expression matched his, then they were doomed. Completely overwhelmed with lust, need and craving, his eyes burned so hot that, somehow without asking, Shannon understood he'd never felt something as strong as this before. Just as she never had.

"Shannon," was all he said as he twined his fingers on one hand with hers, resting them on the pillow above her head, and he didn't have to say anything more. She knew and she agreed.

CHAPTER 10

No matter how much Shannon tried to focus on the work in front of her, she couldn't stop her mind from wandering and replaying the night spent with Matt. To label it mind-blowing was the understatement of the century. Not taking into account her recent lack of exposure in such areas, she'd definitely never experienced anything on that level before and because of that, the one question that remained was how in the hell she was going to walk away.

When she'd left his hotel room that morning, they'd hadn't said much, only kissed and parted ways, but it was no doubt on both of their minds, especially now with Thanksgiving being only a few days away. Matt most likely had plans to head home, even though he hadn't mentioned anything, but it was fine. More than fine, actually. The separation was for the best, really. As much as she wanted to continue seeing him, any relationship with him was an impossibility. They lived in different states on pretty much opposite sides of the country and all of her time was dedicated to work. They'd spend more time apart than together. What relationship could survive that, especially one so new?

If he left soon to head back home to Arizona, that would be perfect. It would take the dirty work out of her hands. Matt would be home for the holidays and soon afterward, he'd head to Spring Training and back into baseball mode, which meant no extra time for him either. This was simply a fun, albeit short, fling, but it was time to move on and remember what their realities were before anyone got hurt.

Then why couldn't she friggin' concentrate on anything? Shannon glanced at the clock on her desk phone and sighed. Perhaps because it was almost four in the afternoon and she'd been going straight since arriving early that morning.

She stood and stretched right as her assistant called her. "Hot and dreamy is here for you."

Conflicting emotions surged through her. She wanted to smile and rush out to meet him as her skin flushed in memory of his touch, while at the same time annoyance and irritation nagged at how she'd given in, making everything a thousand times harder. It frustrated her that she had no willpower when it came to him. All he had to do was smile and she was through.

But she couldn't be rude and ignore him, so she pressed the intercom button. "Send him in."

A few seconds later, Matt walked in with a gym bag hanging over his shoulder.

"Hi." He leaned over her desk to give her a kiss. Shannon tried to resist, planned on only a chaste peck, but again failed and melted into him.

"Hi," she replied when he broke off.

Matt glanced at the scattered papers and folders. "Still working?"

"Yeah, trying to finish up some things with this one case."

"Are you close to being done for the day?"

"Um," she said with a frown. "Why?"

Rather than reply, Matt hitched his head toward the door. "Let's go."

"Again, why and where?"

"It's a surprise," he said with a wide grin.

"Matt," Shannon said in exasperation. "I can't. I have way too much to do and I'm behind as it is. I appreciate it, really I do, but—"

"Not going to let you say no," he interrupted, ignoring her irritation. "You need to get out of here for a bit. Work off some steam."

"Matt…" she repeated, a bit more sternly.

"Do this and I promise I'll let you work tonight afterward. Just take a break for a while…with me," he added with his lopsided grin as he moved in closer to her.

Unable to stop herself, and with a smile tugging at her lips, she gave in. She didn't know what this man had over her, making it so difficult to resist him.

"Fine," she said with a sigh. "Where are we going?" She walked over to her desk to turn off her computer and pack her work up to bring home with her.

He unzipped the bag he carried and pulled out a basketball. "You game?"

* * *

"I can't believe you're making me do this," Shannon complained as they walked into the gym where Matt had reserved a court for them.

"I told you I wanted to see your game. Come on, it'll be fun." Matt smacked her ass. "Go change and I'll meet you on the court."

Shannon rolled her eyes, but grinned at him and ducked into the women's locker room. She quickly changed into her workout gear they'd picked up at her place on the way.

She found Matt in the gym, practicing his shot. He'd removed his nylon workout pants to uncover black basketball shorts topped with a tight black T-shirt, both snug in all the right places. She tried not to stare, admiring how the muscles in his arms and legs rippled as he moved, but it was hard. He was magnificent to watch, even more so than when he was in his baseball uniform. This was much better.

Shannon pulled her hair into a ponytail, then reached down to the floor to stretch, enjoying the view. He dribbled around some more before she finally stood and walked into his field of vision with her hands held up, asking for the ball.

Matt stopped and stared. After a prolonged pause, it made her uncomfortable. "What?" she asked.

He cleared his throat as his gaze lingered on her legs. "Those shorts look amazing on you. I'm not sure I'm going to be able to concentrate."

She rolled her eyes despite being secretly pleased. "Just give me the ball."

He passed it to her and raised one brow when she hit nothing but net from the free throw line. "Nice."

Shannon shrugged as she attempted another, a jump shot this time. "A bit rusty," she claimed, even though that shot went through as well.

"Rusty, my ass," Matt laughed. "You haven't missed yet."

"Just luck," she said with a quick smile in his direction as she ran over to the point, shooting again.

When the ball dropped through, he grabbed the rebound before she could. "I think practice is over."

"Fine." She walked over to the top of the paint. "Check up."

"Well, I guess it's ladies first, huh?" he teased.

"Sounds good to me." She bounced the ball to him, which he returned. She hunched over as he did in defense, and planted her pivot foot. Her eyes stayed low as she tried to determine how she could drive toward the basket. His size was overwhelming, however, and once she committed in one direction or the other, he would be looming over her in an instant and she'd never get around him.

So, she did what she'd always done when faced with a bigger defender. Dribbling as she stepped back rather than forward, she went up and shot over his head. Despite being well behind the three-point line, the ball had the distance. Matt turned just as it swished through the net.

He dribbled the ball over to her with a big smile on his face. "That's how you're going to play it, huh?"

Shannon switched places with him. "I know my limitations, especially when the defender is twice my size."

He laughed, but then he was on the move. He, however, had no qualms about driving for the basket and she attempted one swipe, her fingers flying through air as he blew past her. He jumped for a layup, gently placing the ball in the hoop.

"Where's the defense?" he said with a playful smile.

"Yeah, I'm not getting in front of a Mack truck."

He walked up to her, and leaned down for a quick kiss before handing the ball over. "Probably smart."

The game continued and after a while, Shannon figured out that making Matt cut to his left slowed him a bit, giving her time to run past him. A few times, she managed to squeeze by and break to the net, but he finally discovered her move and grabbed her waist as she darted past.

"Hey!" she yelled as he spun her around. "That's not fair!"

"Are you going to call a foul?" Matt asked as he nuzzled her neck.

"Yes! Excessive use of hands," she cried while laughing.

"I'll show you excessive use of hands." He kissed her again and set her down.

Tied at nineteen and playing first to twenty, Matt was on offense and eyed her calmly as he stood at the top of the key, dribbling. Both of them were sweating and Shannon was more than tired, muscles screaming due to lack of use, but she hadn't had this much fun in a long time and wasn't going to let him win without a fight. He dribbled toward her, but then retreated when she reached out. He teased her back and forth a bit, before he spun to the right, as she'd been anticipating, and she knocked the ball out of his hands when he came out of his turn.

"Shit!" he exclaimed in surprise.

Chasing the basketball down, Shannon snagged it and raced toward the basket. Just as she went up for the layup, Matt grabbed her and pulled her against him, the ball dropping out of her hands and onto the floor. He held onto her as he moved them off the court.

"No way I'm going to let you beat me," he panted, out of breath.

She laughed as she tried to suck in air. "Sore loser."

"Damn right," he said as he lowered his lips to hers.

Pulling back from the kiss, Shannon eyed him. "The game is ending in a tie?"

"Yep, and I'm fine with that. In fact, I'm ready to get out of here and partake in some other forms of exercise."

Her arms went around his neck. "Oh yeah? What kind of exercise would that be? I'm pretty sweaty as it is."

"And you look sexy as hell, but I think I can muss up your hair some more." He pulled on her rubber band.

His mouth came back down on her and he kissed her thoroughly. Even though she had a ton of work to do, she couldn't say no, despite the lectures she'd been giving herself earlier in the day. In fact, she couldn't think of a better way to spend the rest of her evening, especially since he was going to be leaving soon. She'd never felt more alive and she was having fun. She'd worry about work later.

* * *

The next day, Matt stopped Shannon before she walked out the door of his hotel room. "Hey, before you leave, I want to talk to you about something."

Here's where he tells me he's heading home for Thanksgiving. Shannon glanced his way as she shoved her foot in her shoe. "What's up?"

"What are you doing for Thanksgiving?"

"Nothing," she replied haltingly.

"Nothing?" Matt repeated in surprise. "You're not going home?"

"Not this year, no. Since I was home for the wedding, I knew I wouldn't be able to get away again so soon."

"So, you'll be here, alone, for Thanksgiving?" he asked.

Shannon smiled up at him. "Yep. Don't worry. I'm a big girl. I'll be fine."

"I'm not worried. I'm just trying to figure out what we're going to do."

She frowned as she stood and pulled on her jacket. "We? What do you mean, we? Aren't you going back to Arizona?"

"Not yet," Matt said.

"Matt, you should go home. Be with your family. You don't need to waste your time here."

His expression darkened. "Why would I be wasting my time if I was here?"

"Well, I didn't mean…I don't…" Shannon stammered, taken aback by his sharp reaction. They were just having fun, right? "I only meant I know you don't get to see them a lot and I'm going to have to work, so…"

"You've got to have Thanksgiving. You can't not have it. Tell you what, give me a key to your apartment and I'll get everything."

"What?" she asked, thinking he'd clearly lost his mind. "Why would you do that?"

"Because I want to." Matt pulled her close. "I want to spend Thanksgiving with you."

Her heart melted and words failed her. *How do you decline such an invitation? You don't.* Despite the tug-of-war wrestling within her—with half of her insisting this wasn't a relationship and they couldn't be in one, while the other half told her to shut up and enjoy him—she was torn and didn't know what to do. So, she'd listen to the greedy, selfish half and continue seeing him. One day the fun would end and it would be hard when that day came, but she'd get past it. And if a little bit of her heart went with him, so be it. She'd have to live with it. Her life would return to normal, it just wasn't going to be today.

"Okay," she told him with a smile. "I can't wait."

* * *

After Thanksgiving, time flew. Matt stayed in Chicago, getting together with Shannon as much as he could. With her work schedule, that proved difficult and he didn't see her near as much as he wanted, but he did his best to remain patient and understanding. He really liked Shannon, enjoyed every minute he spent with her. He didn't even mind when she'd argued with him over pointless things. She made her opinion known, which he appreciated since so many girls only said what they thought he wanted to hear. She was confident and driven, and he respected her dedication to her job. She had a career and she wasn't looking to be taken care of, which he couldn't say about many of the girls he'd met. Of course, being with a woman who was as career-driven as he was definitely posed some different challenges in a relationship, ones he hadn't dealt with before, but he was willing to try. He was always willing to try.

Time, however, was winding down. The calendar was moving closer to Christmas and him heading home to Arizona. After which came Spring Training in Florida, and any free time of his would disappear. He tried not to stress over what to do next, figuring he'd think of some way to keep things going between them because he wasn't ready to let her go yet.

Spread out on the floor in front of the fireplace, he snuggled closer to her. She'd arrived after work, late as usual, haggard and tired, but her face had lit up as soon as she'd spotted how he'd pushed the furniture out of the way in order to enjoy a romantic dinner in front of the fire, making Matt foolishly proud of the gesture. Anything to put the sparkle in her eye and elicit her beaming grin, he would do. He wanted her happy all the time.

Per the usual, not long afterward, their clothes came off in a rush as if they hadn't seen each other in years. His need for her bordered on insatiable, causing him to worry about when they eventually went their separate ways. They still hadn't broached the subject of the "after" part of this relationship, if you could call what was between them that, and he kept putting the talk off because the outcome appeared bleak. But the discussion needed to happen sooner rather than later, and since Christmas was merely a week away, that meant soon. The pressure from his mother to get home was increasing and she'd stuck Kirby on him as well. He could ignore only so much before the pestering became unbearable.

It was the last thing he wanted to think about, however, as he pulled the naked body, still warm and vibrating from their lovemaking, of this incredibly sexy woman closer. The room was dark, the only light from the fire burning bright. He'd closed the drapes on the large picture windows, shutting them off from the rest of the world, forming a warm, cozy cocoon—one he didn't want to leave from—ever. But they had to face reality, whether they wanted to or not.

Before he drummed up the nerve, his cell phone buzzed on the table behind them. Figuring it was Kirby calling to ride him again about getting back to Arizona, he let the call go into voice mail. He snuggled tighter against Shannon when the buzzing started again.

"What the hell…" he muttered.

"Someone really wants to get a hold of you." Shannon glanced at him over her shoulder. "Maybe you should check to make sure it isn't an emergency or something."

"I'm going to kill whoever it is." Matt sat up and grabbed his phone off the table.

He checked the display and cold shock flashed over his skin before unease settled in his gut. Natalie's name stared right back at him. How in the hell had she'd gotten his new number?

Matt closed his eyes as anger flooded him. He was sick and tired of this. He didn't understand what her problem was, why she continuously pushed, but he was done. He hadn't been able to prove she'd been in Chicago before, but she'd now handed him the proof he needed to show direct violation of the personal protection order.

"Everything okay?" Shannon asked quietly.

He quickly turned off the ringer and tossed the phone down. "Oh, yeah. Sorry about that. No emergency."

She continued to study him and he could tell she didn't believe him. "Who was it?"

He lay back down next to her and kissed her neck. He should say something, but the last thing he wanted to do was scare her away when so much unsettled business remained between them. Once they worked it out, he would tell her everything.

"Just someone who doesn't know how to take no for an answer." He looked her in the eye. "I swear. It's no one important."

"Are you sure?"

A small swell of confidence filled him at hearing her concern, so he smiled. "Yes, I'm sure. There's nobody else besides you and me."

Shannon showed no reaction, remaining silent, and his confidence waned.

"What are you thinking?" Matt asked, needing to know what was going on in her head.

"I was thinking about what you said. About it being you and me…"

"And?" he pushed.

"Christmas is next week…" she started, but said nothing further.

Apparently, her thoughts were running along the same lines as his. The time had come to lay everything out. Matt took a deep breath and cursed the nerves clenching his stomach. Nervous wasn't part of his game and he definitely didn't need anxiety now. He had to be confident or else Shannon would trample all his arguments. It was what she did and did well.

"Are you going back to Michigan?" he asked her.

"No."

"No? How come?" Matt asked as he leaned in to brush her lips with his. He couldn't be around her and not want to kiss her, touch her.

"Work. What else do I have going on?" she said with a muffled chuckle.

He nodded his understanding before he cleared his throat. It was now or never. "Come with me, then."

Her eyes widened. "With you? What? To Arizona?"

"Yeah. Spend the holiday with me."

Shannon sat up, making them separate. She held her knees to her chest and stared at him with what looked like…he didn't know exactly. Fear? "I can't go with you."

Matt sat up too, always making sure to keep his hands on her in some way. He refused to her let build up a wall between them. "I don't see why not. You said yourself that you weren't going home. Come with me. You can relax, see the sun and we can spend some more time together. You can work there."

Heavy silence lingered for a long time as she studied his face, before she slowly tried to edge away from him. "I can't. We can't. We can't keep doing this."

Crap. "Because?"

"You know why. I'm here with my job, and you're in Arizona, then Florida and then Michigan and then all over the place. When would we ever see each other? How would a long distance relationship like that even work?" She shook her head as she answered her own questions. "It wouldn't because I could never get away. You've seen how hard it's been now and you've been in the same city as me. It wouldn't be fair to either of us."

"I know. Believe me I know all of this. I've told myself the same thing, numerous times, but I keep coming back to one thing."

"What?"

"I like you, Shannon. I really like you and I have a great time with you. Tell me you don't feel the same way."

She hesitated, denial almost falling out of her mouth, but she stopped, probably sensing he would recognize the lie. She closed her eyes and gave in. "I do."

At that little crack, he continued to push. "I couldn't live with myself if we didn't at least try. The last thing I want to do is walk away from this and wonder my whole life what would have happened if only we'd tried. I refuse to live with regret."

"Matt—" Shannon started, but he wouldn't let her finish.

"Is that what you want? To wonder? Wonder if perhaps we *could* have found a way to make us work?"

"I course I don't want to," she said as she averted her eyes down. "I just have no idea how."

"We do whatever we can. That's all. But it will only work if we both want it to work. If we both want to try."

Shannon took in a deep breath and seemed to deflate. "No matter what I say, I'm the bad guy in this. If I say no, it sounds like I don't want to try, when that's not true. If I say yes, then it's like I'm giving up on my dreams and myself. Either way, I can't see a way to make this work."

"If you want this, then we'll find a way. You don't have to give up anything. Thankfully, my job gives me enough money to do what I want and I'll fly out here whenever I can. If you don't want to go to Arizona now, then I'll go and come back here after Christmas."

She glanced up in surprise. "You'd do that?"

"Of course I would." Matt cupped the back of her neck. "I feel that strongly about this that I'm willing to do anything. Anything, Shannon."

* * *

Shannon let Matt pull her into his arms because she loved their strength and warmth as they cradled and sheltered her. She'd known each time she continued to see him that breaking away at the end became that much harder. Even now, she swayed toward him and all he promised. She longed for two very different things—she wanted her career, she wanted to make partner and she wanted to be successful, but she also wanted this man in her life more than she'd ever wanted anyone. To have one meant she couldn't have the other—not completely at least—yet she couldn't turn away on either. She had to pick one, but she wasn't ready to do that yet.

She pulled back and Matt studied her with wary eyes, waiting on her decision. "Have you taken anyone down to meet your family before?"

Alarm replaced the wariness before clearing. He hesitated before he simply sighed. "No."

"No?"

"No, I've never taken anyone home to meet them. The last girl they met was a girl I was serious about in college."

"Matt," Shannon said with a huff. "Don't you think they'll wonder about us? Make some assumptions?"

"Don't worry about them. I'll handle them, I promise. They won't make things uncomfortable."

Shannon took a deep breath and even though her brain still struggled to puzzle out the right answer, her heart knew before anything else. She wanted to go to Arizona with him and she wanted more time with him, and foolishly enough, she was quite possibly falling for him. Maybe they could somehow get the impossible to work, although she had no idea how.

"Okay," she finally said and didn't miss his huge grin.

"Seriously?"

"Yes, seriously."

Matt yanked her into his lap and covered her mouth with his. When he finally broke away, he was still grinning at her. "I know you're worried, but we'll figure it out. Everything will work out."

Shannon nodded and gave him a small smile, but it fell short. She tried to swallow past the tight lump in her throat, worried she'd just given up all of her dreams. But at the moment, she couldn't find the will to care. She didn't want to give him up. Not anytime soon, maybe not ever.

CHAPTER 11

As the plane started its descent into the desert, the dormant butterflies in Shannon's stomach awakened and took flight. She'd manage not to fret the entire trip, but now the nerves were unavoidable. Why she'd agreed to visit during Christmas was beyond her. The timing in itself presented unrealistic expectations of her, as well as incorrect assumptions about her and Matt, especially with his family, but here she was. Why? She had no idea. Really, she had no clue. For someone who insisted her career was the top priority of her life, her actions lately indicated the direct opposite. Reality was, despite their agreement to try, a successful relationship between her and Matt was unattainable—he wasn't going to stop playing baseball or ask for a trade from Detroit to Chicago, and she wasn't going to quit her job…if she still had one after this trip.

Her approved request for time off hadn't come without discussion, despite it being over the Christmas holiday when many of their clients were off too. Carol commented that for a junior associate, Shannon sure spent a lot of time away from the office. Shannon assured Carol she would continue to bill hours despite being away, but she'd heeded the message loud and clear—she needed to stop slacking off. This would be her final warning and any signs she wasn't measuring up, she'd be shown out, which was exactly why she'd have to tighten the bootstraps after New Year's, when she returned to Chicago, and put her nose to the grindstone. Nothing else could come between her and work, including Matt.

It wasn't his fault she couldn't say no to him. It wasn't his fault she couldn't get enough of him. No, it was her fault for opening the door in the first place and consequently not being able to control herself, which meant she needed to put some distance between them. After New Year, Matt and Shannon would be no more—although he didn't know that yet.

It was unfair of her to be making these types of plans without discussing them with him, especially since she'd promised she'd try, but even if they tried, they would never work, the differences in their lives being too big for them to succeed as a couple. Their circumstances remained fixed, so why go through the pain of trying and failing if you already know the outcome?

She glanced at him out of the corner of her eye. Relaxed and so handsome as he rested his head against the seat with his eyes closed. He wasn't sleeping, but she took the time to study him unnoticed. She really didn't deserve him. He had his moments where his ego peeked out, and she couldn't blame him when he constantly received praise and accolades as a remarkable ballplayer as well as worship and adoration as a gorgeous man. To his credit, he still somehow remained well-grounded with his priorities straight and considering family to be of the upmost importance.

Which is why he shouldn't waste his time with me. A family didn't wait at the end of the road for them. She had no time to be a girlfriend, let alone a wife and a mother.

Yet here she sat on a plane about to touch down, and his family awaited them. Waited with expectations already set high for her and Matt, and they would crumble as soon as she left. She was a horrible, selfish person, but she couldn't stop herself.

The plane thudded as the tires touched the ground, then the pilots taxied toward the gate. Matt's eyes opened and he turned his head as he grabbed her hand.

"You ready?" he said with a twinkle in his eye.

"As I'll ever be," Shannon replied with a smile she hoped didn't reveal the nerves fluttering inside.

She hadn't succeeded, apparently, since his hand squeezed hers. "Don't worry. It will just be Caitlyn picking us up. I won't throw everyone at you at once."

"Gee, thanks," she said as the plane came to a stop and everyone stood.

They walked through the airport and collected their luggage before stepping outside. The simple pleasure of being outdoors in December and not having to bundle up under multiple layers delighted her as she paused to take it all in. The sun shone brightly, warming the air into the seventies, and Shannon's mood immediately lightened.

"Okay," she said as she took in a deep breath of the sweet air, savoring the comfortable temperatures. "Now I understand what you meant about getting away from the cold."

Matt let out a low rumble of laughter. "I told you. I don't know how you guys live in that crap." He looked around and then hitched his head. "She's over there."

Shannon glanced down the line of cars waiting and spotted a large black SUV. A small woman stood on the sidewalk, and a big furry golden head emerged out of the backseat window. When the dog recognized Matt, it gave a friendly bark, its ears raised and tongue lolled out.

"I take it that's Buddy," Shannon asked with a small laugh. Matt had filled her in about his dog back home.

"The one and only," Matt said with a proud grin before jogging the remainder of the way.

Matt ditched the bags before opening the door, and dropped down to his knees when Buddy launched himself. His tail wagged a mile a minute as his body wiggled and he turned in excited circles, making Shannon dizzy. Matt tried to calm him down enough so he could pet him, but soon Matt fell on his butt and laughed as Buddy continued to throw his weight around.

Shannon laughed, taking in the true scene of a boy, in the body of a man, and his best friend. Buddy was no small dog, but he still managed to tackle a six-foot-five, two-hundred-and-twenty-five-pound man. Buddy finally noticed other humans existed beside Matt and trotted over to greet Shannon.

She knelt down and gave his head a scratch. "Hi, Buddy. It's nice to meet you."

He licked her hand before running back over to Matt, who was brushing off the seat of his pants. Shannon laughed. "I guess you're the only one who matters at this point."

"Matt is his world," the petite brunette said. "When they're together they're inseparable—everywhere."

"You're just jealous because you don't have a best buddy. Isn't that right, Buddy?" Matt cooed as he rubbed the dog's head and ears. "Caitlyn, Shannon. Shannon, Caitlyn."

Shannon held out her hand and resisted the urge to kneel slightly. Since Matt was so big, his sister's tiny stature surprised her and made her feel like a giant. "It's nice to meet you."

Caitlyn gave her a small smile. "You too."

Matt rounded the car to load their luggage into the back as Buddy jumped into the backseat. "Go ahead and get in front with Caitlyn."

"Oh," she said as she glanced at him. "Wouldn't you be more comfortable in the front?"

Caitlyn snorted as she walked over to the driver's side. "He wants quality bonding time with Buddy."

Matt shrugged with an embarrassed smile when Shannon raised a brow for confirmation, and she laughed.

Caitlyn pulled onto the freeway and set the cruise before glancing in the rearview mirror at Matt. "Mom wants you to come to dinner tonight."

"I figured as much," Matt said. "We'll get settled in and head over later. Tell her we'll be there around six or so."

"She's been making quite a fuss about you not being around," Caitlyn told him and Shannon tried not to listen.

"I know. I told her why though," Matt said.

"Did you?" Caitlyn asked and even Shannon couldn't overlook the insinuation behind the comment. They were just as surprised about her as she was to be there.

Matt was unfazed though. "Yep, I did," he insisted and said nothing more.

Trying to ignore the awkward tension because of her, Shannon peered out the car window and admired the big red rock mountains lining the horizon. Saguaros dotted the landscape; some tall with five arms, which made her wonder at all the changes that had transpired over the past hundred years or more. For as far as she could see, it was mostly only flat with brown dirt, but it was in such contrast to the landscape surrounding her on a daily basis, that she appreciated the desert's unique beauty. The majestic mountains impressed and awed her the most and she said as much.

"I'll take you up to them while we're here," Matt replied. "There are some places with great view points, like Mt. Lemmon."

Shannon continued to watch the flat land pass them by until Caitlyn pulled off the freeway, heading straight into the mountains. "You guys live in the mountains?"

"In the foothills of the Catalina's," Matt answered. "We're in a town called Oro Valley."

Shannon rode the rest of the way in silence, but when Caitlyn turned into a neighborhood and Shannon caught a glimpse of the guarded gate and then the first house as they passed through, she let out a gasp. "You live in here?"

"Yep," Matt answered as he started to gather their things.

"So does Jason," Caitlyn informed her.

"Oh," Shannon said, still in shock at the sheer size of the houses. "Seems like a lot of house for two single guys."

"Oh, no. We don't live together. He has his own place. It's right there as a matter of fact." He pointed at a large contemporary house built with pale gray adobe intermixed with a variety of charcoal stones on its sharp angles and dramatic lines.

Shannon quickly forgot about Jason's spectacular abode when Caitlyn pulled into the paved driveway of Matt's home. She simply stared out the car window at the gorgeous, grand house finished in reddish-brown adobe with river rock turrets. Multiple tall windows lined the house to the right of the front door, handsomely framed by one of the turrets, while a three-car garage covered in stone swung down the driveway.

Shannon slowly opened her car door. She hadn't been sure what to expect, but this certainly wasn't it. Buddy rushed past her, happy to be home, as he followed a path around the house and into the backyard.

Matt walked by her with their luggage and nodded toward the garage door Caitlyn had opened. "Come on. I'll give you the tour."

Caitlyn followed behind Matt, leaving Shannon turning in a circle on the driveway. Out of her element, she gave herself a moment for her brain to process this new information. Her family had never wanted for anything, but they definitely hadn't lived in this luxury. Matt made a good living as a ballplayer, but she wondered if his family had wealth to begin with.

Shannon walked through the backdoor and into a large gourmet kitchen with tan stone floors, a massive center island finished in the same mahogany as the cupboards and burnt reddish granite capping the countertops. The appliances sparkled and glistened under the bright kitchen lights, making her wonder if they'd ever been used.

Shannon trailed Matt as he showed her around, the place resembling a model home more than one lived in. Everything appeared picture perfect without a speck of dust. Apparently, Matt had even trained Buddy to shed outdoors as Shannon didn't see one strand of blond dog hair.

When he finally walked into the master bedroom, which actually had a sitting room, she felt she'd seen it all. In the middle of the room sat a king-sized dark wood four-poster bed facing a fireplace situated in the opposite wall encased by black marble. At the far end, French doors opened out to a private patio overlooking a pool and the spectacular view of the mountain range in the background.

Shannon stopped at the doors. "This is beautiful. You weren't kidding when you said you were all about the views."

"I told you, there's nothing better than a great view out your own private window." Matt stopped next to her. "I never get tired of it. I don't know how you guys deal with all that flatness."

"We have a lot of water," she said giving him a side-glance.

"Ah, yes. That we don't have," he agreed with a smile.

Shannon strolled over to the shelves lining both sides of the fireplace to study all the awards and knickknacks on display. In the middle of huge silver bats, golden gloves and large plaques sat multiple baseballs and wood bats, some with writing on them and some not. She inspected each one, but didn't touch in case they held value other than personal.

Matt walked over to her. "Checking out my stuff?"

"What's all this?" she asked.

Pointing to the large silver bats, he said, "Those are Silver Slugger awards. They give those to best offensive player at each position."

"You have four," she pointed out.

"Yes," he answered with a shy grin.

She counted the gold gloves. "And seven Golden Gloves?"

"Best defensive player at each position."

"And you've won for catcher seven times."

He nodded.

"Are you uncomfortable?" Shannon asked with a teasing smile.

He shrugged and shoved his hands in his pockets. "I don't know. I don't want to sound like I'm telling you how awesome I am or something because, you know…" He stopped and lifted his large shoulders again.

"But don't these do that for you?" She waved her hand at them. "I mean, I'm assuming you don't award these to yourself, and your teammates or whomever voted for you. So, not to stroke your ego or anything, but essentially they say that you are. Right?"

"I guess," Matt mumbled and his cheeks reddened a bit.

She pointed to a large octagonal plaque. "What's that one?"

He cleared his throat. "American League MVP."

"Look at you. Most valuable player," she teased.

"Okay, stop. You're embarrassing me." Matt pulled her to him and looped his arms around her waist.

"Why? You should be proud of all this."

"I am, but just not someone pointing out each one and counting them."

"What's that one up there?"

He sighed. "MVP in the All-Star game."

Shannon eyed him over her shoulder. "How many All-Star games have you played in?"

"Uh." His eyes rolled up to the ceiling, counting in his head. "Six, I think."

Her lips twisted. "Baseball stud."

He grinned with a huff of laughter, but still reddened.

"What are those? Autographs of your favorite players or something?" she asked.

"Some of them are. Some have more personal meaning."

"Like?"

"Like…that bat up there." He indicated one in a case on the top shelf. "That was the first wood bat my dad got me." A couple shelves down, he nodded at a ball in a case. "That was my first home run ball in the pros."

"What's that one up there?" Shannon pointed to another one on a high shelf.

"That was the first one I hit off a tee," he said with a soft laugh.

She laughed with him. "That must have been something to see."

"I ran around the bases like an idiot. In my head, I looked like all the big leaguers who hit a walk-off for the win, but really, I just looked like an idiot. It wasn't even really a true home run. I just ran faster than the kids trying to field and they kept dropping the ball, but my mom still asked for the ball. The coaches weren't too happy about it, but my mom promised to buy a replacement."

"Aw. I'm sure you were adorable."

He shook his head. "Nah, I was obnoxious."

Matt turned her, and she placed her arms around him as she smiled up at him. "All little boys are obnoxious."

"Just little boys?" he asked with an arched brow.

"Well, there are those men who are still," she said as she leaned in to touch her lips softly to his. "But you don't qualify."

"Good to know," he murmured, his voice a low rumble. He pressed his lips to hers and kissed her languidly, but thoroughly. When he pulled back, warmth flushed her skin from head to toes.

"As much as I would like to continue the rest of the tour, which includes a personal demonstration of my bed, Caitlyn is still sitting in the other room."

"Yeah, I don't think she'd be up for that part of the tour," Shannon joked.

"Stop," Matt said as he stepped away with a shudder. "Do not include my sister and sex in the same conversation, even joking."

She chuckled as he walked out of the bedroom. Looking around again, she sighed. She sincerely hoped walking away was going to be possible at the end of the trip. If someone asked her right now, however, she wasn't so sure, which petrified her as she stressed over the choices she'd made. In fact, she had the terrifying thought she absolutely didn't know who she was anymore and that scared her the most.

* * *

Matt pulled into his parents' driveway and shut off the engine to his truck.

"You ready?" he asked Shannon as he squeezed her knee.

She took a deep breath as she studied the house in front of her. She swallowed again, he guessed in an attempt to steady her nerves, when Buddy popped out between the seats and snuffed her ear.

Shannon squirmed away with a giggle, which made him smile. "He's invited inside as well?"

"Of course," Matt said with a playful scowl. "Buddy and I go everywhere together."

Shaking her head, Shannon grabbed for the door handle. "Okay, let's do this."

Matt met her at the front of the car and took her hand in his, noting the clamminess of her palm. He understood the reason behind her nervousness and wished he could somehow help her relax and not worry. He gave her a squeeze. "It's going to be okay. Totally casual."

She nodded and tried to smile bravely, but failed. Buddy trotted up to the porch and waited patiently for Matt to open the front door. Another dog raced toward them, tail wagging eagerly, as they stepped in.

"Buddy's sister, Sadie."

"Ah." Shannon eyed Buddy and Sadie as they danced around each other in excitement before running off into another room.

"Well, if Buddy is here, then I have to guess he brought my son with him," his mom said as she rounded the corner. She threw her arms open and went up on her toes. "There you are! I've missed you!"

Matt leaned down and gathered her small frame against his. After holding Shannon so much lately, he'd forgotten how tiny she was and gentled his hold, not wanting to crush her.

"You cut your hair. It looks good."

"And you've gotten bigger, somehow," she said as her arms gave another tight squeeze before stepping back. Her deep brown eyes lighted on Shannon and she smiled as she held out her hand.

"Hi, you must be Shannon. It's so nice to meet you," she said.

Shannon smiled. "Thank you. It's nice to meet you as well, Mrs. Buck."

"Oh, please. Call me Lisa."

Matt glanced up when his dad entered the room with Caitlyn behind him.

"Hey, Dad." Matt gave his father a quick hug. His father stood almost as tall as Matt did, but his frame seemed thinner. "You losing weight on me?"

"Just getting old," his dad answered with a wry smile. "Hair is gray now too."

"Dad, this is Shannon," Matt said as he held out his hand toward her. "Shannon, this is my father, Michael Buck."

"Shannon. My pleasure," his dad said.

"Thank you and the same." Shannon nodded at Caitlyn. "Hi again."

Caitlyn smiled as the door opened behind them and Jason stepped in.

"Whoa! Everybody's waiting for me," he said.

Matt chuckled. "Waiting on pins and needles, bud." He leaned around Shannon to give Jason a one-armed hug. "How you doing, man?"

"It's about time you got here." Jason slapped his back and then turned to hug both of Matt's parents. "Hi, Mom. Dad."

Shannon gave a puzzled frown at Jason's familiarity with his parents, reminding Matt he needed to fill her in on Jason's story, but he'd save that for another day. After Jason had given Caitlyn a quick squeeze, he turned to Shannon and gave her a swift study. His friend's eyes brightened in obvious approval before his gaze perused down her long legs. Jason was a huge flirt and so Matt knew exactly where his thoughts went. When Matt caught Jason's attention, he didn't hesitate to give him a silent warning, which Jason acknowledged with a big grin.

"Jason, this is Shannon. Shannon, Jason," Matt said.

Jason gave her his most charming smile. "It's really nice to meet you. I've been hearing so much from Matt about you."

"Really?" Shannon asked.

"No, not at all," Jason said with a laugh. "Matt's been strangely quiet about you and I'm starting to wonder why."

"All right, all right, all right," Matt said, stopping the conversation before Jason said any more. The evening was going to provide Jason ample opportunity to embarrass him in front of Shannon, and he didn't need the ribbing to start right off the bat. He put his hand on Shannon's back to steer her toward the dining room. "Please tell me dinner is ready, Mom. I'm starved."

"Of course it is," she said as she led them to the table. "I know how your and Jason's appetites work." She glanced over at Shannon. "When they were both growing up, I swear there was never enough food in the house. I would go to the grocery store almost every day."

Shannon smiled as she sat down. "I didn't realize Jason lived here with you guys."

Matt's entire family turned to him in surprise. "What? I'm sorry I don't spend all my time talking about that asshole."

"Matthew, language," his mother chided.

"No problem. I understand you don't want her to be more interested in me than you." Jason turned to Shannon. "That happens. A lot."

"Yeah, that's definitely it," Matt said dryly.

"Well, since he didn't tell you, I will." Jason sat down across from Shannon. "I grew up here. These guys took me in when my father died and my mother didn't care anymore."

"I'm sorry to hear that," Shannon said, her eyes softening with sympathy.

Jason shrugged. "I'm not. My life is definitely a helluva lot better because of it."

"He and I played on the same little league team, which is how I got to know him. He was a walk-on." Matt glanced at Jason and the two started to laugh.

"What does that mean? What's so funny?" Shannon asked.

"It means one day Jason walked by the park where we played, and a ball was hit toward him in the outfield," Matt told her as the scene replayed in his head. It was something he would never forget. "One of the coaches asked Jason to roll the ball back onto the grass so one of us could pick it up. But Jason, the showoff that he is, picked up the ball and threw a strike all the way into the infield with a beautiful throw. The coaches' jaws dropped, and they immediately asked him to join the team. When he didn't have the money, my mom forked it over. She knows a good arm when she sees one."

"I sure do," she said with a smile at her boys. "Even though we didn't know it, Jason became my son that day and I've never regretted it."

"Aw, shucks. You're embarrassing me, Mom." Jason winked at her. "Just don't tell Shannon what you told me the other day."

"What's that, sweetheart?" Lisa asked.

"That you wished I was your real son instead of that big oaf down there." Jason pointed at Matt.

"I don't," Caitlyn disagreed in a quiet voice and the table stopped laughing.

"Why's that?" Jason asked her.

Her face flamed when she realized she'd spoken aloud. "Why what?"

"Why don't you wish I was your brother instead of Matty?"

"I would have preferred a sister," she said quickly and slouched in her chair, trying to get away from the attention.

Jason collected a handful of his curly hair at his neck. "You can do my hair."

"Oh, jeez." Matt's mom waved a hand at them. "Let's eat and not do hair, please."

Everyone dug in and after a few minutes, Matt's father glanced up and cleared his throat. "Shannon, what is it that you do?"

"I'm a lawyer. I work for a firm in Chicago."

Both of his parents' eyebrows raised before slanting their eyes toward him. He knew they were wondering how he could be with someone who lived in Chicago and in a line of work that provided no free time, but he kept his face neutral.

"What type of law?" his father asked.

"Corporate."

"You must be extremely busy, then," his mother said.

"Yes, I am," Shannon agreed. "But I was able to catch a little break and get away for a bit. After the holidays, however, I'm sure things will pick right back up and I'll be back to having no life."

Matt fought to keep his comments to himself, but he didn't miss his dad's sharp scrutiny. He expected to be cornered later and questioned about his expectations with Shannon, since his dad understood firsthand the time commitment required with a firm expecting you to bill over two thousand hours a year—and it wasn't as if Matt had been quiet about his desire to settle down and start a family.

"Matt says you're in law as well," Shannon said to his dad. "What do you practice?"

"General for the most part, but I do a lot of civil litigation. I have my own firm with two partners and I recently took on two more in order to handle the workload. I did the big firm thing for a bit, but it took too much away from the family."

"Yes, it would be hard to balance both. Can I ask you, though, do you regret it?"

"Getting out and starting my own firm?" his dad asked, and when Shannon nodded, he shook his head. "Not at all. I had to choose between my career and my family. I chose my family. I had missed so much early on that I couldn't get back and I didn't want to regret it at the end. I was lucky I was able to get a lot of referrals, build up my client base fairly quickly, and have more control over my time and schedule, and over time it all worked out."

Shannon took a moment to process what his father had said. Matt hoped she was thinking perhaps she could do the same thing, but when she spoke again, her words crushed his wish.

"I never considered doing the private thing. I've always wanted to be a partner in a big firm, so I've prepared myself for the sacrifices I'll have to make in order to do so."

"There will definitely be lots of those," his dad said.

Matt caught his mother's eye and he saw the questions behind them. He smiled, trying to feign indifference, but she wasn't buying it. As much as he wanted to believe Shannon wouldn't bail on them once her visit ended, his confidence was fading. She didn't sound like someone considering trying to make a relationship work with her career. In fact, she sounded like someone who couldn't wait to get right back to it.

He tried not to be frustrated. His eyes had been wide open when he'd asked for this, but still, he resented she wasn't even trying. When his dad mentioned not wanting to have any regrets, he'd hoped the conviction resonated with her, but she appeared to have glossed right over it.

With dinner complete, Matt and Jason remained at the table while everyone else helped to clean up in the kitchen.

"I like her," Jason told Matt in a low voice.

"I like her too," Matt responded. "I just don't know how it's going to work. That's the bitch."

"Yeah, she does seem extremely career-driven, which is surprising to me."

"What do you mean?" Matt asked.

Jason shrugged. "You want a family, Matt. It's no secret. Everyone knows that. I don't see how you're going to get that out of her. At least not right away."

"We don't need to get ahead of ourselves," Matt said. "We just started seeing each other."

Jason tilted his head and gave Matt a scowl. "Don't try to pull that on me. I know you've been thinking about it. It's how you work. It just seems like you've put yourself in a no-win situation and I can understand why. She's beautiful and she seems perfect for you, except her career. I don't want to see you get the short end of the stick again, bud."

"I know, I know," Matt agreed. "I have to try, you know?"

"Did you tell her about Natalie?"

Matt shook his head. "No, not yet. I haven't had the chance to dump that bit of fun information on her."

"Matt," Jason hissed, his voice laced with exasperation. "You have to tell her. She has to know what's going on in the background."

Matt scratched at his hair in frustration. "I know and you're right. With everything being so unsettled between us, I didn't want to throw that at her. That will definitely cause her to run."

"Then she fucking runs," he said. "At least you know where you stand with her."

"What are you guys whispering about?" Shannon asked as she walked back in.

Jason stood and smiled at her. "I was telling Matt what a lucky son of a bitch he is."

Shannon's cheeks blushed a pretty pink. Matt pulled her to his side and pressed his lips to her temple. "Damn right I am."

"Don't mess it up or I'll be there to pick her up," Jason said with a smirk as he walked into the kitchen.

Matt leaned down to give her a kiss. "I don't plan on it."

CHAPTER 12

Shannon walked into the master bedroom after they'd returned from dinner and sat on the edge of the bed, toeing off her shoes. She liked the Bucks—really liked them. A close-knit and supportive family, they cared about each other and didn't hesitate to say as much.

The story of how Matt's parents had taken in Jason was heartwarming and reminded her that there were still people in the world who cared about others. One day Shannon wanted to do pro bono work for those who needed someone to speak for them, but didn't have the necessary funds. With her current schedule and lack of free time to volunteer, however, it wouldn't be any time soon and would most likely have to wait until after she retired since she didn't think Bickles, Bickles and Barnes would be too keen with her taking side work.

Shannon couldn't say enough about Matt's parents. His mother obviously loved her children and thrived on having them all back together in the house. Matt's father reminded her a bit of her own, very driven with a passion for law, but the resemblance ended there. He didn't mind talking shop, but would much rather discuss the events happening in his kid's lives. Making the shift in order to balance his career with his family had worked for him, and she respected the decision he'd made.

The dynamic between Caitlyn and Jason was intriguing. Jason treated her like a little sister, but Shannon swore she'd caught him occasionally stealing glances at Caitlyn, his brown eyes warming considerably in what appeared to be attraction. Even though Caitlyn had managed to remove her foot from her mouth, she'd been clearly embarrassed at having spoken aloud and Shannon was pretty sure a preference for a sister wasn't what Caitlyn had really meant. Interesting.

But, as much as she liked them all, she wasn't going to be a popular person within the family after the holidays. Shannon hadn't missed the quick glances thrown Matt's way when she'd discussed her career, but having everything out on the table now would save a lot of shock, heartache and surprise in the end for everybody.

Spotting a large photograph hanging on the wall over the bed, Shannon walked over to get a closer look. The picture captured the sun coming up over a mountain range, throwing the sky into a riot of different shades of pinks, yellows and oranges. The cactuses in the foreground glowed an electric green against the reddish brown mountains muted by the brilliant colors surrounding them. It was a magnificent photograph.

When Matt walked in after letting Buddy outside one last time for the night, Shannon said, "This is a great photo. Where did you get it?"

"It's Caitlyn's," he answered.

"What do you mean?"

"She took it. She's a photographer."

Impressed, Shannon turned back to the photo. "Wow! She's really talented."

"Yeah, we all keep telling her she needs to open her own gallery and sell her work, but she keeps shying away from doing it for some reason."

"She definitely should," Shannon agreed as she studied it again. "She has an amazing eye."

Matt pulled her into his arms. "I think tonight went well, don't you think?"

"Of course, how could it not? Your family is awesome."

He smiled. "Thanks. I can tell they liked you too."

She tried to ignore the guilt his comment elicited. "Jason certainly did," she joked.

Matt laughed. "He's an idiot. It's best just to ignore him and not encourage him." He gave her a gentle kiss. "I know you were nervous when we got there, so I appreciate you dealing."

She shrugged. "It was inevitable coming down here."

Matt nuzzled her neck, his lips paving a warm trail down. "I'm glad you're here. I like having you in my house and I especially like having you in my bedroom."

She smiled as she pulled him closer. "Oh yeah? And why's that?"

He glanced toward the big bed beckoning them and gave a slight shrug. "I can think of a reason or two."

"And what would be the other reason?"

"Did you happen to see the Jacuzzi tub I have? It's quite nice." He took her hand in his to lead her into the bathroom.

"I did happen to see that before as well as your astronomically sized bathroom."

She leaned against one of the sinks lining the wall next to the bathtub as he set the plug before starting the water. Picking up a remote, he flicked on the see-through fireplace. Fire blazed up instantly, dressing the room in a soft glow when Matt dimmed the lights.

"Why are you still dressed?" Matt asked as he came back over to her.

"I'm just watching you and all of your toys."

"Toys?" He reached out to pull her shirt over her head. "I haven't even gotten started on the toys."

"Okay, okay," Shannon chuckled. "We can keep those safely tucked away for now."

She removed his T-shirt and ran her fingers over the dips and curves of his perfectly chiseled chest. Placing her palms flat, she marveled at his rock-like physique. Glancing up, she found his blue eyes hot on her. Matt ducked down, taking her mouth with his as his large hands cradled her head, his tongue pushing through to tangle with hers.

The steam rising from the tub heated her already flushed skin and added to the pleasant sensation of being cocooned within a bubble of warmth. She leaned back, letting his soft lips trail down her neck, suckling and nibbling as he unbuttoned her pants and tugged them down along with her underwear. He unlatched her bra and let it fall to the counter before stepping back to shed his jeans and boxers. Simply the sight of him standing before her completely naked had her knees going weak and her mouth going dry.

"Come on." Matt pulled her to the Jacuzzi and held her hand as she stepped in. He hit another button and multiple jets came on as she sank down into the soothing water.

She settled back, a padded headrest supporting her head, and closed her eyes. "Oh, man. This is nice."

"The view's nice too," he said from where he sat across from her.

Shannon caught him staring at her breasts where they floated just above the waterline. "Perv," she said with a laugh and a light splash in his direction.

He gave her his megawatt smile as he moved toward her. "If enjoying the sight of a beautiful woman naked in my bathtub makes me a perv, then my name is Matt and I'm a perv."

Pulling her onto his lap so she straddled his hips, his lips found hers again. Their skin, slick from the water, moved across each other with a slippery friction. She rocked her hips, drawing a sharp inhale from him before he tightened his grip, urgency replacing the slow and languid seduction he'd started.

Shannon let herself sink into him as his hands explored her shoulders, down her spine and into dips of the small of her back before settling on her ass and grabbing a handful to urge her against him. The intensity of his desire for her only caused hers to spike, leaving her blind with need.

Lifting up on her knees in order to guide him into her, she started to sit, but he gripped her thighs, his fingers digging to stop her.

"No, not yet," Matt gritted out. "I don't have a condom on."

Her body trembled and she fought his hold with a groan, burning need making her impulsive and careless, but he held her too tight to resist. Just when she thought he purposefully was prolonging her suffering, he shifted, lifting her by the waist to place her on the outside lip of the tub, causing water to surge over the edge and splash onto the tiles below. Her wet butt skidded across the cold fiberglass, and goose bumps broke out over her heated skin as it encountered the cool air, but her discomfort didn't last when he spread her legs wide enough to accommodate his broad shoulders.

"Hold onto the spigot," he rasped before his head ducked down and his mouth covered her.

Her mouth opened as a rush of pleasure racked through her, but no sound emerged. His tongue worked over her, never pausing in any one place as he laved and suckled.

"Oh, God. Please, Matt," Shannon begged. What she asked for, she didn't know, but whatever it was, he understood because he hooked one arm around her waist to hold her while he continued to devour her.

Her fingers threaded through his hair and she gripped a handful before she gave herself over to the surge within her. Pleasure exploded out from her center in a rush that peaked and ebbed before cresting again. Matt sat up on his knees in the tub as her legs dropped down from the edge with a splash, and she collapsed against him. Her head rested on his shoulder and his arms circled her as he took one of her nipples with a gentle nip. A new wave of hot heat pulsed through her. He moved and gave the same attention to the other one before his lips slid up, exploring along her shoulders and up her neck. One hand skimmed up her back and cupped her nape as his lips sought out hers.

As Matt kissed her with slow, drugging kisses that rocked Shannon all the way down to her toes, he stood and dragged her up with him. Water sluiced down his body, trailing over the hard, sharp ridges of his muscles, and she'd never seen anything sexier. And the fact that this man was all hers—at least for the time being—made her weak and breathless. Need darkened the color of his eyes and the heat from his body radiated off him as his chest moved up and down with choppy breaths. Shannon's desire ramped up again simply from the look of pure lust on his face.

He stepped over the edge onto the mat and held her hand as she climbed out as well. He tugged her to him, wrapping a fist in her hair. His other hand moved over her hip and around to one cheek before his longer fingers ran down the cleft of her ass and lower over her folds.

"Fuck, you are still so wet," Matt said, his voice low and husky. "Get down on your knees."

He guided her over to the large slate-colored circular rug in the middle of the bathroom and pushed her down by her shoulders.

"On your hands, ass in the air," he demanded as he reached into a drawer.

She started at first before leaning down so her breasts brushed against the soft rug and her arms ran alongside her head. Submissive she was not, but she didn't mind a little dominance from Matt. The sound of a wrapper ripping filled the air before he positioned himself behind her.

"You have no idea how amazing you look right now," Matt murmured as he kneaded her butt before gripping her waist and pushing inside her, his thick, muscular thighs hitting the back of hers.

His fingertips roamed up the ridges of her spine and back down while a hand held her in place, his fingers digging into her hip. She pressed into him and moved her hips to match his hard thrusts.

Their wet skin slapped loudly against each other but their heavy breaths carried over the sharp contact. Her orgasm snuck up on her and she groaned into the carpet, her hips jerking and pitching as sensation exploded within her, but Matt held her tightly, keeping her in place as he continued to batter her.

Panting and sweaty, Shannon braced herself up even though she wanted to collapse. Matt pushed into her one final time with a long groan before stilling. He bent over her, his hot breath heating her skin before he dragged his nose along her spine to place a soft kiss on her lower back. She fell to her side and curled into a warm, complacent ball in the middle of the rug as she closed her eyes.

Matt chuckled a second before he said, "Goddamn it!"

She jerked upright, but he was already around the corner and shutting the door to the water closet. Shannon waited for what seemed like forever, but soon the toilet flushed, and he stepped out and took a deep breath.

"The condom broke," he announced.

Her throat squeezed shut and her heart did a double stutter before settling into a hard, thudding rate.

"I'm sorry." He walked over and sat down next to her on the rug. "I don't suppose you're on the pill too?"

She shook her head. "No. No, I'm not."

Matt sighed as he closed his eyes and ran his hand over his short hair. He turned and pulled her to him, placing a kiss on her temple. "We'll deal with whatever happens, but there's nothing we can do about it now."

She tried to take a deep breath, but she couldn't stop the panic welling up within her, threatening to overflow. She couldn't have a baby, especially not now. They weren't even officially dating, never mind the fact she couldn't keep her job if she had a child. Her plan to have fun with Matt didn't include this, but that was no excuse and she was stupid to overlook the risk, the possibility, once she decided to have sex with him.

"You don't need to worry about diseases or anything." Matt held her close to him and rested his chin on her shoulder. "I'm clean."

Shannon hadn't even been thinking along those lines, fretting only about what she would have to do if she ended up pregnant.

"Thanks," she mumbled. "Me too."

"Hey," he said and gently shook her. "We'll be all right. I know it's hard not to focus only on this and worry, but I don't want this to ruin our time together this week. Okay?"

"It's just a shock, you know?"

"I know, but we'll deal together with whatever happens. You can trust me on that."

Despite his assurances, Shannon couldn't wrap her mind around how this could change everything. All of her plans killed with one shot. She couldn't let that happen.

"I'll need to get to a drugstore, to buy a morning-after pill."

Matt's expression hardened a bit. "Are you sure—?"

"I can't do this now!" she interrupted, afraid he was trying to talk her out of it, and unable to hold back the panic. "We haven't been together long, my job, your job, everything…it won't work!"

"Okay, okay," Matt said as he draped his arm around her shoulder, pulling her to his side. "I get it, I do. If that's what you want, then we can do that. We can go tomorrow, right? I mean, we don't have to go right this second, do we?"

"No, no, you're right," she said, trying to be as calm as him. "I think you have up to five days."

"Okay, then that's what we'll do," he said, giving her a squeeze before nodding toward the tub. "Want to get back in and warm yourself up? I'll let you relax this time."

Relieved with their decision, she nodded. "That would be nice."

She let him help her up and together they climbed in. He turned on the warm water and fired up the jets again. Resting his arm along the edge behind her, he tucked her into his side and she laid her head on his shoulder, gazing at the flames flickering in the fireplace.

Surprisingly, relaxation settled over her, so comfortable and at peace next to Matt that she soon found herself wondering what she was so worried about, questioning why she had panicked. Would it be so bad if she did end up pregnant with Matt's child? Sure, a lot would change and her plans would have to be altered, but having a baby wouldn't be the end of the world. In fact, she thought as she let her eyes drift closed, a family with Matt might be pretty wonderful.

CHAPTER 13

The next morning, Matt and Shannon enjoyed breakfast together outside by his pool. Despite the big, bright sun lighting up the sky, the air remained cool, but would eventually reach almost seventy, resulting in another glorious day.

"I'm going to be spoiled with all of this sunshine," Shannon said with a smile at Matt, who sat next to her reading the paper and petting Buddy, who never left his side. "Not sure how I'm going to be able to deal with the winter in Chicago after this."

Matt didn't take his attention away from the newspaper article when he asked, "Who said you have to?"

"What's that?"

"Go back," he replied, still not looking at her.

She studied him for a moment, taking in the entirety of what his simple statement encompassed. The idea of her and Matt making a life together did make her breath catch and her heart thump erratically, there was no denying it. It was all too much, though; everything so strong so quickly that she didn't know how to handle it, what to think or what to do. Toss in the scare from the night before, which had progressed to almost acceptance, and overwhelming confusion swamped her. But her life and her job, all she'd worked very hard for, were back in Chicago and she couldn't forget that, couldn't just give up on that.

And because of her determination to stay the path she'd laid for herself, she laughed. "Right, like that could happen."

Matt finally put the paper down and sat back in his chair, his blue eyes hard on hers. He had an irritated, almost mad, scowl and she wasn't sure why. "Is it that bad?" he asked.

"What? Here?" she clarified and at his nod, she shook her head. "No, but this isn't my life, Matt."

"And you don't want it to be?"

"Matt, come on. We barely know each other—" she started.

"Are you telling me you don't feel what I feel?"

Her throat tightened. She so did not want to be having this conversation. She had intended to come down here, spend a wonderful time with Matt, but then move on. She couldn't add this to her life now. As much as she wanted to, she simply couldn't. "What are you saying?" she whispered.

Matt's shoulders raised and he took in a deep breath, staring out over his backyard at the mountain range in the distance. His gaze finally came back to her and he leaned toward her, resting his elbows on his knees. Buddy plopped down with a huff, as though realizing Matt had turned his attention elsewhere. "Look, I know we have a lot to work through and there are multiple complexities that make this difficult, but I don't know, Shannon. I really feel as if I'm—"

The ringing of her phone on the table interrupted whatever he'd been about to say. She wanted to ignore the intrusion, but she'd promised work she'd be available.

"Sorry," she said as she picked up her cell. Apprehension washed through her when she unlocked her screen and saw the call wasn't work but rather her father. "Hi, Dad."

She didn't miss Matt's grimace in annoyance as he leaned back in his chair and picked up the paper. Standing, she walked away from the table toward the pool.

"What the hell is going on?" her dad said right off the bat. "How am I supposed to react when Marcus calls me and says you're not in the office, but you're on vacation? Then I find out from Karen that you're in Arizona. Why are you in Arizona?"

"Like you said, taking a vacation," she answered in a low voice, hoping to keep her conversation from carrying back to Matt. "How did Mr. Barnes know?"

"He was checking on you as a personal favor to me and someone told him you'd requested time off. Again," he stressed. "Why would you think this is okay? I don't need to tell you this isn't a good reflection on you or your work."

Shannon closed her eyes and took a deep breath, reaching for patience, but also trying to ward off the hard ball of guilt forming. "I'm still working. Hours are being billed."

"Why are you even in Arizona?"

"Um," she said, not even sure how to explain things with Matt since she hadn't planned to need to. "This guy lives down—"

"Guy? You're flitting around with a man?" her father yelled. "This is ridiculous. So, not only are you not at work, which is where you should be if you want any chance at making partner, but you're spending Christmas with some boy you can't have known for very long, since we just saw you at Karen's wedding and you didn't mention you were seeing anyone."

"I met him at the wedding," she mumbled. She hated how he made her feel like a small child at times.

"Shannon," he said with a blustery sigh. "You don't have time for a relationship, especially a long-distance one. Why are you risking your career for this? You've worked so hard and now that you've finally gotten your first opportunity, at a firm most people would kill to get into, you're going to throw it all away? And for what? Someone you barely know?"

Shannon looked across the patio at Matt, who still sat at the table. Shadows clouded her view of his face, but the rigid lines of his body clearly signaled his frustration. Even mad at her, however, he rendered her breathless simply by being. A sweet, fun and caring guy who exemplified perfection in everything he did and how he made her feel, and that was why she was there.

Her father was right, though. She'd put too much in, given too much up to get to where she was today only to risk her success by making foolish decisions with her heart rather than her head. Sacrifices. She'd told herself more than enough times to understand they had to be made…whether she liked them or not and regardless of fairness.

"It's simply a quick break, and he's just a friend," she said. "I'm keeping up with work and I'll be back after Christmas. I needed to see the sun, that's all."

"I don't need to tell you—" he started, but she cut him off, growing tired of his lectures.

"No you don't. I told you, everything is fine. I have it under control. Once I get back to Chicago, it will be like I never left."

"Fine, but please remember a lot of eyes are on you and they know when you are not around. Questions asked, comments made. You don't want to give them anything to use against you. You can't afford to screw this up over a trivial affair."

Shannon glanced back over her shoulder, but the seat stood empty as Matt had retreated into the house along with Buddy, leaving her alone outside. Trivial? *Trivial* did not describe her feelings for Matt, never mind the fact she could be pregnant, which definitely wasn't inconsequential, but she couldn't tell her father that. Her admission would lead to more lectures about things he didn't understand nor did he care. He certainly wouldn't accept it, so trying to gain as much from him would be a pointless and upsetting exercise. He only cared about one thing—her success as a lawyer.

Nevertheless, she reminded herself—her father's voice now added to the mix— Arizona and a life with Matt wasn't her reality. She couldn't fall into the trap of questioning whether she actually wanted to return to Chicago, as she'd started to. Of course she did. Chicago was where her life was, where her job was; the job she'd worked her butt off in order get through school with a high GPA as well as editor on Law Review so she'd be attractive to such a competitive firm, regardless of her dad's pulls. To think she'd never be resentful if she gave it all up was irrational and foolish.

The longer she stayed in Arizona, the harder it would be to leave, which meant she had to return as soon as she could. She'd originally planned to stay until after the New Year, but now new plans had to be made. The more she put her departure off, the higher chance she could talk herself out of it and put her job at further risk, which was unacceptable.

Telling Matt was going to be hard, probably the hardest things she'd ever had to do; she wasn't naïve enough to believe it would be easy. Even now, she still wavered, wanting to give in and convince herself there was a way to make it work, that they could figure out something without anyone having to give up anything, but it was false hope. Staying would only prolong the eventual pain. As hard as it was going to be, she was going to have to put it all behind her and pretend she hadn't fallen in love with him.

* * *

Christmas night, Matt and Shannon were hosting his family for dinner. Matt had told Shannon not to worry about trying to get anything together, promising the responsibility of preparing the meal was all his. She only needed to focus on work and be ready when everyone showed up. She appreciated the gesture and started to take advantage of the opportunity, but found she couldn't concentrate on anything. Guilt washed over her every time Matt banged something around in the kitchen as she imagined him struggling to boil water.

Getting up, she walked out of the office toward the noise, patting Buddy on the head when he stood to follow her. The scents drifting from the kitchen smelled amazing and her mouth started to water. Shannon stopped right inside the doorway, the scene before her quickly dispelling any notion cooking was foreign to Matt. He stood in front of the island chopping up onions with a dishtowel over one shoulder and the sleeves of his navy button-down shirt rolled up to his elbows, revealing his thick forearms and the heavy platinum watch circling his left wrist. On the stove, water churned and bubbled while peeled potatoes waited next to the pot to be submerged. A dish of breadcrumbs stood next to the cutting board along with some celery and mushrooms.

"Wow! Look at you," she exclaimed. "I had no idea."

Matt gave her his winning smile as he continued to chop. "I can't let out all of my secrets now, can I?"

Can't there be one *thing unappealing about you.* He was not making things easy.

"Seriously," she said as she sat on one of the stools lining the opposite side of the island. "You'd give Karen a run for her money. I must have missed this while I was at work on Thanksgiving."

"I doubt it since Karen is a trained professional," he said as he deftly transferred the now chopped onions to the same dish as the breadcrumbs before pulling a couple stalks of celery onto the cutting board. "I enjoy cooking though. It relaxes me."

"I can't think of anything more stressful," Shannon said with a laugh. "But what can I do to help?"

He eyed her as she moved over to the sink to wash her hands. "You done with work?"

"I'll never be done with work, but the brief can wait. I should be in here helping you and so that's what I'm doing."

"I've got everything covered, Shannon. It's all right."

"Nope, you're not getting rid of me." She planted herself next to him and hit the counter with her palm. "Now give me something to do."

His blue eyes studied her for a moment before he leaned down to place a soft kiss on her lips. "Thank you," he said quietly.

She smiled back at him, forcing herself to ignore the roll her heart wanted to do in her chest, and maintain neutrality since everything was going to change very shortly, and not for the better. "You're welcome. Just don't yell at me when I burn something."

Matt pulled out a cutting board. Turning around, he grabbed a knife from the wood block on the counter behind them and handed the blade to her handle first. "Then we'll give you something you can't burn. Chop up these mushrooms, please."

"I think I can handle that." She took one from the bowl and placed it on the board.

They worked in companionable silence and Shannon tried to ignore how comfortable and right being with Matt felt. Her decision was made and she'd even purchased an airline ticket for the next day, but doubt still lingered and niggled at her. She had to ignore it and stay focused on her dreams.

All that remained was getting through the dinner with his family and then somehow telling Matt.

* * *

Sitting at the head spot at dinner, a sense of peace fell over Matt. Everyone important to him sat in his house, around his dining room table, which was all he ever wanted. His parents, his sister, his best bud, Jason, and now the woman who fit perfectly into the mix. He didn't like others helping in his kitchen as he had his own rhythm and methods, but he'd appreciated Shannon's help, especially since she had so much on her plate that she was willing to put it aside, and he liked how they had worked easily around each other. Granted, she wasn't anything to write home about as far as cooking, but she chopped and stirred just as well any anybody else.

Matt took a sip of his wine, relaxed back in his chair, and let all the noise wash over him. Buddy inched over when Matt shifted, waiting patiently for Matt to pet him. Matt couldn't resist, as always, and rubbed his head, even though his mother hated to have Buddy so close to the table especially with food around. Everything was perfect.

Following a lull in the conversation, Shannon started to gather the dishes and then held out her hands when his mother did the same.

"Oh, no, Lisa. Please, sit and relax. Matt and I have this. You are our guests."

All eyes turned to Matt and he grinned. "I guess that's my cue to get off my ass."

"I want to help," his mother insisted as she reached out for a plate, but Matt grabbed it before she could.

"You heard Shannon, Mom, and you don't want to get her mad at you," he teased as he kissed her forehead. "Go into the other room and relax. We'll only be a second and then we'll open gifts."

Matt shooed them all from the dining room into the family room before following Shannon into the kitchen where she'd already started to load the dishwasher. He stacked the dishes on the counter and stood behind her, shifting her long hair to the side to expose the slender column of her neck. He wrapped his arms around her waist and for one instant she tensed before she relaxed. Assuming he'd misread her reaction, he placed a kiss just under her hairline.

She glanced at him over her shoulder and smiled. "What was that for?"

He shrugged as he leaned in and his lips bussed her nose. "Do I need a reason? How about just you being you." Stepping beside her, he took a dish from her and loaded it in the dishwasher, and soon they had a flow going. "Thanks for helping out."

"Of course," Shannon said. "I may not be able to cook, but I can clean with the best of them. It's the least I could do."

"I think we work pretty well together," he said and this time her flinch was obvious. "Something wrong?"

"Nothing. Why do you ask?" she asked with a frown, keeping her attention solely on her task.

"I don't know," he said as he placed a plate in the lower rack. "You seem tense or something."

"No," Shannon said before finally turning toward him. She smiled, but the light didn't reach her eyes. "No, everything's fine."

"You thinking about your family?" He'd wondered if being with his on Christmas made her miss hers, but she hadn't said anything.

She shrugged as she turned back to the sink. "I don't know. I guess it is sort of weird. I talked with them this morning, though…" She broke off.

"Were they upset you weren't there?"

She sighed and turned off the water. "Karen and my mom were. My dad's still annoyed I'm not at work. Same conversation as the other day."

What is with that guy? Her father seemed insistent she work herself to death. Why he pushed Shannon the way he did didn't make sense to Matt, but he kept his opinions to himself since Shannon obviously cared about her father's view on things. She'd proven as much when she'd taken his phone call right when Matt had been about to divulge his true feelings for her.

"Well, hopefully you assured him you're still getting a lot done while you're here," he said. "I wouldn't want him to think I'm letting you slack or anything."

Shannon laughed as she shook her head. "I told him I'm working. Who knows? He gets uptight about stuff sometimes. He knows how hard I've worked for all this and he only wants what's best for me. It's fine. I'm fine," she said as she squeezed his hands. "We should get back to the rest of them."

She walked past him out of the kitchen and Matt leaned against the counter as she disappeared around the corner. She worried about work constantly and once she returned to Chicago he didn't doubt she would submerge herself again.

If she did that, who cares if he could travel wherever, whenever. They would never see each other and he had no idea what she thought about that. She didn't appear to want to make any changes in her life, which pretty much sucked.

Stepping in the living room where the tree had been set up in the corner, he leaned against the doorframe. The scene in front of him was one he'd wanted for a long time, minus a couple of kids, but that still seemed out of his reach, unfortunately. This life wasn't what Shannon had in mind for herself and she didn't seem to be able, or want, to deviate. Sure, she'd agreed to come down here and spend time with him, but nothing she'd done or said had given him any confidence in her desire to try past this little trip. He didn't doubt her attraction to him, no question the sex between them was amazing, and she might even care for him, but in the list of her priorities, he wasn't anywhere near the top, and he'd just about run out of ways to try to at least get in sight of the top runners. He hated to give up, in fact almost never did, but a guy could only put himself out there so many times before his self-esteem started to take a beating.

"Sweetie, come sit down," his mother said as she grinned up at him from where she sat, beckoning him into the room.

Matt smiled, trying to push aside the melancholy bringing him down. Right now, everything was perfect and would have to be good enough. He would deal with the rough stuff when he needed to, but now he wanted to enjoy the moment.

He sat on the loveseat next to Shannon and gave her a small smile as he squeezed her knee. "Who's first?" Matt asked the room.

Everyone went at once, wrapping paper ripped off the gifts and strewn around. Buddy even had his own gift to unwrap, and everyone laughed as he bit into the paper and pulled off as much as he could, desperately trying to get down to the hard chew toy inside. Shannon opened the gifts his family had given her—an oversized coffee table book filled with pictures of Arizona from his parents, for which she thanked them profusely, and a simple black sweater from Caitlyn. When another gift landed in her lap and she read his name on the tag, she glanced at him. Matt didn't miss the wariness, which cut at him because he didn't understand what was behind it, but he gave her an encouraging smile, prodding her to open the small box. She let out an almost audible sigh of relief when she spotted the scarf inside. He'd picked the silky accessory because the vibrant cobalt-blue fabric matched perfectly with the color of her eyes.

"It's beautiful. Thank you," she said to him.

"You're welcome."

Matt kept his gaze on her, thinking she'd never looked so beautiful before. A pretty pink flush highlighted her cheeks from the warmth of the room, and the reflection of the multi-colored lights on the tree glittered in her eyes. Shannon appeared relaxed and content, almost carefree and soft. He wished he could keep her happy all the time, but soon she would start to worry about work again and the hard lines would reappear, tightening her jaw and her temple. No question she was still beautiful, but the stress she tried to hide from everyone produced a hardness to her and he hated that she did it to herself.

Shannon handed a gift to him. "Open yours."

"You didn't have to get me anything," he said as he leaned to the side closer to her, their shoulders touching.

"I wanted to. It's a bit difficult getting someone who has everything something he doesn't already have, but I tried."

"You already gave me what I wanted," he said in a low voice.

A creased formed between her brows. "What's that?"

Matt picked up her hand and kissed her knuckles. "You."

She hitched in a breath and sadness crept into her eyes before she shoved it out. "Stop."

He shrugged. "I'm serious, but if you don't want to believe me, okay."

"Just open it."

Matt pulled off the paper and opened the nondescript box. It was heavy and when he lifted the tissue, he understood why.

"I noticed you didn't have one like that. I thought it was pretty neat…" She stopped, obviously uncertain.

He reached in and pulled out a perfect replica of a baseball, even down to the stitching, made out of silver. Most likely meant as a paperweight—an expensive one at that—but his wouldn't end up on his desk. His was going on his shelf in his bedroom with the rest of his baseballs, all of them holding a special meaning to him. "It's awesome," he told her, touched she'd been able to pick out something so perfect for him.

"You probably already have one—"

"No," he interrupted. "No, I don't. I mean it, Shannon. I love it. Thank you."

She gave him a small smile and let him pull her to him in order to touch his lips gently to hers. "Thank you," he said again in a whisper.

She reached down and plucked up another gift. "Here's another one for you," she told him.

He frowned. "You didn't need to do that."

"I didn't," she told him with a small grin. "I found it on the front porch the other day."

"Oh."

Grabbing the tag, he turned it over and had to check his reaction. He recognized the handwriting as Natalie's, and he absolutely did not want to open the gift in front of everyone, if at all. Instead, he calmly placed it behind the couch, trying to act as if nothing was wrong even though he would have preferred to stomp on it before tossing it in the trash.

"Why didn't you open it?" Shannon asked.

He shrugged. "I didn't want to."

"Why not? Who was it from?" his mother said, the entire room curious now.

"Nobody," he insisted.

"Matt," Jason warned, catching on very quickly.

"It's from one of my sponsors, that's all," Matt told them with a warning glance at Jason. "It's probably batting gloves or something equally boring. Nothing exciting," he assured them.

A gasp from the couch captured everyone's attention from Matt. Caitlyn had turned beet red as she held a bracelet in her hands.

"Oh," Shannon said as she leaned closer. "Is that one of those charm bracelets?"

Caitlyn didn't answer, only stared at Jason, who sat at the opposite end from her looking uncomfortable.

"Jason?" Caitlyn eventually said.

"What?" Jason replied with a shrug, trying to detract the attention away from them. He ran a hand over his curly hair before sitting up a bit. "I heard girls like those, so I thought you might…" He dropped off with another awkward shrug, obviously embarrassed.

"Jason, these are…I don't know, personal," Caitlyn said.

He frowned. "Personal? What do you mean?"

"The charms. You pick ones that mean something."

"Okay. It isn't like I don't know you. I grew up with you, for God's sake."

Caitlyn went through them and Matt studied his sister and his friend, the tension palpable between them. If he had to guess, Jason had most likely pissed her off and hoped the gift returned him into her good graces. Although a good guy, Jason sometimes did idiotic things and didn't use his head. What he'd done to Caitlyn, Matt had no idea, but he'd guess probably slept with one of her friends and wasn't calling her back. Whatever had caused the rift, Matt wasn't getting involved.

"What does this one mean?" Caitlyn asked Jason as he she held up a small key.

Jason turned an interesting shade of red as everyone waited for him to respond. "I don't know. Maybe it was on there already. I don't remember." He quickly stood and feigned a stretch. "I'm going to head out. Love you guys. Merry Christmas!"

Jason leaned down and embraced Lisa before walking over to pull Shannon into a hug as well, but he avoided Caitlyn. Matt stood and patted his friend on the back. "You sure, man?"

"Yeah, it's cool. We'll talk," he said pointedly at Matt under his breath before retreating and Matt knew he meant about the gift from Natalie. "Thanks again for everything," he said as he shook their dad's hand on his way out.

Soon after Jason had gathered his things, his parents and Caitlyn headed out as well. Once the door shut behind everyone, Matt and Shannon eyed the mess left behind, paper and ribbons everywhere, but cleaning was the last thing on his mind. Shannon, apparently of the same mindset, collapsed back on the couch, stretching out.

"Why are holidays so exhausting?" she asked.

Matt lifted her feet and dropped down, putting them in his lap as he rubbed them through her socks. "I don't know, but they are, that's for sure."

They sat in silence for a bit, both of them staring at the tall evergreen covered in decorations from top to bottom, not a branch remained empty. Matt usually didn't decorate, but Shannon had insisted. He hadn't had many ornaments and so they'd bought some, and Shannon picked out one of everything in every color. To his surprise, he'd enjoyed trimming the tree with her, especially afterward when he'd laid her out on the floor and made love to her under the twinkle of lights. If he had his way, he would make it a yearly tradition.

Reaching behind the couch, Matt pulled out another gift.

"I got you something else, but I didn't want to give it to you in front of everyone."

Shannon jerked up as she eyed the long, thin package with apprehension. "You didn't have to get me anything else."

"I know, but I wanted to. I saw it and I wanted you to have it." He placed it on her lap. "Open it," he said when she made no move to do so.

She gave him another long look before she ripped the paper off. When she opened the blue velvet case, her breath caught. "Oh my…"

Shannon pulled out the platinum diamond tennis bracelet with multiple large diamonds set between equally large sapphires. He didn't miss how her hands shook. "I can't accept this."

"Why not?" he asked, having a feeling he wasn't going to like the answer.

She laid the bracelet back in the case before she placed it on the coffee table in front of them. She clasped her hands in her lap and took a deep breath. "I'm leaving tomorrow."

He'd expected not to like what she said, but he definitely hadn't anticipated that. "What?"

"I need to get back," she said in a rush. "I have so much work to do and I have to get back. To Chicago," she added lamely.

Matt stared at her as disbelief washed through him before he pushed himself up and paced around the room. "You're just telling me this now? What happened to staying until after the New Year?"

"I have to get back," she repeated. "We all knew this was just a vacation. If I'm going to get the partnership, then I need to take things seriously and I need to be there. In the office."

"No, I didn't know this was *just* a vacation," he told her, anger lacing his words. "I personally thought it was much more than that." He narrowed his eyes at her. "Is this your decision or are you doing what your father wants you to do?"

Her shoulders immediately stiffened. "Of course it's mine. I've been saying the same thing since day one. You've just refused to hear it."

"Yes, you've been *saying* as much but your actions have been very different."

Her mouth gaped opened as she tried to find a retort, but came up empty.

He shook his head. "You're very quick to throw in the towel on this."

"Matt," she said with pleading eyes. "We both know this isn't going to work and so why keep going with the charade? Why make it harder for both of us? My life, my career, is in Chicago. I know that and you know that."

"I do know that," he said unable to stop his voice from rising. "But I thought we said we were going to try. This doesn't seem like trying to me."

"We did try," Shannon said.

"This?" he cried as he threw his hands out. "This wasn't trying. This was the easy part, Shannon. We both knew after the holidays it was going to be difficult and now it seems you're wimping out from actually trying."

Her back jerked straight and a hard expression fell over her face. "I'm not wimping out on anything. I'm being realistic. You, however, refuse to admit this impossible situation will not work."

"Maybe because I *want* it to work, I want us to work, no matter what," he exclaimed as he pointed at his chest with his finger for emphasis. "I can't say you feel the same way."

Her throat moved as she swallowed and then retreated within herself. At that exact moment, Matt knew he'd lost her. "You're right," she finally said. "I can't say I feel the same way. I've wanted one thing for so long that I can't walk away from that, no matter how good things are with you."

He stared at her, at a loss as to what to say before he understood nothing else remained unsaid. Did he really want to be with someone he had persuade to be with him? No, he didn't. And with that realization, he gave her one last look before walking out of the room.

CHAPTER 14

Shannon slouched down in her chair, exhausted. It was almost eight o'clock—no, scratch that, it was nine o'clock at night and she was still at the office. The last time she'd glanced at her watch, it'd been six and she'd told herself only one more hour…three hours ago. She'd missed dinner, but given her current level of stress, hunger didn't even register, which was the theme lately.

Ever since returning to Chicago, she'd dove headfirst into work. She slaved all day and night, only going back to her apartment in order to fall into bed, repeating the routine the next day. Leaving work at a reasonable time was out of the question because if she did, all she did was sit and dwell…about him. Drowning herself in work equaled survival.

She couldn't think about Matt. To do so made her miserable…more than she already was. They hadn't spoken one word in six weeks since he'd dropped her off at the airport in Arizona, and his only words to her then were to ask what airline and flight time. As he drove out of her life, she'd fought the urge to call him back and tell him she'd lied when she'd told him she didn't want things to work out between them. The lie had been a necessity, a means of survival, to preserve and protect her dreams. The look on his face had torn her apart, pierced a gaping hole in her heart, one with no hope of healing. She'd been convinced time away from him doing what she'd said she wanted would make the pain and hurt disappear, so certain the out-of-sight-out-of-mind logic would work, but no. Separation made everything worse and only full submersion to the point of exhaustion provided the escape she needed, by not allowing her thoughts to wander because, truth be told, she absolutely regretted what she'd done and what she'd said. Her only defense for her actions was she was a big fucking wimp. A big fucking wimp who was unable to admit to having second thoughts. Matt had absolutely been right to call out how her actions spoke louder than her words. They did.

The fact of the matter was she *did* have misgivings around some of her life decisions, clear evidence of such being the stabbing disappointment when she'd started her period. Had she truly wanted to turn up pregnant with Matt's child? Was that why she'd never revisited getting the morning-after pill? The timing still would have been terrible and the situation less than ideal, but yes. As twisted as it was, yes. With the need to worry removed, sorrow settled into its place.

Now Shannon didn't know how to turn it all around, didn't know how to stop, rethink and re-plan with this new information. She didn't know what she even wanted to do anymore, and she definitely didn't know how to tell her father. And if she was being *completely* honest with herself, he was what held her back.

Yep, she'd gotten herself into a fine mess; one she really had no idea how to get out of. Nor did she know if she had it in her to even try. Which only irritated her even more because she'd believed herself to be a strong person, but she didn't know anymore.

Shannon leaned her elbows on her desk and picked up her pen. She needed to get this brief done and to Carol before eight in the morning, which meant getting her head back in the game. But, just as she started to write down some notes, her phone buzzed. Recognizing the number as the security desk in the lobby, she frowned as she picked up her handset.

"Shannon Morrison," she answered.

"Good evening, Ms. Morrison. This is Dwayne from Security. We have a Karen Smutton who is here to see you."

What the hell is she doing here? Not only had Shannon not spoken with Matt in six weeks, but she'd also turned away her family. Karen had called her multiple times, but each time Shannon had an excuse at the ready as to why she couldn't talk before finally ignoring Karen's calls altogether. She didn't want to discuss Matt, which is what Karen wanted details on ever since finding out about them. Her plan to ignore Karen long enough in hopes she would eventually get the hint and leave her alone had failed, but really she should have known better.

Before Shannon could respond, Karen's voice said, "Let me talk to her," before some shuffling sounds came across the line, clearly indicating Karen had grabbed the phone from the poor man.

"You can't ignore me now, can you? Get your ass down here," Karen said without any prelude. "She's my little sister," Karen told Dwayne in a sweet voice.

Shannon gave a small chuckle even though the visit was going to be anything but friendly. "I'm on my way."

"You better be or I swear—" Karen muttered over some more shuffling as she handed the phone back to the security guard and told him, "She's on her way."

Hanging up, Shannon slipped her feet into her heels and ran her fingers through her hair as she stepped into the elevators. Karen really had to be ticked off to show up unannounced, and now Shannon had to hear all about it, which she really did not have time for.

Stepping into the lobby, Shannon headed toward the security desk. The guy sitting behind the counter, who must have been Dwayne, spotted her and pointed toward a cluster of chairs. Only the back of Karen's head was visible, but when the click-clack of Shannon's heels sounded on the tiled floors, Karen straightened and turned.

"Oh, your ass is mine now," she said as she used one of the arms of the chair to hoist herself up.

When Karen faced her, Shannon let out a small gasp. "Oh my god! Look at your little stomach! You look so cute."

"Nuh-uh." Karen strode past Shannon toward the elevators. "You are not going to try to get on my good side now by telling me how cute I am pregnant. You will save that for later, after I've bitched at you."

Shannon grinned at the security guard overhearing their conversation and gave a small shrug. "Sisters."

Pushing the button for her floor, she turned and found Karen glaring at her. "I can tell this is going to be a fun visit."

"Six weeks," Karen fumed. "Six weeks and I've heard nothing from you. What the fuck, Shannon?"

"I know, I know." Shannon sagged against the back wall. "I've just been really busy."

"Not eating too." Karen eyed Shannon's thin frame. "You are too tall to be that skinny."

"I eat enough," Shannon huffed as she exited when the doors slid open on her floor. She passed the empty reception area and Karen followed her to her office in the far corner. Collapsing behind her desk, she waited as Karen tossed her jacket into a chair before sinking down into its partner. She glanced around, her gaze falling over the piles of papers on every surface, and towers of files and books on the floor before she gave a small nod.

"So this is where you live. Nice," she said.

Shannon rolled her eyes. "Okay, let's skip the preliminaries, shall we? Let's get the bitch session started so I can get back to work. I have deadlines."

Karen's eyes widened before narrowing. "Are you seriously going to sit there and tell me your work is more important than a surprise visit from your sister?"

Shannon instantly regretted what she'd said and her shoulders drooped in defeat. "I'm sorry, Karen. I'm under a lot of stress right now, and I know this isn't a pleasure visit. I know you came here to ream me out."

"Of course I did, but I would still like to believe that after that unpleasant-ness, we can get to the pleasant part of the visit," she said sweetly, her blue eyes bright and innocent.

Shannon smiled and leaned her elbows on the desktop. "Okay, let's get the unpleasantness out of the way."

Rather than launch into a full-out bitch session, which Shannon would have preferred, Karen simply titled her head and said, "What's going on, sis?"

Her sister's concern was all it took for Shannon's eyes to flood with tears. "I don't know," she whispered.

Karen scooted her chair closer to the desk and reached out to take Shannon's hands in hers. "Tell me what happened."

Shannon took a deep breath and wiped hastily at her eyes with one hand. "I told him we couldn't continue, that there was no way things could work between us. I left the day after Christmas and I've been working ever since."

"Trying not to think about him," Karen added.

Even though she didn't ask as a question, Shannon nodded. "Yes."

"Which means you don't really believe what you told him."

Frustrated, Shannon stood and started pacing. "I do, but I don't. If I'm going to keep this job and continue pursuing partnership in this firm, then yes, I do believe. But..." She broke off unwilling to actually speak the words.

"But if you don't want this job, then..." Karen let the rest hang in the air unsaid. "Is that what you're struggling with?" she asked, cutting right to the chase.

Shannon leaned against her bookshelf and crossed her arms. "Yeah, I guess," she admitted quietly.

"And what's wrong with that?" Karen asked.

"It's not that easy," Shannon said as she sat back down in her chair.

"But it is," Karen stated.

"No, it's—"

"Shannon, I've said this before and I'm going to say this again. This is *your* life, not his. You're always trying to make him proud and I get that, believe me I do, but if you do everything for him and not yourself, you'll be miserable for the rest of your life. If you're having second thoughts now, then you'll always have them."

"It's not so simple, Karen," Shannon insisted. "I've worked so hard to get here and now I'm just going to throw it all away? For a guy? This is what I've wanted for so long and now I don't? It doesn't make sense, not even to me."

Plus, she could already see the look of absolute disappointment on her father's face if she told him that not only did she not want to be a partner in a prestigious law firm, but also by doing so, she felt like the life was being sucked out of her. Her father was a very serious and often difficult man, and Shannon had worked so hard to make him proud of her. Now she was going to destroy that pride simply because she had doubts about how much she really wanted to follow in his footsteps.

"I didn't say it wasn't going to be hard. You are so against the possibility you might be changing your mind that you won't listen to yourself." Karen stopped and shifted. "Let me ask you this. Before Matt, were you having any second thoughts about any of this?" She caught Shannon's shifty eyes and added, "Be honest with yourself."

Shannon sighed. "Some," she muttered.

"So adding Matt to the mix upped it a bit?"

"Yes, I guess you could say that."

Karen sat back in her chair. "You really like him. Tell me about it."

Unable to sit still, Shannon stood and started pacing again. "I don't know what to say. He's great and amazing and perfect."

"Is he serious about you?"

"Yes, I mean, I think so." Shannon strode around the small space. "He was always telling me how much he wanted things to work out between us. He took me to meet his family, for crying out loud. He told me the last girlfriend they'd met was some girl he dated back in college." She stopped and faced Karen. "He wasn't very happy with how we left things."

"And neither are you," Karen said simply.

"Aagghh," Shannon cried in frustration. "No, I'm not, but I don't know if I want to change things either. I'm a conflicted mess."

"Look," Karen said as she walked over to her. "If you want to try things out with Matt, do it. Just because you're changing, it doesn't mean you're changing *for* him. You're trying to find yourself and he's part of your journey. Don't you want to at least try instead of always wondering what if?"

Shannon gave her a small smile. "You sound like him now."

"Then I like him. He's smart."

Shannon laughed as she glanced around her office, recognizing it for the first time as the jail cell it was. "Oh, what a mess this is going to be. I don't even know where to start."

"What would tell me to do?"

"Huh?"

"If I was going around and around about Jerry and my job, what would be your advice to me?"

Shannon mulled it over even though she knew without a doubt what her guidance would be. But she wasn't so sure she wanted to follow the same for herself. "Quit your job and find him."

"Well?" Karen said. "If that is what you would tell me, then why can't you do the same?"

"Quit? I don't know about outright quitting..." She broke off as panic flooded through her. Mr. Barnes had been a strong advocate for her within the firm as a favor to her father, which had landed her the job, and her quitting would definitely put a dent in their relationship, something else her father would blame her for, rightfully so. Any way she turned, she was going to be leaving a big mess.

"How else are you going to make the change? You already said this job doesn't leave you time for anything else. If you don't quit, what changes?" Karen asked. "Seems like we're still in the same spot."

"I don't know," Shannon said with a shrug. "Maybe I can try to work something out," she suggested even though the possibility was slim, but she still couldn't get her head around completely quitting either.

"When you thought about yourself as a lawyer, is this what you envisioned?

"I don't know. I guess."

"Shannon…"

"Fine." She blew out a breath. "Not really. I mean, not in a big firm like this, representing crooked executives."

"Then why would you stay in a job you don't even like?"

"Because I need to be doing something!"

Karen raised a skeptical brow and Shannon pressed on, attempting a different angle. "Besides, I'm not even sure Matt even wants to see me. It has been six weeks. Who knows? He might be seeing someone else now. Seems like I should figure that out before quitting my job."

Karen didn't seem concerned. "Nope, he isn't, and of course he does."

"Karen…"

"So it seems the only part of your advice left is to find Matt. And I'm pretty sure we know where he is…"

Shannon glowered at her sister. "Florida."

"Correct!"

Shannon hesitated. Was she seriously considering going to Florida? Apparently she was because she had no other ideas. If she wanted to see Matt, then heading south remained the only option since Spring Training had started. Besides, this definitely wasn't a conversation to have over the phone.

"I can't believe I'm actually considering this," she finally said.

"If he truly wanted things to work out with you guys, then I don't think you have anything to worry about. He'll be ecstatic to see you."

"It's not only that." Shannon walked away and swept her arms out. "Everything, all of this, it's…crazy."

"No, it's different. It's different than what you had planned and so it takes getting used to." Karen smiled at her. "You know, when I was so adamant I didn't want anything more from Jerry than hot sex, there was one thing you said to me that always stuck."

"What was that?"

"What's so wrong with liking him, with wanting more from him? And I say the same to you now, what's so wrong with wanting to be happy with your life, with wanting to be with Matt?"

"Nothing," Shannon said.

"Exactly." Karen brushed a hand up Shannon's arm. "So, we'll go with *your* plan of quitting and then go to Matt. You can come down with me. I'm heading down to Florida the day after tomorrow."

"Wait, what? Why are you going?" Shannon asked, confused. "Plus I don't have a ticket."

"I only have a short time left where I can travel, so I'm going to head down to surprise Jer. Once things get going with their games, I won't see him much. So, I made plans to visit him and I got you a ticket as well. Just in case."

"Well, that was pretty cocky on your part? So sure I was going to go?" she said with a grin, which Karen returned with a shrug. "So I'm just supposed to show up with you?" Shannon asked and at Karen's nod, she grimaced. "Yeah, I don't know."

"Why not? How else would you do this?"

"What if he doesn't want me back?" she whispered, putting voice to her biggest fear.

Karen titled her head. "Aside from being his loss and a drastic change in my opinion of him, then you'll move on, but you tried, and that's what matters. But what's most important is you're learning something about yourself and what you want and don't want."

Shannon eyed her unusually subdued sister. "How did you get all calm all of a sudden? Where's the bitch session in this?"

"Oh," Karen said with a wave of her hand. "I'm mad about you ignoring me, don't get me wrong, but I'm working on keeping myself calm. This baby doesn't need to hear me swearing all the time. I slip every once in a while and Jerry gives me a look, but I'm trying." She collapsed back in the chair with a gusty sigh. "Plus, I'm starting to get so tired that I don't really have the energy to yell at anyone for too long."

Shannon smiled. "Well, that's a good thing, I guess."

"Yeah, good for everyone else, but I'm the one bottling everything up inside." They made eye contact and started laughing. "I just want you to be happy, little sis, and I can tell you're not."

"I know," Shannon said. "And I appreciate it, I really do. It's just scary, especially when I think about telling Dad."

"That's why I'm here," Karen said. "I'll help you through this and dealing with him, and then you get to help me through this kid. I'm going to need all the help I can get, I can tell. If this baby is anything like his father, then I'm in deep trouble." She kicked back and propped her feet up on the chair next to her. After a few moments of silence, Karen broke it. "Well, finish up what you need to so we can get out of here and get something to eat, and then you can get back to telling me how cute I am with my little belly."

Shannon laughed, feeling much better after talking with Karen, which only emphasized how idiotic she'd been for pushing her off for so long. Karen only wanted the best for her, and she'd forgotten that. Now Shannon needed to put things into action. She had to figure out how to break the news to her father, which downright terrified her, but Karen was right. Shannon had to think about herself and only herself. This change didn't mean she wouldn't stay in the field of law. It just wasn't going to be in this law firm nor in some other big, prestigious firm. She needed a balance as she had other dreams, some she hadn't even realized, and she refused to give those up. She was determined to find a way where she could have everything.

CHAPTER 15

Crouching behind home plate, Matt eyed where Jason stood in the infield. Throwing drills took priority on the agenda for the day, and Matt was working on his throws to second with Jason, who was working on covering second base from his position at short in a steal situation.

The pitch came in away from the left-handed batter. Matt shifted his weight as he caught the ball and threw it to Jason, who moved toward second base. Jason fielded the toss cleanly, placing his body in front of the bag in order to prevent the imaginary runner from being able to sneak in a hand or foot, as he dropped his glove to simulate the tag.

"Nice and quick, Buck, and right on the money. Perfect," Jason yelled out.

The next one crossed inside the plate, causing Matt to step back to throw behind the hitter. His momentum carried him too far, however, and he fell toward the dugout, causing his line to be off.

"Goddammit." He grimaced as the ball sailed between Jason and the third baseman into the outfield.

"Come on, Bucky. You've got it," Jason said in encouragement.

"Of course, I do," Matt yelled back as he arranged his mask over his head. "Make sure you're ready, Kirb."

"Always ready, baby. Ready is my middle name," Jason replied. "You just need your fat ass to get it down here."

Some of their teammates chuckled and Matt sent Jason the middle finger, triggering Jason's hoot of laughter, before crouching down. This time, he made sure to tighten his shuffle as he threw hard. As promised, Jason stood ready and waiting. He leaped to snatch the ball out of the air above his head, before dropping down to graze the ground with his glove.

Jason popped upright with a big grin on his face. "You're an asshole. I know you threw it up there so I'd have to jump."

Matt chuckled as he bent down to pick up his helmet. "Don't worry, Kirb. You're still growing." Jason stood a tad under six feet, a good deal shorter than Matt did, and Matt loved to tease him about it.

"Girls, girls," Jerry said as he wandered over to them from the dugout where he'd been watching. "Do I need to separate you two?"

Matt and Jason met in the infield and grinned at each other. They'd been giving each other shit for years.

"Nah, Matt just has his panties in a bunch. Girl problems, you know," Jason said to Jerry.

Matt's smile immediately dropped. "Fuck you."

"Things not going good with Shannon?" Jerry asked.

Matt glowered at Jason for opening his big mouth. "I'd rather not talk about it."

The last thing he wanted to do was think about her, let alone talk about her. He'd come to Spring Training determined to put everything behind him. Embarrassed, pissed and hurt, he simply wanted to move on. His story was something had come up at work requiring her to get back to Chicago, but Jason knew him better than anyone else and called his bullshit. He never asked directly, however, instead made the occasional snide comment, trying to trick the story out of Matt. So far, Matt wasn't biting.

Jerry glanced at Jason. "He's not saying."

Jason nodded as he narrowed his eyes at Matt. "Yeah, he's good at that. Stubborn ass."

He wasn't saying because he still couldn't wrap his head around what had happened. He didn't understand how she claimed she wanted to try only to suddenly declare she'd tried, it wasn't going to work and she would be returning to Chicago. All this before things truly got hard. He could handle all of it and quite possibly learn to accept it, except the not wanting to try. That he didn't understand at all.

But it didn't matter that he didn't understand. It didn't matter that they got along great, connected and enjoyed each other. It didn't matter that he loved how passionate she was, how dedicated she was or that she was just as competitive as he was. It didn't matter that he respected the hell of out her, that he loved that she had her own goals, dreams and aspirations. He'd said what he'd needed to say, and she ignored him. Time to move on.

Spring Training had been the perfect answer. Away from the house and any reminders of Shannon, entire days filled with baseball, leaving no room for anything else. Most nights he simply collapsed into bed, exhausted, not allowing any moments for his mind to wander. The last thing he needed was these guys trying to stir up some gossip.

"We still going to dinner?" Jerry asked Matt.

"Yep, sounds good," Matt said as they all walked together off the field and into the locker room.

Leaving the stadium with his duffel bag slung over his shoulder after they showered and changed, Matt put his aviators on as he headed out into the afternoon sun. Jason walked next to him as Jerry followed behind, all of them slowed a bit as they made their way down the sidewalk lined with fans asking for their autographs. They tried to oblige as much as possible, signing bats, balls, even stopping long enough to have their picture taken, before stepping over to the other side of the fence, which separated them from the autograph seekers.

"Oh, man." Jerry turned his face up the sun. "I was so ready for this warmth. It was a brutal winter this year."

"I have no idea how you guys deal with that winter crap," Jason said.

Jerry shrugged. "Hey, man. My baby wants to live in Michigan, so we live in Michigan."

Matt glanced at him over his shoulder as he walked around to the driver's side of his truck. Since a few of them had rented apartments in the same complex, they had driven together in Matt's car. "Karen won't move?"

Jerry opened the back door and tossed his bag onto the floor before climbing in. "I don't know, to be honest. I've never asked, but I assumed she wouldn't want to move. I mean, that's where Maddie is and that's where her mom is. Plus, I'm fine with Michigan."

"I don't know," Jason said. "If some girl I was with wanted to live in a place where the temps dropped below sixty degrees, I think I'd have to leave her."

Matt chuckled as he started the car. "Says the guy who's never been in a relationship."

Jason gave an easy shrug as Jerry laughed from the backseat. "Never saw the need. There are a lot of women out there who have yet to enjoy my company."

Jerry gave another hoot. "Ah, man. You're priceless. I can't wait to see the one girl who's going to bring you down on your ass. That's going to be beautiful."

Matt laughed and nodded in agreement. "That is going to be entertaining and we'll be right there calling you whipped just as you do to us."

Jason only grinned. "Whatever. Not going to happen."

Pulling into the complex, Matt parked in his assigned spot. Each apartment had their own private entrance, which sat back from the road, and you had to pass through a landscaped courtyard to get to them. When they came around the corner, Jerry exclaimed, "No way!" before he pushed Matt off the sidewalk.

Jerry rushed ahead and caught a female throwing herself at him with a squeal. It took Matt a second before he recognized Karen.

Jerry tried to hold her in his arms, but with her protruding stomach, he struggled for a minute before he finally set her down. "What are you doing here?" he asked ducking his head again to catch her mouth with his.

"I wanted to surprise you," she said when they broke apart.

Swallowing the jealousy building within him, Matt tried to disappear quietly, allowing them a private moment. He stepped around them to head to his place when Jason cleared his throat.

"Uh, I'm guessing she's here for you," Jason said.

Following Jason's gaze, Matt started when his eyes connected with Shannon's. She stood behind her sister, hovering near the door to Jerry's place.

He was floored. Having not expected to cross paths with her anytime soon, if ever, a gamut of emotions rolled through him—surprise, happiness, excitement, anger, frustration, and resentment all being the first he recognized.

A hand clamped down on his shoulder. "Guess I'm on my own for dinner. I'll catch you later, man." Jason turned up the sidewalk to his place and went through the front door.

Matt gave a distracted nod, not able to look away from her. She walked slowly toward him, her steps short and timid as she sidestepped Jerry and Karen, who were still wrapped around each other. Her eyes passed over him, taking in his long-sleeved navy athletic shirt and training shorts, and he didn't miss the way they darkened before coming back to his face.

"Hi," she said quietly.

Shannon was dressed in a slim pink T-shirt topping white skinny jeans, which made her legs look somehow longer than they already were, and with her hair pulled back into a messy bun, he could tell she'd lost some weight. She was too thin, the lines of her face too sharp, her blue eyes almost too big, and her collarbone too pronounced. Anger pushed through at what she'd done to herself, but she was still so beautiful that it took his breath away.

"Hi," he finally said.

She glanced over her shoulder at Jerry and Karen before turning back. "Can we go to your place? I think I'll be in the way right now. Besides, I'm sure you're wondering what I'm doing here and I'd like to explain."

He nodded and pointed to the door straight ahead. "That's me."

"Okay." She returned to the small patio in front of Jerry's place. "Would you guys get inside? You're nauseating."

Karen and Jerry finally separated. "You okay?" Karen asked her.

Shannon nodded as her eyes flitted over to Matt's for a second before she embraced her sister. She smiled and gave Jerry a hug before she headed toward Matt.

Opening the front door, Shannon stepped in behind him and glanced around. The apartment was nice and furnished, but small. All Matt cared about was the privacy the place provided at the end of the day.

"Can I get you something?" He shoved his thumb toward the cubby of a kitchen.

"Water would be great, thanks," she said.

Matt watched her as she walked around the small living room twining her hands together, clear evidence of her nerves. He wasn't exactly at ease himself, but curiosity as to what she had to say won over any nervousness.

He handed her the bottle of water he'd pulled from the fridge and drank out of his own. "What are you doing here, Shannon?" he finally asked. No reason to beat around the bush.

She had just taken a sip and half choked. "Right to the point, huh?"

He shrugged. "Sure, no reason not to."

Shannon nodded. "I honestly don't know where to start," she finally admitted.

"Wherever you want," he said as he sat on the arm of the brown leather couch that filled most of the room.

"Okay, um, where to start." She started to pace in the narrow space. "Let's see, I guess that would be when I got back to Chicago…"

"Shannon." He put his hand on her arm, stopping her in mid-pace. "There's nothing to be nervous about. Just tell me what's on your mind."

Relief passed over her face. She turned to him and straightened her shoulders. "I've really missed you."

There was no point in denying the surge of pleasure warming him at her words. However, it didn't mean she'd changed her mind about her career being the number one priority in her life, in which he didn't fit.

"I have too," Matt said simply. She needed to reveal more of her hand before he showed his.

She took another deep breath. "All right. I've been miserable. I've done nothing but work since I left Arizona so I wouldn't have any time to even think… about you."

"And yet you're here," he said.

"Yes," Shannon said. "I quit my job."

A jolt of surprise hit him as that was the last thing he'd expected her to say. "What? Why did you do that?"

"Well, it was either quit or be forced out. I tried to talk to the junior partner I worked with, Carol, but once I asked about reducing my workload, she made it perfectly clear it'd be better if I left." She let out a gusty sigh. "It was hard and, I'll admit, I'm still not quite comfortable with it, but I decided I needed to take some time to figure out exactly what is going on in here," she said as she tapped her temple.

"But I thought your dream was to be a lawyer?" he asked her.

Shannon smiled. "It is and I do, but it turned out I have other dreams I was ignoring and I was starting to resent all the sacrifices I was making. One of them being you."

Matt narrowed his eyes, not quite believing his ears. "What about your father?"

"What about him?"

"Shannon," he warned, giving her a hard look at her attempt to avoid. "Does he even know? He's the one who got you the job."

"Not yet." She at least had the decency not to lie to him.

"And what's going to happen when he does?"

"He'll be upset, but I'll deal with him," Shannon insisted. His doubt must have been obvious because she became adamant. "I will. I just have to work out what I'm going to say to him."

Matt sighed, unsure what to think. On one hand, he was very happy to see her. The fact that she'd left her job said a lot. It definitely showed she was willing to make changes she'd hadn't been open to before and perhaps her priorities were now different.

On the other hand, however, the situation with her father left him unsettled. He didn't quite believe she would handle his disappointment as easily as she did. Although, since she'd quit, even if her father did become pushy, she couldn't go back. He'd take that as a win and the rest they'd figure out together.

"So you quit and came down here," he said.

"I figured it would be better now before the season started. But..." she dropped off and he followed what she left unsaid.

He smiled and reached out to tug her closer to him. "I'm really glad you came."

Relief washed over her face again and she let out a breath. "Yeah?"

Matt pulled her flush against him. "Very much," he said as he ducked his head to take her mouth with his. He proceeded gently, wanting to savor having her in his arms again.

His hands ran up and down her back, tracing the bones of her rib cage, her shoulder blades as well as what felt like each vertebrae. His tongue did one more tangle with hers, before he released her.

"You are way too skinny, Shannon," he said.

She gave an embarrassed one-shoulder shrug. "I was stupid, I know. I totally immersed myself and if I ate, I ate but I didn't go out of my way to find food."

"We're going to get some food in you," he said as he started to head toward the kitchen, but stopped when she tugged on his hand. He glanced back at her and she gave him a small smile.

"In a bit, okay? I'm not done saying what I wanted to say."

"Okay," he said, interested in what more she had to say.

Shannon took his other hand in hers and studied his fingers for a moment before she cast her gaze back to his, her blue eyes wide and searching. "I want to tell you what tipped it for me and then you can tell me if it freaks you out or not. You promise me you'll tell me the truth?"

A small ball of uneasiness grew in the pit of his stomach, not liking the direction the conversation was going, especially if she worried he would freak out. "Okay, I promise."

"Remember what happened in Arizona? In the bathroom with the…"

He knew exactly what she was referring to, as he'd wondered himself, figuring she'd let him know if there was a need. "Yeah, I know what you're talking about." All of the sudden, panic rippled through him. "Wait, are you trying to tell me—"

Shannon held out a hand and quickly shook her head. "No. Not that. I'm not pregnant."

"Okay," he said and took a deep breath. Not that he didn't want a family, but he definitely didn't want one with someone out of wedlock or with someone who, up until a few minutes ago, hadn't wanted to be with him. "Okay, good."

She eyed him for a second, unsure whether to say anything more, before finally blurting out what she was trying to tell him. "But I was disappointed."

Matt puzzled over her words before he stepped back and sat down on the edge of the couch again. "You were disappointed you weren't pregnant?"

"Yes, and before you freak out, let me explain." She eyed him and whatever she saw must have told her he was listening, even though his mind was very muddled. "I know we're not in any position to start a family or anything, and it would be ridiculous to believe otherwise, since we really are not even dating, but it told me this was something I wanted and something I was ignoring. I don't want to ignore it anymore and I don't want to ignore how I feel about you anymore." She paused and took a steeling breath. "I'm in love with you."

Silence fell between them as he processed her words. Everything had taken such a drastic turn from believing he had to move on and that Shannon was no longer an option. But here she stood before him, telling him they were still a possibility and not only that, but she loved him. He shook his head as if trying to clear out the cobwebs.

"Tell me what you're thinking, please. I'm dying here."

He cleared his throat before grabbing her to place her between his legs. "I'm honestly stunned, Shannon. One second I thought whatever chance we had was gone, that you didn't want it. Then you show up, tell me you've quit your job, and not only do you not want that job anymore, but you want a family and you love me. Honestly, I can't keep up."

She swallowed thickly as her eyes dropped. "I understand."

"Hey," he said and waited until her gaze lifted. "I'm not done. Remember, I did just say I was glad you're here. I knew in Arizona I had fallen in love with you and that hasn't changed."

"Yeah?" she asked with a shy smile.

Whenever she smiled at him like that, he would do anything in the world for this woman. Anything. "Yeah."

She reached out to run her hand over his cheek, scruffy since he hadn't bothered to shave in a couple of days. His eyes closed and he let the pleasure of her touch wash over him. Her fingers threaded into his hair before trailing down his neck, and she pressed her soft lips to his temple. When she leaned back, he opened his eyes and the love in her expression made his heart swell with happiness. Everything was finally right.

CHAPTER 16

A few days later, after Matt left for the ballpark, Shannon had to get off her butt and do something. Sitting around the apartment complex was getting boring and she needed to put her mind to a task. Matt had gotten a ride with one of his teammates, leaving her his truck, so she set out from the apartment to find the closest grocery store. The cupboards in the kitchen were bare since she and Matt had been holed up with him only emerging for practice.

As she drove, she thought about how not only was she going to take the time to find out who she and Matt were as a couple, but she also wanted to figure out who she was. She'd changed so much in the past few months and she had to make sure she was at peace with her choices. No regrets, as Matt always said, and she needed to be solid in her resolve because when she talked with her father—which she'd put off until she got her mind settled, though once the news spread from Mr. Barnes, he would surely blow up her phone—it was going to be difficult to avoid the pressure from him. She wanted to be with Matt and had no doubt in her decision to be with him. She had his full support in everything and he would never do anything to put what they had together in jeopardy. She was so lucky to have him and so thankful she hadn't lost her chance with him.

Parking in a spot in front of the store, Shannon walked in and grabbed a cart. Wandering through the produce section, she was considering a clamshell of strawberries when she glanced up and a brunette standing next to her gave her a hesitant smile. Shannon had never seen her before, but she gave the stranger a friendly acknowledgement.

The woman's smile grew as she closed the remaining gap between them. "Hi. I didn't want to come at you out of the blue, but you're Matt Buck's girlfriend, right? Shannon?"

"And you are?" Shannon asked, trying not to be creeped out and figuring there was a good explanation as to how this woman knew her.

"I'm Shelly." The woman held out her hand in introduction. "I'm Brian Woodsey's wife." At Shannon's obvious confusion, she continued. "He plays right field."

"Oh, sorry," Shannon replied sheepishly. "I don't know all the players yet."

"Oh, that's okay," Shelly said with a peal of laughter. "He's one of the quieter ones, doesn't quite get all of the attention like Matt does."

"Oh, I don't know about that…" Shannon stammered.

Shelly laughed again with a wave. "It's okay. We're all used to it. We know who the stars are on the team. It doesn't hurt that Matt is *so* gorgeous as well."

Shannon wasn't quite sure how to handle the wife of Matt's teammate calling her boyfriend gorgeous, so she kept her mouth shut.

"Well, I wanted to introduce myself," Shelly said. "Maybe we can get drinks or something one night. Hang out while the guys are at the park."

"Yeah, great. That sounds nice." Shannon reached into her purse for her phone. "I'd been hoping to meet other people. Let me text you my number."

"Oh, no bother. I have Matt's. I'll give you a call, okay?"

"Oh, okay." Shelly seemed to know a lot about Matt, which Shannon found odd, but perhaps dating a player on a team meant being included in a tightknit family of the teammates and their significant others, something new and foreign to Shannon. She had much to learn. "It was nice meeting you."

Shelly smiled and walked out of the market, which was peculiar in and of itself since she didn't appear to have purchased anything, but Shannon didn't think any more about it as she moved deeper down the aisles to finish her shopping. She returned to the apartment and started to unload the car when Karen walked out of the one next to theirs.

"Where'd you go?"

"To the store, to pick up some groceries. Come on in. I'll make us some lunch."

"Thank God. I'm starving and there's nothing in Jerry's place."

"Figured as much. Matt's was pretty sparse as well. I didn't think to ask if you wanted to go. Sorry."

Karen waved her hand as she slowly lowered herself into one of the chairs around the small kitchen table. "Don't worry about it. If I need anything, I'll make Jerry go out when he gets back."

"I met one of the player's wives today, Shelly," Shannon told her sister.

Karen frowned. "Shelly? Who's Shelly?"

Shannon shrugged as she walked over to the fridge to put the milk away. "I don't know. She said she was Brian's wife."

"Oh, Shelly," she said with a nod. "Yeah, Brian's wife." Then she frowned again. "I didn't know she came with him. I asked Jerry who was around and he didn't mention her. She's nice. I've met her before."

"Where are they from?"

"Texas," she answered.

"Texas." Shannon replayed the woman's voice in her head. "She didn't have an accent at all."

"Really? I remember her having a distinct twang."

"Maybe, but I didn't notice any. Who knows. She's here since I met her today." Shannon loaded a carton of eggs in the fridge. "She seems nice and she suggested we do drinks or something when the guys are busy. It will be good to have someone to do things with, especially when you go back."

"It's good for you to meet some of other girls. It helps to have others relate to what's going on. Having Maddie was a godsend, that's for sure. Both of us learning the ropes together, otherwise I would have gone mad with the guys' moodiness when things don't always go so well. Now you can commiserate with us," Karen added with a smile.

"It looks that way," Shannon agreed as she took out the fixings for turkey sandwiches.

"So I take it the surprise went well?" Karen asked with a mischievous glint in her eyes. She and Shannon hadn't any time to catch up since arriving. "Not much talking happened, I'm going to guess."

Shannon laughed. "There was some talking and some…not."

"And?"

"And," Shannon said with a one-shoulder shrug as she rinsed off leaves of lettuce, "we'll see how it goes. We're both kind of trying to figure things out as we go. We both want to be with each other, so I guess that's as good a place to start as any."

"Matt wants a family. He wants to get married and settle down," Karen said with what sounded like a warning in her voice. "That's what he's going to be looking for, he's never hidden that, so if that isn't what you want, then better to cut your losses now."

"I know," Shannon said, "but that doesn't mean we have to run out and do it tomorrow. We have time, which we need. I'm still trying to process the changes happening inside me. He knows that too." She pulled two plates out of the cupboard. "One day at a time. That's all I can take right now. It helps that we're open and honest with each other. No games and no hidden agendas. No secrets." Shannon picked up both plates and headed toward the small outdoor patio. "Let's sit outside since it's nice out."

They ate in silence and as she sipped her iced tea, Shannon studied her sister. Glowing with happiness, Karen was finally at peace, the negativity built from past anger and hurt, which had hung like a dark cloud over her, finally gone, and Shannon was so thankful for Jerry since it was because of him.

"You look amazing." Shannon leaned forward to pat her sister's stomach.

"I look like a whale." Karen slipped off her sandals to put her feet up on the chair next to her. "And I'm only going to get bigger. Ugh."

"You do not," Shannon laughed. "Do you know what it is? Did you guys want to find out?"

"It's a pain in the ass, just like his father. He can't sit still for five minutes," she sneered before she smiled. "No, we don't want to find out, we want to be surprised, but he's adamant it's a boy."

"What do you think it is?"

"I honestly don't have a clue, but if it's a girl, Jerry's not going to know what to do with her."

"Oh, he'll be great," Shannon said. "She'll totally be daddy's little girl."

"Oh, I have no doubt, but he'll be paralyzed with fear at first. He knows what to do with a boy, but has no idea when it comes to girls. It might be funny." Karen gave her a long look. "You do, too, you know? You finally look relaxed. Happy."

"I am," she decided. "Very happy."

"You and Matt look good together. Do you love him?" Karen asked bluntly.

"Karen!" Shannon exclaimed.

"What? It's an easy question really. You do or you don't."

"Omigod, this is coming from the Queen of Feeling Denial," Shannon teased.

"That was the old Karen," her sister insisted. "This is the new, matured, overly emoting one."

Shannon laughed before she gave a small shrug. "Yes."

"You should. He's a great guy." Karen eyed her for a second before she said, "Have you talked to your dad again?"

The smile fell from Shannon's face as she shook her head. "No. I need to get my thoughts straight before I deal with him. It's not going to be easy, as you know."

"They're your decisions, Shannon. If this is what you want, then fuck him. It's your life, not his."

"I know, I know. I just hate disappointing him."

"You're going to have to get used to it and he's going to have to get over it," Karen said.

Shannon sighed. "It's just weird. I'm not used to conflict with him. I'm used to him being proud of me, not angry with me."

"Girl, he's been disappointed with me since the day he married Mom and I'm still here," Karen told her. "He'll get over it eventually. And if he doesn't, then he doesn't."

"He's my father," Shannon insisted. "I can't just write him out of my life."

"I'm not saying you should write him out," Karen said. "But if he's being an ass and he can't be supportive, then you have to accept this is how it is going to be. The only way he'll be happy is if you go back to Chicago, get back into some snooty law firm and work to death, but that means no Matt. Is that what you want?"

"No," Shannon said firmly.

"You can't make everyone happy, Shannon. You can only worry about yourself and Matt. Everyone else will fall in line if they sincerely have your best interest at heart and not their own."

"You're right," she sighed. "It's just so hard."

Karen reached out and squeezed her hand. "He'll come around, I know he will. Just give it time."

"I hope you're right."

"Of course, I am," Karen said with a smile. "Have you forgotten your older sister knows all?"

Shannon grinned. "Nope, and I'm glad she's here."

"Me too."

* * *

"Let's go!" Matt said from the doorway of the apartment.

Shannon gave herself once last glance in the hallway mirror before grabbing her purse. "I'm ready."

He smiled at her and before she strode out the front door past him, he grabbed her hand and brought her closer to him. He leaned in and gently laid his lips on hers. "Have I told you how beautiful you are and how much I love you?"

She linked her arms around his neck. "It doesn't get old hearing it and I love you too."

He kissed her again before giving her butt a smack. "Shall we?"

"Absolutely."

They met Jerry, Karen and Jason out on the sidewalk, where they stood waiting on them. They climbed in Matt's truck, heading to a local Mexican restaurant for dinner with the team.

Sitting in the front seat next to Matt as he drove, Shannon smiled when he reached over to hold her hand. She loved the way hers looked so small and fragile in his. She wasn't a giant, her exaggeration of her size drawn from insecurity, but she hated how she seemed so much bigger and awkward next to women who appeared petite and dainty.

Matt gave her a squeeze. "What are you thinking?" he asked quietly under the drone of the voices in the backseat as Karen and Jerry bickered about something while Jason laughed at them.

"How happy I am thanks to you."

He smiled and even though his aviator sunglasses hid his eyes, she could envision how the blue of them warmed as they usually did. "Me too."

At the restaurant, they found some of their teammates already seated at a long table in a large room with walls filled with sombreros and Mexican blankets, intermixed with paper flowers in every shade of the rainbow. Colorful *papel picado* stretched from corner to corner and piñatas in every shape and size hung from the ceiling. Matt took the time to introduce Shannon to each of his teammates even though she was never going to remember everyone's names, but she smiled and tried her best.

At the end of the table, Matt slapped the shoulder of a man who had just taken a sip of his beer, causing liquid to slosh over the rim. "Jesus, Buck," the guy cursed with good humor. "Take it easy with those paws of yours."

Matt grinned. "Just reminding you of your place in the pecking order." He motioned toward Shannon. "Brian, say hi to my girlfriend, Shannon. Shannon, this is Brian Woodsey. He plays right field."

Shannon, recognizing the name instantly, smiled and stuck her hand out while Brian stood. "It's nice to meet you, Brian."

"You too," he said with a firm shake before he sat back down. "Not sure how you put up with this one here, but good luck to you."

Shannon chuckled and dropped into the seat next to Brian while Matt sat next to her. He didn't seem to be familiar with her name, but perhaps Shelly hadn't mentioned their meeting to him. "Oh, he's not so bad most of the time." She glanced around, but didn't spot his wife. "Where's Shelly?"

Brian frowned. "How do you know Shelly?"

"I met her the other day," Shannon said.

"You met her? Shelly?" Brian asked, still clearly confused.

His perplexity made Shannon pause and question her memory. She was certain Shelly had said her last name was Woodsey and Brian was her husband.

"Yeah, at the grocery store…" she started to say, but Matt interrupted, introducing her to another teammate who sat on the other side of him.

When Shannon turned back, only an empty seat remained.

Well, that was strange. Brian stood at the opposite end of the table talking to Jerry, but an eerie air settled around her, leaving the impression something wasn't quite right. His reaction to her asking about his wife, not to mention how he never answered where she was, combined with Karen's surprise to hear Shelly was in Florida, all left a notion of things being off-kilter, but even that didn't make sense.

Maybe there's trouble in paradise, she supposed, trying to get rid of the uneasy sensation in her stomach, which she didn't understand.

"You all right?" Matt reached out to grab her hand.

"Yeah, yeah. I'm good."

A waitress appeared a few minutes later, placed an overflowing basket of chips with salsa on their table, and proceeded to take their order. As everyone nursed beers or margaritas, or water in Karen's case, a constant stream of conversation continued around Shannon. She tried to keep up as best as she could, before giving up, since she couldn't follow most of it, and letting the noise flow all around her. Brian had returned to his seat, but had yet to say anything more to her and appeared to be avoiding her. Perhaps she was being sensitive, however, as he was in a deep conversation with the player sitting on his other side about diving for balls and how the guy apparently needed to leave his feet more in the outfield.

Hector. Shannon tried to remember the player's name. *No, Jorge. Center field.* She'd never get everyone down.

Some movement behind Jorge, who sat with his back facing the front of the restaurant, caught Shannon's attention, and she recognized Shelly as she walked purposefully toward the table. Shannon moved to nudge Brian, since he hadn't noticed, when the expression on Shelly's face stopped her. The bright smile and perkiness were gone, and in their place was…a wildness, almost. No, madness and she hadn't even glanced at Brian, her supposed husband. Instead, her focus was intent and solely on Matt, as if he were the only person in the room.

Things took a full turn toward the inexplicable when Matt glanced over and all the color drained from his face. A bad taste entered her mouth that Matt acknowledged Shelly, not Brian.

Matt jumped up, causing his chair to topple over. "What are you doing here?"

Shannon's attention volleyed between them before noticing Jason's quiet presence behind Shelly, his eyes wary, as if expecting her to do something. The entire table stopped, all eyes on the exchange, unsure what it was they were witnessing but sensing something was off. Shelly continued to stare at Matt, and her eyes welled up.

"Why?" was all she said.

Shannon shoved her chair back and stood, finally finding her voice and needing to understand what in the hell was going on. "Matt?"

He put a hand on her arm as he stepped past her and over to Shelly. "You need to get out of here, Natalie. Now," he warned in a low and guarded tone.

Natalie? Who the hell is Natalie? And why did she tell me her name was Shelly?

Natalie rushed him, throwing her arms around his waist as she started to sob. The restaurant had dropped into unnerving stillness, the silence somehow loud, everyone watching the bizarre scene unfolding, drawn to its peculiarity like a house fire. Matt clenched his jaw and squeezed his eyes shut for a second as he took a deep breath, obviously steeling for patience, before he pried her off him. Shannon didn't comprehend anything, but she needed to show her support for Matt somehow and stepped around the table to stand next to him.

"Now, Natalie. Leave," he said again.

Jason stepped forward and made to grip Natalie's arm but stopped when she reached into the waistband of the back of her shorts and pulled out a gun. Jason instinctively took a step away from her as she pointed the gun at Matt. Shannon's blood froze in fear, everything playing out in slow motion even though chaos surrounded her.

"No," Natalie said to Matt.

Jason's eyes widened, understanding dawning of what Natalie was going to do. He hurried toward her while at the same time multiple people jumped up from the table in order to rush her, but it was all too late. Ignoring everyone, Natalie raised the gun steadily, but at the last second, she shifted her aim toward Shannon.

Shannon gasped as the sound of a gunshot rang out. What felt like a Mack truck slammed into her, launching her through the air, her shoulder and back connecting with the hard corner of the table as she fell. The table collapsed from the weight and she crashed to the floor, her head taking a horrendous bounce before stomach-churning, conscious-losing pain flooded through her. She heard a deep grunt that she didn't think came from her. The pandemonium of crying, screaming and yelling, along with a whirlwind of commotion, circled around her, and then her world went black.

CHAPTER 17

Matt lay in the hospital bed staring at the ceiling. He couldn't get his head around how everything had drastically changed in a short span of time. One second he was enjoying Spring Training, enjoying the surprise of having the girl he loved by his side, enjoying a team dinner. In the next, an ex-girlfriend shoots him in the leg and throws his life in an upheaval. So many questions jumbled in the air without any answers. His brain wouldn't cooperate, reluctant to process or comprehend the meaning of what had transpired, leaving his emotions in a chaotic, tumultuous mess.

Through the chaos, however, one scenario refused to escape his attention. The possibility of his season being done before even starting. To focus on baseball was stupid given the fact he'd been shot, but despite everything, all he could singlehandedly concentrate on was what might happen with his career. Nothing else mattered.

The door opened and Jason rushed in with Matt's mom and dad right behind him. They had gotten on the first plane to Florida once they'd heard what had happened.

"Matthew," his mother cried as she rushed over to the bed. "Omigod, are you okay?"

He hissed in a breath as she jostled him a bit. "Leg hurts like a bitch."

Her hands fretted in the air over his braced leg as if she wanted to ease his pain in some way but was afraid to touch anything. "I don't understand. Who is this girl? Why would she shoot you?"

Matt glanced at Jason, who shook his head, indicating he hadn't told them anything. "She's an ex-girlfriend."

"You dated her?" his father asked, standing on the opposite side of the bed from his mother.

"Yes, and things ended badly. She refused to move on, following me and calling me all the time." He took a deep breath as he leaned back into his pillow. "I ended up filing a restraining order against her. Guess that didn't work."

Both of his parents exclaimed with shock, but then his father said, "Why didn't you tell us any of this? I could have helped."

"Because I didn't want you to worry. I had everything under control." Their faces blanched. "It's all right, guys. I've talked to the cops already. She's locked up and they're gathering the evidence they need in order to press charges. We won't have to worry about her anymore."

"Omigod," his mother said again as she paced away from the bed with her hand covering her face. She struggled to pull herself together and when she finally did, she cleared her throat and straightened her shoulders. She tugged at the blankets over him, smoothing out the wrinkles. "Okay, it's in the past now. We'll let the legal system do its job and she'll get what's coming to her. What we need to focus on is you and getting you better. What have the doctors said?"

"Not much, just that I have a fracture in the femoral shaft," Matt admitted, struggling to find a comfortable position, which caused him to grimace. "They want to take me to surgery in order to determine the extent of the damage, but that's all I really know right now."

"Okay, okay." She ran her fingers through his hair and fussed over him, her eyes glistening with tears. "We're here and we're going to help."

"Mom," Matt sighed. "I'm okay."

Her face crumpled, making him feel even more like shit. "Let me be. You don't know how it feels to hear your child's been shot, so let me fall apart. And don't tell me you're okay when I know you're not."

His father came over and put his hands on her shoulders. "You scared the hell out of us, Matthew," he said, with a sheen of tears in his eyes as well, which shocked Matt as his father didn't usually get emotional.

"I'm sorry," Matt mumbled.

"Don't you be sorry," his mother said ferociously despite the tears running down her cheeks. "This is not your fault."

Matt shifted uncomfortably, his leg throbbing. His mother caught the pained expression on his face and sprang forward. "What is it, honey? What do you need?"

"Leg really hurts and it's very uncomfortable," he admitted.

"Let me go find a nurse and see if they will give you something," she said. "Come on, Michael. Maybe we can find a doctor who can fill us in." She pulled her husband out of the room with her.

Jason, who'd been standing in the corner, out of the way, came forward. He stood off to the side with his hands in his pockets. "This sucks, huh?"

"Pretty much," Matt agreed. "How bad is it outside?" The media had camped in the parking lot of the hospital desperate for the story about the MVP catcher from Detroit shot by a crazy ex-girlfriend.

"They're still hanging around, but the hospital is working to keep them away as much as possible. Nobody's saying anything, only what the cops have been willing to share, which isn't much. The team and your agent are still saying, 'No comment.'"

Matt shook his head. "I still can't believe she did this…"

"Shannon's still—" The door opened and a doctor strode in, interrupting Jason.

"Mr. Buck," the doctor said as he thumbed through his chart, brusque and all business. "We're taking you into surgery right away. We're going to place a rod here." He pointed to an x-ray hanging on the wall next to the bed. "Place a screw here and here. We might even place a rod here, but we'll know more when we get in there and see the damage with our eyes. Essentially we're going to put the bone back together to allow it to heal properly."

"Okay," Matt said. "What's the prognosis? Am I going to miss the entire season?"

The doctor crossed his arms. "Right now it's hard to say. Everything depends on how well the bone heals. I would expect you to be out for the season, but there is the slight chance for more."

"More?" Matt asked with a frown, refusing to understand what the doctor was implying. "What do you mean, *more?*"

"Matt," the doctor said as he stepped closer, his face filled with compassion. "Injuries like these are tricky for the average person. Combine that with your profession…well, everything becomes much harder. You might never get the strength back in your leg that you need in order to catch or endure the stress of playing at a major league level. Of course, we'll do all we can, and you're going to need to do all you can with therapy afterward, but there's always a chance the bone, even healed, may not allow you to perform at the level you need."

Speechless, Matt stared at his doctor, unable to believe how his world had crashed around him. Never play ball again? He couldn't even contemplate the possibility. In fact, he refused to. A season he was reluctantly willing to give up, but his career… No, he couldn't. If he didn't have baseball, he had nothing. Without baseball, he *was* nothing.

* * *

Opening her eyes, Shannon cringed at the brightness. She moaned and squeezed them shut against the pain as her stomach rolled. She'd been in and out all night, never able to stay awake for longer than two minutes.

"Take it easy, sweetheart," a soft voice said to her. "Just take it easy."

She squinted and tried to figure out where she was. From the stark whiteness of the room and beeping noises, she had to guess she was in the hospital.

"What happened?" she croaked.

"You have a pretty bad concussion, a dislocated shoulder and lots of bruises. You probably feel like you got hit by a truck."

Shannon took a quick assessment of everything and had to agree that was an accurate statement. "Was there an accident?" she asked, trying to recall why she was here.

The young nurse stood closer so her friendly face came into Shannon's direct field of view. "Do you not remember what happened? What do you remember, sweetie?"

"I…can't…" she started to say before everything came rushing back. Shelly… no, not Shelly, someone named Natalie had come in and started shooting. "Matt! How is Matt?"

The nurse frowned. "I'm not sure who Matt is. Was he with you?"

"Yes, he's my boyfriend. Buck. Matt Buck. He was there too. She pointed the gun at him. Did she shoot him?" she asked, her mind jumping all over the place as flashes of what had transpired whirled through her head.

"I'll see what I can find out, but there are some policemen who are going to want to talk to you. We need to tell them when you're okay enough to talk. In the meantime, your sister has been here all night."

"Karen," she said and tears flooded her eyes at the comfort her sister would bring to this horrible situation.

The nurse walked out and a few minutes passed before Karen hurried in with Jerry right behind her.

"Oh, thank God," Karen said as she rushed up to the side of the bed, her eyes full of concern and worry. Reaching out to brush some of the hair off her forehead, Karen eyes were roaming all over her sister's face. "How are you feeling, honey? We were so worried."

"I hurt like hell. Concussion, something with my shoulder and who knows what else." Her eyes passed over her sister and then Jerry, and the relief at seeing them both okay rushed out of her as the tears started to fall. "I'm so glad you guys are not hurt. The baby's safe."

Shushing her, Karen squeezed her hand hard. "It's okay, Shannon. We're okay. Nothing to worry about."

"What happened? What the hell went on?" Shannon said between gasps as she tried to calm herself down.

Karen glanced over at Jerry and he gave her a small shrug. Karen cleared her throat. "We're not exactly sure, but from what we've gathered, the girl was an ex-girlfriend of Matt's."

"What happened to Matt? Where is he? Is he okay?" Shannon asked all in one breath.

Karen paused as if in preparation of sharing bad news. Dread surged through Shannon like a tidal wave and sharp, cold panic flashed over her skin. Before Karen could say anything, Shannon shook her head. "No! No…"

"No, Shannon. Calm down," Karen said. "Calm down. He's here, he's was shot, but he's going to be okay. All right? Do you hear me? He's going to be okay."

"Then why the look? Why the hesitation?" Shannon demanded.

Karen took a breath. "He was shot in the thigh and, from what we've heard, the bullet did significant damage."

"What do you mean?" Shannon asked.

"We don't know," Jerry said quietly. "That's all we know. There's been speculation he might not play ball again, but we don't know."

"Who cares?" Shannon exclaimed, not understanding why anyone would be concerned about baseball right now. "He's alive, isn't that all that matters?"

Jerry started to say something, but Karen shook her head sharply before turning back to Shannon with a tight smile. "You're right. Absolutely. We'll take it one day at a time. You just worry about getting yourself better."

"I want to see him," Shannon said but found she was having trouble keeping her eyes open.

"Go to sleep. You need to rest and get better. I'll be right here," Karen's voice said to her. "I'll be right here and then we'll see about Matt."

Shannon started to drift off, letting Karen's soothing voice float over her. Suddenly another voice came into the room and she struggled to wake back up.

"Is she okay?" the low voice asked.

"Yes, no thanks to your friend," Karen hissed. "Why didn't he ever fucking say anything?"

"Karen," Jerry cautioned.

"No, don't Karen me. He knowingly put her in danger. I mean, seriously, what the fuck? He didn't think it was something she should know?"

"I know, I agree with you," the voice said.

Jason. It's Jason. Shannon wanted to talk to him, ask him about Matt, but her eyes wouldn't budge and she was losing the battle of staying awake.

"I told him he needed to tell her, and he said he would, but…" Jason broke off, clearly not knowing what more to say. It was obvious he wanted to stick up for his friend, but didn't know how.

"But now they're both in the hospital," Karen finished with disgusted sigh. "I don't know what's going to happen, but once Shannon's father gets down here, all hell is going to break loose. There's no telling what he'll say or do."

"I know," Jason said bleakly. "He's already a mess mentally and things are only going to get worse."

"She's asking to see him," Jerry said.

Jason let out a heavy sigh. "After the news he just received, he doesn't want to see anyone, so I honestly don't know if he'd welcome a visit from her right now. He threw me out, as a matter of fact, and he won't even listen to his parents. I tried to tell him about Shannon, but we were interrupted."

"What's going on?" Jerry asked him.

"They're taking him into surgery, but they told him the prognosis might not be great. He might not play ball again."

"Oh shit," Jerry said as he paced in the opposite direction. "What a fucking mess."

"I know," Jason agreed. "Once they told him he might never play ball again, they might as well have signed his death certificate with the way he's taking it."

The room went silent and Shannon lost the battle against sleep.

CHAPTER 18

Two days later, Shannon's doctors released her from the hospital. The severity of her concussion had them keeping her a couple of nights, but they'd finally discharged her to the care of her parents, who were on their way to pick her up and take her back to the condo they'd rented. Her release instructions consisted mostly of getting plenty of rest, keeping her arm in the sling to prevent jostling, and avoiding traveling by plane until her concussion symptoms abated. Until then, she would stay in Florida.

Which was fine, as she wanted to remain close to Matt and help him with his recovery, even though she had yet to see him. Every time she'd asked, Karen had convinced her to wait, insisting Matt was still groggy from surgery or with his doctors and nurses or with his therapist, or whatever excuse she came up with. After a while, that was exactly what they were—excuses. But now she wasn't at the mercy of others and could visit him like a normal visitor and nobody could stop her.

She didn't know why they were all trying to keep her from him, but it didn't matter. She was going to see him and she was going to see him now. She was going to find out what the hell was going on.

A nurse came in with a wheelchair and smiled at Shannon. "You ready to go?"

"Yep," Shannon said as she sat down.

Holding her purse in her lap, the nurse wheeled her to the elevator and pressed the button for the first floor. They exited the hospital into the bright Florida sunshine and Shannon immediately nodded toward a bench by the doors.

"I can sit here while I wait for my parents. They said they would be here shortly."

"Are you sure, honey? I can wait with you."

"That's not necessary. I'm fine, really. Besides, they'll be here any minute, I'm sure of it. Thank you."

Shannon climbed out of the wheelchair and seated herself on the bench. She smiled at the nurse, who sauntered back into the hospital. Shannon waited five minutes before she got up and walked back through the same doors.

Despite the dull ache in her head and shoulder, along with sluggish movements, determination propelled her. She approached the information desk and tried to appear bright and alert.

"Hi. I'm looking for Matt Buck's room, please?"

"Name, please," the older man sitting at the front desk asked.

"Shannon Morrison."

After pulling Matt's information up on the computer, he glanced at her before picking up the phone. He told whomever answered the other line in a low voice that a "...Shannon Morrison was here to visit Matt Buck."

His shrewd eyes studied her as he waited and Shannon smiled at him, hoping to hide some of her nervousness. She'd forgotten the situation, forgotten Matt's status as a well-known athlete, and the restrictions likely in place as to who could visit him, given the crime. Surely the media had gotten ahold of the story by now and wanted the grisly details. She was definitely off her game not remembering the unique circumstances of the situation, but she had to be on the approved list, and if not, then someone was going to get an earful.

Thankfully, whomever the gentleman had been speaking with confirmed Shannon's approval. He hung up and smiled at her, while giving her a visitor's badge with instructions on how to get to Matt's room.

She took the elevator up to the fifth floor and took a deep, calming breath before letting her feet carry her to his room. Rather than overwhelming excitement to see him, to touch him and talk to him, consuming apprehension almost made her turn around. She'd been so confident beforehand, but insecurity now settled in its place. He hadn't attempted to reach out to her. What did that mean?

Did he even want to see her? Had he even been asking about her? Would he ask her to leave?

She scoffed, telling herself she was being ridiculous. Of course he would be happy to see her. Why wouldn't he be? Matt loved her. This wasn't *her* fault. There had to be a perfectly valid explanation why he hadn't been able to see her…or call her.

She stood outside his closed door, battling to steady her thudding heart as it tried to pound its way out of her chest. She cleared her throat and adjusted her arm in the sling, still not used to the contraption, causing her to wince. She wished she'd taken the time to make herself somewhat presentable, but she was here now.

Reaching out, Shannon pushed the door open and the sight of Matt lying on his bed, his left leg straight and stiff immediately greeted her. His hair was messy, most likely from him running his fingers through it, hard lines of strain showed in his face, and his body remained rigid. He stared out the window, but his head turned at the sound of the door. When his eyes landed on her, he didn't appear happy, but he didn't seem upset either, rather bland, emotionless and detached. His face was drawn and haggard. His bright blue eyes, usually full of warmth and a spark, were flat and dull.

She smiled at him and stepped in, letting the door close behind her. "Hi there, stranger."

"Hey," Matt answered in an impassive tone.

"How are you?" She stopped next the bed near his head.

"Been better."

Shannon nodded and tried to overlook that he'd yet to ask her how she was, but she wrote it off to the shock of the situation he'd been thrust into. He'd never been so closed-off and distant, and she struggled with what to say, how to snap him out of it.

She glanced down at his leg, noticing the bandages covering his incisions as well as the metal frame in place to keep it stable. There was obvious swelling and deep purple bruising along the leg, which looked painful to her.

"How's the leg? What's the prognosis?"

"What are you doing here, Shannon?"

Her head snapped back sharply at the harshness in his voice, and her eyes immediately welled up. Why wasn't he even happy to see her?

"Matt," she whispered. "What's going on?"

He sighed and leaned back, closing his eyes. "Just leave, Shannon. I don't want to talk about my leg."

She stood in shock as he effectively turned his back on her without actually doing so, alarmed at the drastic change. One day they were planning a life together and now it was as if they were strangers. He acted like she'd pulled the trigger, that she was the one who did this to him. She was a victim just as much as he was, so why was he punishing her? His dismissal pissed her off and she swiped angrily at her tears.

"I don't know what your problem is, but you're going to talk to me." Shannon waited, and when he continued to ignore her, she pressed on. "If you truly meant what you said when you told me you wanted to be with me, that you loved me, then you owe me this much."

Matt opened his eyes and glared at her. "I don't know what you want me to say. Things are a bit fucked up now, as you can see. There's not much more to say than that."

"You don't even want to tell me why? Why you never told me about her or anything?"

"What's the point?" he exclaimed. "I didn't, all right? There's not much I can do to change that now. It doesn't matter anyway. Not anymore. Nothing does."

"Nothing?" she repeated. "Nothing matters? Not even me?"

"Just go," he said, his tone weary. "I can't do this now."

"When then? If not now, when? It's not like you've tried to reach out to me since we've been here. I had to come down here, concussion and fucked-up shoulder and all. And you know why? Because you're important enough for me to do that."

His cool blue eyes locked on hers. "And there's your answer."

Shannon gasped as the tears started to fall again and she didn't try to stop them.

Matt finally appeared distraught and he swallowed hard. She could tell he was fighting some emotions, she just didn't know which. "I'm sorry. I didn't mean to say that. I…I just can't think straight right now."

"Then what did you mean?"

"I…just…" He stopped and dropped his head with his eyes closed. When his gaze met hers again, in it was a deep, gut-wrenching ache that tore at her heart. "Look at me," he whispered.

"I am, Matt. Tell me what I'm supposed to be seeing, because I am looking at you and I see the same man as I did before." She reached out to grasp his hand.

"No." He pulled his hand away. "No. I'm not the same man and I don't know if I will ever be again."

"No," she said. "You may not play baseball again, but you *are* the same man. Someone who's caring, fun, loving…that's still you."

He shook his head. "No, I'm not. I'm not the same man you fell in love with. He's gone. You couldn't…you can't be…" He stopped, took a deep breath as he collected himself and his eyes turned hard. "It doesn't matter. My life has been turned upside down. I may never play ball again. Never."

Shannon faltered, stumbling slightly as she backed away from the bed. "I see," was all she said as she finally comprehended the underlying message. Baseball was all that mattered. Nothing else, not even her. "I understand that is all you care about right now. I'm sorry if I thought I somehow was included, but I guess I was wrong."

With her shoulders stiff, she stepped out of his room. She continued straight to the elevators, ignoring the tears streaming down her face and the bone-aching hurt threatening to weigh her down. She retraced her steps through the hospital back to the wood bench outside in the sun without seeing anything. She plopped down and sat in a daze, replaying the conversation in her head. Never before would she have characterized Matt as self-centered, but he certainly was acting like a selfish asshole now, and if he only wanted to focus on his issues then she wouldn't get in his way. She'd given up everything believing he was a different person and now she had nothing. No job, no boyfriend, no direction. Nothing.

When her parent pulled up to the curb, Shannon caught her father's sharp eye when he climbed out, a clear sign her life was about to get harder. A lot harder.

* * *

Matt lay wide-awake despite it being well past midnight. Darkness filled the hospital room with only a slim beam of light passing between the slits of the blinds. The occasional soft thud of footsteps as someone passed by his closed door broke through the quiet. But even with the dark and the silence, sleep eluded him.

It might have been expected, given the extreme discomfort with his leg. His movements were restricted and the throbbing unrelenting, the pain, although somewhat dulled by meds, never truly disappearing. But he'd deal with the physical pain, never shied away from it before and, in fact, he spent the majority of his seasons hurting in one way or another. Most catchers did given the physical demands of their position. No, this was a different pain in the form of a big fucking hole in his chest.

Even if he couldn't get back with the team this season, he'd been confident he would return to the field next year, but four little words from one of his doctors killed what hope he'd had—*never play baseball again*. Forget the fact his doctor had said *might*; it didn't matter because Matt hadn't heard anything else.

Everything else had faded away afterward, leaving him focused on and obsessing over the loss of the game he loved. Simply put, he lived for baseball. If he didn't have baseball, he didn't have anything; he didn't *want* anything. He wanted to go out on his terms and only then, not a second beforehand. He didn't want to hear he'd be a great coach or he'd find something else to do in the game. No, fuck that. He was a baseball player, he was a catcher, he was the manager on the field, and he was a goddamn great hitter…that was who he was and he wasn't ready to change. Not yet, damn it.

All he could do now was wait. They allowed him to do some minimal leg motions, but they insisted he use crutches because they didn't want him putting too much weight on his leg yet. As soon as evidence of new bone formation appeared, they would take the crutches away—or at least limit their use—and go from there. Literally one agonizing day at a time with no way of telling what lay ahead. Nobody knew anything and it was all so fucking unfair.

His only fault in this was getting involved with Natalie. That was it. Everything else, he'd been by the book and look where that got him. He vacillated between being pissed beyond belief and overwhelmed with grief for all he might lose. More MVPs awaited him, a Triple Crown, the award for leading the league in three batting categories, lingered just out of his grasp waiting for him to get his batting average up, and the Rockets still had a pennant to win. All of those accomplishments and more remained for him in the game of baseball, and it was what he was going to do, even if it killed him.

He'd failed in getting Shannon to understand this, unable to convey how distraught he was. She deserved answers to everything, especially about Natalie, but he didn't even know what to say given the circumstances. Sorry? That was a weak and lame apology. So instead, he avoided the conversation just as he had from day one when Jason told him to tell Shannon everything. Telling her everything now would only make him look even more like a failure to her. He would rather have her hate him than think he was weak and a big disappointment. That would absolutely kill him.

Plus, so much anger swirled within him at Natalie and what she'd done. It wasn't fair to Shannon to have to deal with what he almost couldn't handle, especially when it wasn't focused at her, but he lacked the ability to separate one from the other. With so much negative energy surrounding him, he had no room for anything else, had no desire to feel anything else.

Despite fantasizing about ways to retaliate against Natalie, Matt would let the justice system do its job and, in the meantime, he would do his, which meant getting back on the field as quick as possible. He hoped Shannon realized he still loved her, wanted to be with her, even if he didn't exactly know how to tell her as much in his messed-up state. He should have handled her visit better, should have been more excited to see her, should have asked her how she was feeling. He simply wasn't able to focus on anything other than his fierce rage at Natalie and the three words screaming in his head day and night—*baseball career over.*

His throat tightened with emotion.

Matt glanced at his cell phone on the table and, as he had multiple times before, contemplated calling Shannon. He missed hearing her voice, talking to her and being with her, but he couldn't. What stopped him each time, he couldn't say, but whatever it was, it overwhelmed him, and he wanted to stay hidden in his hospital room. He didn't want to face anything. He didn't want to deal with anything. He only wanted one thing—baseball.

CHAPTER 19

Shannon sat in a chair on the small porch attached to the condo her parents had rented, staring across the courtyard, but unfocused. She tried to think about things, to figure everything out and understand what had happened. But all she could do was stare. She couldn't concentrate and she definitely couldn't put the pieces together. All she knew was she'd made a life-changing decision in order to pursue a relationship with the man she'd believed to be the love of her life only to end up empty-handed. And no matter how she tried, she couldn't understand how the blame had landed on her shoulders.

Yes, Matt's current situation was horrible, and she understood the devastation he had to be experiencing, but why was he taking it out on her? Why was he turning his back on her when they needed each other now more than ever? The threat Shannon hadn't even known about no longer existed as Natalie waited behind bars, but Shannon didn't understand the reasons behind it all, and the lack of answers left a lingering fear. The details provided by the police when they'd spoken with her in the hospital were sketchy at best, but they weren't enough. She needed more from Matt and she didn't know what hurt most—how he'd kept it all from her or how he'd pushed her away.

Perhaps their relationship, too new and too fragile, could never survive something such as this. Even though they loved each other, this was too much to overcome. As much as his dismissal hurt and as much as it went against what she wanted, she wouldn't force herself on someone who didn't want her. Message received. Now what?

Now she needed to figure out how to put her life back together, what she was going to do and where she would go from here. Trying to make any decisions, however, was daunting since all she wanted was Matt. She struggled with thinking about anything else.

The screen door opened and her father stepped out, stiff and formal. The time for their "talk" had finally arrived. They hadn't said much to each other since her release. Their conversations had centered on safe topics such as her health and recovery or speculations on the charges against Natalie, most likely first-degree attempted murder. He never asked about Matt, her job or how she'd ended up in Florida. Her father had to be livid with her choices of late, but he'd continued to keep his disappointment from her.

Dressed casually, for him, in gray slacks and a white dress shirt without a tie, he sat down in the chair next to her, tugged at his pant crease and crossed his ankle over his knee. He didn't say anything, but he was only taking the time to choose his words carefully. She glanced behind him and her mother stood inside on the other side of the door, wringing her hands.

Awesome. Shannon took a deep breath in preparation.

He cleared his throat. "We need to talk about some things."

"Things?"

"Yes, things. For one, why did you quit your job? Secondly, why would you quit for a young man who obviously doesn't care at all for you?"

"I didn't quit my job for him. Well not entirely," she amended.

"Of course you did. You've been working your whole life for this opportunity until he came along and somehow smooth-talked you into resigning."

She frowned. "Smooth-talked me? I do have a brain, you know. I know my own mind."

"It doesn't appear that way."

"Excuse me—"

"I can't understand how you would turn your back on all your dreams like that. All that work you did, for what? Nothing, that's for what."

She slouched down in her chair as her head started to pound. "I'll figure it out, okay?"

Without a job, her place in Chicago was no longer affordable, but she didn't want to live in the city anyway. With her new niece or nephew on the way, Shannon wanted to remain close, which meant moving back to Michigan, but she would have to move in with her parents until she got her life together—if her father would even let her. This was probably not the best time to ask.

"Mr. Buck is lucky I can't file a civil suit against him, or else I'd take him for everything. The negligence he's shown by not informing you he'd filed a restraining order against that girl is abhorrent."

"I'm sure there was no malice on his part…"

But part of her did blame Matt for putting her in this situation by failing to tell her anything. There had been plenty of opportunities to inform her about Natalie, but he'd never once broached it.

"Why are you standing up for him?" he demanded. "He obviously had no thoughts toward your well-being. The fact of the matter is he'd filed a PPO against her, so he knew she was a possible danger. Did he tell you about that? No, he didn't and now look at where you are."

She didn't believe in evil intent on his part, but simply negligence and outright stupidity. But Matt wasn't stupid and he wasn't careless, so she just couldn't make sense of it.

"Yes, this sucks, but I think he got the short end of the stick on this one. He did, not me."

"I don't care about him. I care about you, my daughter. Not some lowlife baseball player."

"Dad…"

"Stop." He stood and scowled down at her. "He's done enough damage to your life, and now we're left here picking up the pieces. Somehow he convinced you to quit your job and give up all your dreams, and this is how he repays you?"

She started to shake her head, but stopped when the movement only made it throb more. "No, he didn't. I did that on my own. I've told you that."

"We'll get you back to Michigan as soon as we can," he continued as if she hadn't said anything. "We'll have to discuss whether we should press charges against her, obviously, but we'll get you back on the right track," he said, ignoring her attempts to interject. "Unfortunately, you've ruined your chances at Bickles,

Bickles and Barnes, but I have some other colleagues I can call on. Some equally well-known firms in Michigan. Not quite the same scale as BB&B, but nothing to frown upon either."

"Please, stop..." she protested, but he held up his hand, stopping her.

"That's it, Shannon. There's nothing more to say. I'm not happy with your decisions lately, but you're my daughter, and so I'll make this right. I won't have you giving up on the dreams you've worked so hard for. I won't sit by and watch you be unhappy."

He gave her his back and walked inside, putting the conversation to bed. Shannon's mother whispered to him as he stepped past her, but he shook her off, declaring everything was set.

No, it wasn't set. This wasn't what she wanted. She didn't want to be without Matt. She didn't want to get a job in some other law firm that sucked the life out of her. She didn't want to leave without answers. All of that would make her unhappy, the one thing he said he didn't want.

But it didn't matter what Shannon wanted. Nobody wanted to listen to her or give her the answers she needed. Her dad didn't and Matt certainly didn't. No matter what she said, her father wouldn't listen. All he cared about was how he was going to fix everything, and she could do nothing but watch as the storm blew by.

Maybe she shouldn't even try to stop him. Maybe her decisions with Matt had been too on the whim and dictated by a simple attraction blown out of proportion. She'd simply been at a low point in her life, looking for something to provide spark, a distraction to the negativity and discontent muddling within her. Maybe her father really did know best.

But Matt was the most caring person she knew and that was what made everything so much harder to understand. She was so confused and all she wanted to know was why.

Unfortunately, answers didn't seem to coming any time soon. Shoved away by Matt, she didn't know how to reconnect with him or even if she could. The one person she'd believed she could have it all with had turned her world to nothing, sending her back to square one with no idea where to go from there.

* * *

Collapsing on the couch in his condo, Matt launched one crutch across the room into the vertical blinds. He took a deep breath and fisted his hands in his hair, barely restraining himself from pulling a hunk out of his head.

Six weeks had passed and he still couldn't walk without a limp. The bone had healed enough, allowing him to put some weight on his leg, but only for a short amount of time. He'd foolishly believed everything would be a breeze once he got here. Sure he'd known therapy would be difficult, since he had to rebuild the strength in his leg again, but he understood the hard work ahead of him and he wasn't afraid of physical pain or putting in the hours needed. Because, in his mind, if he got through the difficult part, then he could play ball again, which was all that mattered.

But he couldn't even walk without gimping and the pain made him grit his teeth. He was weak and sweating after only ten minutes, which pissed him off even more. They wanted him to take his therapy slow and easy, while he wanted to push his leg and make the damn thing heal itself. He was done waiting; any longer and he would go out of his mind.

Working on getting back in shape was all he had, and he needed it in order to keep from focusing on how crappy his life was now. He didn't have baseball and he didn't have the girl of his dreams.

The front door opened and closed, and Matt glanced over his shoulder as Jason walked through the door. Matt had remained in Florida, wanting to stay near the team, but Spring Training was now over. The season opener was in Kansas City, but at the end of the series, everyone would be back in Michigan, including him, as he'd arranged to continue his PT up there.

Jason nodded at him as he stepped into the room. "What's up?"

"Nothing. Just got back from therapy."

Jason eyed the crutch leaning against the window and the vertical blind now threatening to come off the hook as he sat down on the opposite end of the couch. "I take it it didn't go well."

"My leg is all weak and shit. Can't even walk without a fucking limp."

"You got shot, man. You had a fucking broken femur. It is going to take time to heal."

"I don't have time."

"If you want it to heal right, you do. Don't fuck this up by being a stubborn idiot and pushing yourself too much."

"I don't need this now," Matt said on a hiss through his nose as he pinched the bridge, squeezing his eyes shut. "I just need things to move faster than they are."

"You can't force this. You're going to have to take one day at a time, as much as that pains you."

"And do what, Jay?" Matt jerked upright. "Sit here on my ass and think about what a shithole my life is?"

"Matt," Jason said, his voice equally rising. "You need to stop the feeling-sorry-for-yourself shit. It's getting old."

"Oh, I'm sorry. I think I'm allowed some amount of self-pity when my life has taken a dump."

Jason stood. "Yes, this sucks. Nobody has said otherwise. It really sucks that Natalie took control away from you and dealt you a crappy hand. Yes, I get all that and yes, you are allowed some self-pity, you're allowed to be angry, pissed off—but, Matt, buddy, you've got to see what you're doing to yourself."

Matt frowned. "What do you mean?"

"You're pushing everyone away. Me, your parents, other teammates…everyone who wants to help you through this, you're pushing us away, and I can't figure out why. We're trying to help, do whatever you need us to, but you'd rather sit, bitch, be a dick to everyone and mope about things. Shannon, the girl you were crazy about—I could see how crazy you were for her—is suddenly gone. Why? Where did she go? What did you say to her?"

Shannon. Simply thinking her name made his chest ached. She'd upped and returned to Michigan without even saying good-bye. Matt had finally asked Jerry about her during one of his visits and had found out she'd gone back with her parents. He'd kept waiting for her to come back and demand answers from him, and when one day turned into the next without any word from her, it became that much harder for him to pick up the phone. So, he didn't and, apparently, they were over. Shannon had simply given up on him.

"Who said I said anything? Maybe she just cut her losses and got out. Didn't want to deal with all this." He waved his hand at his leg stretched out in front of him.

Jason scowled. "I seriously fucking doubt that. What did *you* say to her?"

"I told you, she stopped by the day she was released and I didn't see her after that."

"What did she say to you when you saw her?" Jason pressed.

Matt shrugged. "She asked how I was. Wondered about Natalie and the story behind that."

"And what did *you* say?" Jason asked again.

Matt glowered, realizing his friend was going to force him to say it. Admit he was the one who'd fucked up. "I told her I couldn't deal with it at the moment and all I was focused on was getting back to baseball."

"That was it?" Jason asked, his face the perfect picture of disbelief. "You didn't say anything else? Didn't answer any of her questions? Didn't ask about her, how she was doing? Didn't apologize for not telling her?"

"Nope. Pretty much that's all I said." Listening to himself, Matt agreed he sounded like an asshole.

Jason closed his eyes as he shook his head. "Jesus, you are an idiot. Why wouldn't you tell her about Natalie? Why wouldn't you tell her you needed her? Why would you let her leave?"

"I didn't *let* her leave." Matt swiped at his hair in frustration. "She just fucking left without saying anything. If I'd known she was going to, I would have asked her not to."

"Did you try to call her or anything?"

Matt cleared his throat and paused before he said, "No." When Jason threw up his hands as if to say "What the fuck?," Matt took in a deep breath. "Jesus, all right! I know, I know! I should have and wanted to, but I didn't know what to say. Everything was upside down and I was trying to get my head around all of this, and I didn't know what to say to her. Besides, it's probably better, for her own good, to be away from me. Safer."

"Cut the dramatic bullshit," Jason said with a roll of his eyes.

"Well, whatever. I still don't know what to say to her. She probably thinks I'm a big-time loser.'

"Yeah, she probably does," Jason agreed, "but not because of what happened. No, because you need to get your head out of your ass and stop feeling so god-damn sorry for yourself. You have it all, Matt. A great family, a great girl and a great life. Not everyone has that. All you need to do is look at me and you know it's true. We're not all as lucky as you, so stop being a dickhead."

With one last glance, Jason stalked out, slamming the front door behind him. Matt rested his head against the back of the couch and took a deep breath. It was hard to hear, but Jason was right. If anyone knew what it was like to have nothing, it was Jason and he had every right to ride Matt as he had. He'd acted like a self-centered idiot, was still acting like one, so caught up in the fucked-up state of his life that he ignored everyone else. He'd even told his parents to leave because he couldn't handle them being around, even though they'd only been trying to help.

Shannon was a victim just as much as he was and the situation had thrust her life into disarray and all he could think about was himself. Not only should he be pissed at Natalie because of everything she'd done, even before the shooting, but also because she'd planned to hurt Shannon, pointing the gun at her at the last second. He'd conveniently forgotten that in his self-absorbed state. He was an ass.

His negative frame of mind didn't help his recovery either. He expected nothing less than game-day shape immediately, which made him overlook the progress he had made. He needed to take things slow, he needed to do things right and he needed to start celebrating the positives.

And as much as Matt was reluctant to admit it, there was more to life than baseball. He knew that but the unfairness of his situation made the potential loss of the game he loved a bitter pill to swallow. But it wasn't everything and if he didn't get his head of his ass, just like Jason said, then he would be left with nothing. He had to try to get Shannon back, because if he didn't, then he'd end up regretting everything and be disappointed in himself for the rest of his life. And that was truly unacceptable.

CHAPTER 20

Toward the end of April, Shannon rushed down the highway to the airport to pick up Jerry. The call from Karen stating she was in labor had come in, and her mother had shot out of the house to the hospital quicker than Shannon had ever seen her move.

Shannon drove toward baggage claim, trying to hurry while at the same time not hit any of the travelers who stepped into oncoming traffic with their trail of luggage without even looking. She spotted Jerry at the end, waving his hands above his head, as he tried to ignore the people who recognized him, attempting to snap photos with their phones.

She pulled up to the curb, and Jerry sprinted over and climbed into the passenger seat, tossing his bag into the backseat.

"Go! Go!" he said.

"Have you talked to her?" she asked as she headed back toward the highway.

"No. She left a voicemail and now I can't get anyone to answer. Why is your mom not answering?"

The panic in his voice was evident and Shannon quickly tried to reassure him. "I'm sure everything's fine. Really. They're probably getting her settled in a room and talking with the doctors."

"I don't know, Shan. I don't know what to think," he said, clearly going out of his mind and she realized no matter what she said, he wouldn't be at ease until he heard Karen's voice.

She picked up her phone. "Let me try my mom's phone. Maybe she doesn't have Karen's phone near her."

"She's supposed to! That was the plan in case I wasn't back yet. Your mom is supposed to have Karen's phone so I can be in touch."

Shannon quickly dialed her mom's cell. Her mother's cheery voice came across the line after only two rings. "Hello, honey. Where are you? Have you picked up Jerry yet?"

"Mom, Jerry's been trying to get ahold of you ever since he landed. Why haven't you answered?"

"I had my phone on me the whole time—"

Jerry reached across the console and grabbed the phone from Shannon. "Linda, where is Karen? How is she doing?"

Shannon missed what her mother said, but a look of relief crossed Jerry's face and a big grin broke out. "Hey, baby. How are you? Are you cursing me yet?"

Shannon turned her shoulders slightly, trying to give him some privacy and not pay attention to their conversation. The love in Jerry's voice rang strong and her own throat tightened with emotion. She longed to hear a man talk to her with that much love. She'd once believed she'd found it, but she'd turned out to be dead wrong.

She stopped before she delved into anything more with Matt. Once she returned from Florida, she'd put him out of her mind and moved on. He'd been clear about his priorities and none of them included her. So she'd forged ahead and started to put her life back together the only way she knew how, the only path of which she was sure. She'd gotten out of her lease in Chicago, not without paying a hefty price, and was living with her mom and dad temporarily until she found a job. She pretty much felt like a loser, but her father had put out some feelers for her while she inquired into other local firms. So far, no bites, however. While she almost resented jumping into the same lifestyle again, it was what she needed to do. It was what she was supposed to do.

Jerry hung up and handed her the phone with an embarrassed grin. "Thanks, Shannon. Sorry to flip out on you like that."

She gave his hand a squeeze. "Don't worry about it. You have a right to be freaking out…Daddy."

He beamed. "That's so awesome. I can't wait. She's in her room and they're watching her. So far, she's only dilated about two centimeters. So let's pick up the speed. I'll pay your ticket."

Shannon laughed, but she did accelerate. She wanted Jerry to be at Karen's side as their child entered the world. When they arrived, she pulled up at the front entrance and let him jump out before she parked the car. She found her mother in the waiting room outside the delivery area.

"Jerry get here in time?" she asked her.

"Oh yes, good timing. I think they were going to take her back soon, but he definitely got there in time."

"Good." Shannon sat down and held her mother's hand. "I can't believe Karen is going to be a mom."

Her mother chuckled. "Me either. She's definitely grown up since being with Jerry. She's going to be a great mother."

"That's for sure."

Her mom squeezed her hand. "You know, I always thought I'd be here with you way before Karen."

"Really?" Shannon said in surprise. "Why do you say that?"

"You always loved to play house when you were little. You always had all your baby dolls and for the longest time you said you wanted to have lots and lots of babies."

"All little girls say that."

"Well, maybe, but Karen never did and you were so adamant," her mother said with a smile as she thought back on the memories. "You always asked me when I was going to have another baby, and whenever we saw a baby anywhere, you would stare in fascination."

Shannon frowned. "I don't remember that. When did all of that change?"

Her mother let out a sigh. "When your father decided he wanted more for you than that. You craved his attention and when he started to show it..." Her voice trailed off as a sad expression crossed her face.

Shannon glanced over at the regretful tone of her mother's voice. "Mom?"

She shook her head. "Oh, it's nothing. You're a grown woman now and I know you know your own heart. I once worried you were only doing what your father wanted you to do. You always were trying so hard to get him to notice you, but I know you're past that. You're doing what you want to be doing and if that makes you happy, then I'm happy for you."

"Yes, of course," Shannon said, but without much conviction.

Why hadn't her mother said any of this before? Shannon shook her head slightly. Had she been so desperate for her dad's approval she'd been completely willing to ignore everything else? She didn't even remember her dreams of having tons of babies. Not that it was realistic, but still.

Her father spoke of sacrifices in order to purse her dreams, but they were different for him than her. Why hadn't she recognized this before? While her father worked and put in long hours, her mother took care of the home and family. He didn't have to put anything on hold because her mother had taken care of it. Shannon didn't have that. It was different for her regardless of what he said, and she wasn't sure if she believed now that it was worth it.

The sound of feet rushing into the room interrupted her contemplation and Shannon glanced up to find Jerry standing in the doorway still dressed in green scrubs with a huge grin on his face.

"Come on, you guys! Come meet Zachary Ryan Smutton."

At least others can follow their dreams. Shannon jumped up with her mother to follow Jerry down the hallway to meet her nephew. Maybe vicariously through others, she would find hers.

CHAPTER 21

Matt walked slowly up the front steps of the Morrison's home and paused on the stoop.

He took a deep breath, bolstering himself, before pressing the doorbell. Soft chimes rang inside the house. He waited and his heart rate multiplied when footsteps moved closer. The door opened and an older version of Karen stared at him.

"Mrs. Morrison?" he asked and at her nod, he said, "I'm Matt Buck. I'm a friend of—"

"I know who you are," she said without much warmth. "What are you doing here?"

Matt couldn't blame her. Three months had passed without a word from him, and even though he missed Shannon tremendously, he'd needed the time to get past the blinding rage he hadn't been able to control, and get his head straight.

It also gave him a chance to collect his thoughts and work out what he would say to Shannon, and while he lacked a clever argument or smooth explanation, the time had come when he had to do something and couldn't wait any longer to produce the perfect speech. The more he waited, the higher the chance of losing her completely, if he hadn't already, and he really wanted to prevent that. Even if he'd lost his chance, she still deserved answers and he would give them to her.

"Hoping to talk with Shannon, if she's available. Only for a second," he added when she appeared to be contemplating slamming the door in his face.

She studied him for a moment before sighing. "I can't promise you anything, but let me see if she's willing. One second."

She closed the door and left Matt standing on the front porch like the un-
wanted guest he was. He debated whether he should turn around and walk away,
trying to gauge if she'd lied and had no intention of getting Shannon. He'd wait
a few minutes and if nobody appeared, he'd figure out another way to get Shannon's attention.

Matt glanced around at the neighbor's houses in the quiet, upscale neighborhood, feeling stupid standing in front of the closed door, and turned to step
down off the porch when the door opened again and Shannon stood before him.
Surprise had him momentarily at a loss for words, since he'd been expecting her
mother to return telling him to get lost.

"Hi," he said finally.

Shannon eyed him before stepping out onto the stoop with him and shutting
the door behind her. She crossed her arms. "What are you doing here?"

He tried not to let her coldness bother him since he deserved nothing less. "I
was hoping we could talk for a minute."

"There's nothing to talk about. I believe you said all you needed to say in
Florida."

Despite her resistance, Matt refused to give up. He would do whatever necessary in order for her to hear what he wanted to say.

"Please, Shannon. You know I didn't, and I want to clear the air between us.
I'd never forgive myself, otherwise. If after that, we have nothing more to say, I'll
leave, but please let me say what I've come to."

Her blue gaze coolly assessed him, but she finally slouched, giving in. "Fine."

"Thank you." He shifted his weight, needing to take some of the pressure off
his leg, which sometimes ached after being on his feet for too long. He no longer
required the assistance of crutches and finally noticeable progress had been made
in his rehab. His leg was stronger, allowing him to do more in therapy to start the
rebuilding and re-strengthening of his muscles, a major milestone on his path to
recovery, but some caution remained since the bone was still healing.

"I was an idiot the last time we talked. I don't know what my issue was…
Well, I do," he corrected. "I couldn't get past the fact I might be losing my baseball career and it was completely out of my hands. I was angry, distraught and

everything else in between. I didn't want to think about anything else, which was extremely selfish of me."

"Sounds like an excuse," Shannon said, doubt coloring her tone.

"No," Matt said with a shake of his head. "It's not an excuse, it's an explanation. It doesn't excuse my behavior at all. Nothing does. All I can do is apologize and that's what I'm doing. I'm sorry."

Her face revealed nothing, but she nodded. "Apology accepted. I can appreciate how hard it was for you to face the possibility of not playing the game you love again."

Her voice, so flat and monotone, like she was speaking to a stranger, ripped at him, but Matt wouldn't throw in the towel. He had to keep pushing.

"Stop, please. I know I hurt you. I told you I loved you and that I wanted to be with you, but then I didn't act like it and I told you to go away. I know you're pissed at me, so please don't act like this. Let it out and let me have it. I deserve having you scream at me."

Her eyes flashed, but otherwise she kept her emotions in check. "I don't need you to tell me how I'm feeling or how I should be reacting."

"I'm not. I'm telling you I want you to tell me all the things I didn't give you an opportunity to say because I wimped out. This is your chance."

Shannon walked away from him. She stood stiff and straight, but when she turned back, the pain and hurt he'd been expecting filled her face. Her eyes shone with unshed tears. "Why didn't you call me or anything?" she whispered.

Gratitude filled Matt at this small opening, this proof she still felt something for him. He stepped forward and gently touched her arm. "I know. I was an idiot. I know I keep saying that, it's weak and it's stupid, but it's all I have. I thought about calling you so many times, actually grabbed the phone, but I just couldn't do it." He stopped and swallowed hard before continuing, ready to divulge what had been going on in his head. "I was afraid I wasn't good enough for you anymore."

Her eyes widened. "That's ridiculous. Why would you think that?"

"Because I wasn't the same guy you said you wanted to be with. I was this broken-down version of him, a guy who'd lost the one thing he was good at. What would you see when you looked at me? Not the All-Star or the winner of Silver Sluggers, or an MVP. No, all you would see was a loser. A broken-down loser."

Shannon shook her head at him, compassion starting to show in her expression. "Matt, that's absurd. You're still the same man. Yes, you're a great baseball player, but that's not all you are. You're a great man. Kind, caring, compassionate. You're still the same person I quit my job to be with. The same guy I wanted to be with whether you're playing baseball or not. I wanted to be with you."

"I know that now. I had some help removing my head from my ass, so to speak."

"Why didn't you ever tell me about her?" she asked, changing the subject.

Matt took a deep breath and ran a hand through his hair. "Kind of for the same reason, I guess. Jason told me repeatedly I needed to, and I agreed with him, I never intended to hide it, but I could never do it. I didn't want you to think I hadn't been able to handle the situation, that I let her control my life. I was afraid it would push you away, especially when our relationship was so new, when we were still struggling to figure us out. I didn't want to risk telling you and have you leave me because of it."

"I had a right to know—"

"You absolutely did. I was wrong to keep it from you. I don't know that you knowing would have prevented what happened, but you could have had your guard up more."

"And I might have known it was her when she approached me." He frowned. "She approached you before?"

"Yes, but she told me her name was Shelly."

"Jesus." Matt closed his eyes and rubbed at his temples. He had no idea Natalie had actually made contact with Shannon. Had she'd been aware of the situation, her suspicion might have been raised, preventing things from progressing as they had. His existing guilt ramped up to staggering levels at this new information. "I'm sorry. I really fucked this up." He took her hand in his. "There's nothing I can say to tell you how sorry I am and I have no excuse for not telling you. None."

"Did you ever trust me?" she wondered, her eyes filled with pain.

"What do you mean?"

"You keep telling me all these reasons why you didn't tell me or why you pushed me away was because you were afraid that was going to be my reaction anyway. Did you ever trust me to stay with you, no matter what? That I wanted to be with you, no matter what?"

He started to insist he did—how could she think otherwise? But then had to admit perhaps he hadn't. Not completely, anyway. He took in a deep breath and let it out. "I guess I didn't."

"Why not?" Shannon asked as a single tear escaped down her cheek. "What had I ever done to not make you trust me?"

He hissed out a breath, pained to see her tears, but he would suffer because he deserved all the pain, guilt and blame she threw at him. "I don't think it was only one thing. I think it was a bunch of things. The situation with Natalie probably had me subconsciously assuming things, putting me in a dark place to begin with, even though I didn't want to admit it because, again, that meant she had control. It had a little bit to do with you and your job. You'd been saying your career was all you wanted for so long and then you just gave it all up. Could I trust it was what you really wanted and you wouldn't regret your decision later? But it's also me and how I tick. It's one of the reasons I'm a catcher. I don't just call pitches and catch balls. I see everything on the field, I direct what's going on and I coordinate. I need to be on my guard and in control. That's who I am and that's who you came to know. So, how do you think I felt when I had these situations where I was very much *not* in control? Of course, I'm going to think it makes me weak and...I don't know, undesirable. Why would you want to be with someone who couldn't get some girl to leave him alone and he can't do anything about it except ask the law to protect him? I didn't trust that you'd love that guy just as much as the other one."

She went soft. "Matt. My God. That's...so stupid."

He chuckled. "Tell me how you really feel."

Shannon put her arms around him. "I loved you and I wanted to be with you...all of you, the good and the bad. I never thought any of that stuff. If anything, I think you've managed everything as best as you could, given the circumstances. You've done admirable." She stepped back. "I mean, look at you. You're standing without crutches and you really can't tell anything's happened to you.

You're working hard to get back to where you want to be, where others would have given up a long time ago."

"Well, I guess it's a good thing you don't hate me," Matt said

She smiled at him. "I don't hate you. I was hurt and angry, but I never hated you." An awkward pause fell between them, neither of them sure where to take the conversation next, before she cleared her throat. "So, I'm assuming you are preparing your suit against Natalie?"

"Um. No, I'm not."

She cocked her head as if she had misheard him. "You're not? Why wouldn't you sue her?"

"Because what would it solve?" Matt said to her. "It's not going to change the past, make things better between you and me or get me back in the game quicker. She's a mentally ill girl who obviously needs help. If I sue her, it's only going to drag things out and hinder everyone's ability to move on, and that's all I want. So, I'll let the law do its job and then let it go."

Shannon stared at him in disbelief before a small smile lifted her lips. "That's really…great of you. Most people wouldn't see it that way and would want to make her suffer as she's made you suffer."

He shrugged, uncomfortable with the praise. "I'm not trying to be nice. I just want what's best for everyone involved. I just want to move on from all of this."

"And have you? Are you going to be able to play?"

"I'm getting there," he replied to her first question. "I won't be able to completely until we're good." When she averted her eyes, clearly not ready to discuss them yet, he continued. "But, yeah. I hope so. I'm not going to be able to catch this year, but I can run the bases, so I can be a bat off the bench. Whatever I can do to help my teammates, get back into the lineup before the end of the season, I'll do."

She nodded. "That's awesome. I'm so happy for you. That's what you wanted and—"

"I was wrong," he interrupted, his eyes strong on hers.

"About what?"

"Baseball isn't the most important thing. It definitely isn't more important than you."

Her blue eyes searched his, seeking out the truth and when she found it, clear and sure, she took a staggering breath. "Matt…"

"Loved?" Matt said as he eyed her for her reaction.

"What?" she asked with a slight frown.

"You said 'loved' me? Is it past tense now?"

"No, it isn't past tense, but I…I don't know…" She stepped away from him and crossed her arms across her middle.

"I never stopped wanting you, wanting to be with you," he said, forging ahead, unwilling to give up. "I never stopped loving you, even when I implied I didn't."

"I…" She stopped and shook her head before turning back to him.

"This recovery has been one of the hardest things I've ever had to do, but I made it even harder by pushing you away. I've needed you more than I've ever needed anyone, Shannon. I know I don't deserve a second chance, but I'm here, begging you for one."

"I…I don't know what to say."

"Say you want to try again," he said as he crowded her, refusing to let this opportunity slip through his fingers. He leaned down and placed a gentle kiss on her neck. "Say you want to be with me. Say you still love me."

Shannon sighed as she tilted her head and leaned into him. His hands went to her waist and pulled her tightly to him. His lips hovered a hairbreadth above hers, waiting and letting her make the decision to close the gap between them. Her lips parted on a small gasp before touching his. The kiss started out light and tentative, but soon familiar heat spiked and her mouth opened to his as his tongue sought out hers. He plastered her against him, missing the softness of her, and her arms went around his shoulders. She moaned into his mouth when his fingers threaded through her hair. They separated and the same desire surging within him swam in her eyes.

"Is that a yes?" Matt asked with a hopeful grin.

She smiled. "I guess it is."

He leaned in for another kiss. "What do you say you come back to my place with me?"

"Hmm…" Shannon murmured against his lips. "I wish I could, but I can't."

He stood back. "How come?"

"I have a job interview later on."

"Oh?" he said. "Where at?"

"A local law firm. My dad knows one of the partners."

Matt paused. He didn't want to jump to conclusions, but he didn't like the sound of this. "What kind of firm?"

"A corporate law firm. I think there are over two hundred attorneys. It's a great firm, one of—if not the—top firm in the area with lots of recognition, and if I can make partner—"

"So you're getting back into a big firm again, even though you said you didn't want to?" he interrupted, annoyed at the circle they seemed to be turning in.

Shannon's eyes narrowed. "I have to do something."

"I understand that, but I didn't think you wanted to get back into a demanding firm."

She let out a huff. "I need a job. I lost the one I had to be with you, remember?"

"Whether you're with me or not, you should be doing what you want to do. Not what others want you to do."

"I'm not," she insisted, but her shoulders went rigid. "This is what I know, what I do."

"So, then you've changed your mind about what you want? Again?"

"No…I…it's not…" she stammered, looking irritated and frustrated.

"Then what is it? You want to be a partner in a big firm or not?" he pushed, anger tinting his tone.

She stepped back from him, mouth gaping in shock before she snapped it shut with anger. "I'm trying to figure everything out. I quit my job so we could be together, but then that fell apart—"

"I never asked you to quit your job. You did that yourself."

"Because I thought it was what you wanted! I thought you wanted us to be together!" she cried.

"I do. God, I do more than anything, Shannon," Matt said with pleading eyes. "But not at the expense of your happiness. I want you to do what *you* want, be what *you* want, but not if it is one or the other. I couldn't live with that."

Defeat weighed on him. He couldn't do this. He loved her and he wanted to be with her, but he couldn't continue to go back and forth with her while she figured out what she wanted out of life. She had to understand who she was, be faithful to herself before committing to anybody else. He needed her to be one hundred percent happy with her decisions, not forever questioning them. He couldn't live with her resenting him because he'd kept her from following her true dreams.

"I can't do this," he said in a low voice, unable to believe he was actually uttering the words.

Panic and fear crept into her bright blue eyes. "What are you saying?"

Matt slowly backed away from her. "I don't know. I don't know if I can continue to battle like this. I expect to have to work on things with you, but we seem to be going in circles with what you want. What you want your priority to be. You need to figure that out before we can ever work. I don't want you to be bitter, believing I made you choose something you didn't want."

"I would never...it wouldn't be like that..." she faltered, realizing he was right.

"You just said as much..." He stopped with a shake of his head. "And this thing with your father...I...I don't know. I can't compete with that," Matt told her. "You have to live your life, the way you want. Not the way he wants. I understand you want to make him proud. Hell, I want to make my dad proud, but I have to do what's right for me. His happiness shouldn't dictate your choices."

"He's not," she insisted, but the weakness in the declaration was clear.

"Yes, he is. I thought when you'd quit your job in Chicago that you'd finally started to step away from him, but I was wrong. You're still putting his wishes ahead of your own. You said yourself you didn't want to work in one of the big law firms he keeps pushing you toward, and yet you have an interview with one this afternoon rather than telling him 'No thanks.'"

Matt placed his hands on his hips and hung his head. He couldn't believe this was where they ended up. Grief emanated from her that matched his heavy heart, but he wouldn't let it change his mind. He had to do what was right for himself.

"I'm sorry, Shannon. I can't do this if it's always going to be like this. I need…" He paused and took another deep breath. "I need you to be happy with yourself and your decisions, and you're just not there yet. God, I want you to be, but you're not. It isn't fair to you and it isn't fair to me."

"But…" Shannon started to say as her tears overflowed.

He held up his hand, stopping her. "I'm sorry," he said with a hoarse voice as his throat tightened. He leaned forward to press his lips to her forehead, and closed his eyes, drinking in her light citrusy scent and storing it to memory. "I'll see you…around."

Even though it was the hardest things he'd ever had to do, he turned and walked away.

CHAPTER 22

Needing a dose of baby cuteness to cheer her up, Shannon called Karen to ask if she wanted company for lunch. Since Karen was in desperate need of some adult companionship, she almost begged Shannon to come over.

Shannon let herself in and moved into the kitchen, where she was certain she'd find her sister. Sure enough, she spotted Karen digging through the refrigerator.

"Hey," she said.

"Hey, yourself," Karen's voice answered from within the fridge.

Shannon strode over to the bassinet in the corner and peeked down at the bundled lump nestled inside. "He's conked out, huh?"

Karen dumped a load of vegetables from her arms onto the counter. "Yeah. I just fed him."

Shannon pouted as she brushed a light fingertip across her nephew's full round cheek. His little fingers flexed, but otherwise he remained fast asleep. She gently ran a hand over the shock of dark hair on top of his head that stood out in stark contrast to the white sheet of the bassinet. He was definitely a miniature Jerry. "Bummer."

"He'll be up in a while and I'll even let you take diaper duty," Karen said with a big grin.

"Gee, thanks," she said as she sat on the opposite side of the counter. "What are you making?"

"I've got some chicken and bacon, so I thought I'd make a Cobb salad for us. That good?"

"Yes, perfect. Anything you make is perfect." Shannon glanced back over at the bassinet, striving to ignore the jealousy storming through her. This was what she wanted, where she wanted to be in her life, even though for some reason, acceptance of this continued to evade her. "I bet Jerry can't wait for them to done with their road trip so he can get home."

"When he had to leave after we brought Zach home, he about cried. The man is more of a mess than I am with my hormones all over the place."

"Aww, how cute. He was over the moon at the hospital. I didn't think he was going to let anyone else hold him."

"He wasn't going to," Karen said. "I had to remind him I was the one with the boobs and therefore, I had to hold Zach in order to feed him."

Shannon laughed. "That's awesome. You got a good one, Karen."

An expression of pure love filled Karen's face and her eyes misted. "I do, don't I? Now stop or you're going to make me cry like a fucking sap. Oh, I forgot to tell you. Guess who's preggers?"

"Is she?" Shannon said, guessing who immediately. "Oh, that's wonderful! I know they've been trying."

"Yep. She's only about a couple months along, and they didn't want to tell anyone yet, but I guess Chase hasn't been able to stop smiling, and I pulled it out of Maddie since she's been dragging so much lately. She's due in the beginning of November."

Envy surged through her again. Her turn would come one day, she kept telling herself. Maybe. "I'm so happy for them."

"I'm jealous since they have a built-in babysitter with Bree. She'll make an amazing older sister," Karen said. "Anyway, enough of the baby talk. It gets old, even to me. So what have you been up to?"

Shannon shrugged. "Just trying to find a job. I really need to get moving on that and get out of Mom and Dad's. I have the money for my own place, but still figuring out location. Waiting to see if we get any bites on some of the firms we've contacted."

"Are you only looking here in Michigan?"

"There's a couple back in Chicago that Dad knows, but yeah, mostly here. I would prefer to stay nearby so I can spend time with my gorgeous nephew."

Karen eyed her and Shannon could tell she wanted to make a comment about the job search, but, thankfully, she kept her mouth shut for once. Instead, she said, "How are things with Matt?"

"Matt?" Shannon asked. "Who said anything about Matt?"

Karen paused as she studied her and then she sighed. "I take it you're still avoiding him?"

"I was never avoiding him," Shannon told her with huff. "He made it loud and clear what his decision was. He basically put me in the position of having to choose him over a job. Sorry, but I'm not going to do that, especially given everything that has gone down between us. It's not like he's Mr. Trustworthy."

"I thought you loved him and wanted to come up with a compromise? You both have very demanding jobs, but there's got to be a middle ground somewhere."

"Wait a minute," Shannon said as she held up her hand. "I thought you were mad at him?"

"Of course I am," Karen said. "But I'm sure he had his reasons for not telling you about Natalie, which I'm sure he told you about. If you're okay with it, than I am. I never thought he kept it from you because he wanted you to get hurt or anything. I was just pissed that it had to get as far as it did before it all came to head. It was scary as hell and I'll never forget it for the rest of my life, but it's because of Matt that you're weren't more hurt than you were. You might not be here today if it wasn't for him, so I have to remember that."

Shannon froze. "What are you talking about?"

"What do you mean?" Karen said. "He pushed you out of the way. He basically threw his body in front of yours when bat-shit crazy chick pulled out the gun." When Shannon continued to look at her with a puzzled expression, Karen's eyes widened. "You did know he took the bullet for you, didn't you? How else did you think you got hurt? I thought you remembered everything."

"I…I didn't know," Shannon said, stunned. "I assumed I got caught up with people rushing her."

She recalled the weight of something heavy landing on top of her, and the searing pain in her head and shoulder, but she hadn't known Matt had thrown his body in front of hers. He'd stepped between her and Natalie, and because of her, his career was in jeopardy. She hadn't pulled the trigger, but the bullet had been meant for her. She'd clearly seen Natalie change her aim in her direction. Matt had risked his life for her and this was how she paid him back. Being wishy-washy about what she wanted and afraid to take a stand for who she was. She hadn't even said, "Thank you." No wonder he walked away from her. She would have too.

* * *

Stepping up to the reception desk of the law firm of Danner, Honeyman and Wagner, Shannon introduced herself. "Hello. Shannon Morrison here to see Mr. Walters."

The receptionist smiled brightly at her. "I'll let them know you've arrived. Please have a seat."

Shannon smiled in thanks, turned and sat in a dark mahogany leather club chair. She tucked her briefcase next to the leg and crossed her feet at the ankles. Her third interview in as many days, and so far, she'd left each one less and less excited about the prospect of joining another large firm. She tried to come across as eager and enthusiastic, but failed, and, as a result, there'd been no callbacks. She had to do something, however. She couldn't remain jobless forever.

Her phone buzzed from within her purse, indicating an incoming text. Karen had sent her a picture of Jerry sleeping on the couch with Zach in his arms. Both of them had their heads thrown back as they slept hard and Karen captioned the photo with, "Like father, like son."

Shannon started to grin at the sweet picture before the smile quickly fell. She couldn't get upset before she went in for the interview—a sure way to blow it—so she put her phone back into sleep mode and placed it out of sight. She wouldn't think about how the adorable picture of Jerry and his son tugged at her heartstrings, making her want things she couldn't have. She couldn't let it distract from what she had to do, and that was secure a job.

A well-dressed woman walked up to the receptionist's desk and slouched down with a huff. She had on an expensive black suit with a three-button blazer cinched at the waist, and a narrow skirt that hit right above her ankles. She leaned against the front desk to relieve some of the pressure off her feet, which were stuffed in three-inch black heels. A tight bun held her blond hair, and her makeup was flawless, but stress and exhaustion lined her face, evident even from where Shannon sat across the room.

"Oh, man. What a day," she bemoaned to the receptionist.

"Tough day in court?" the young woman asked.

"Omigod, yes," the lawyer said in a low voice. "I hope this trial wraps up soon."

"You're going on vacation with your family afterward, right?"

"Oh, no. I'm not able to go. My husband is going to take the kids."

The receptionist frowned. "You're not even going to meet them?"

"No can do. I can't leave here. Too much to do."

"Well, that's great your husband is willing to take them all by himself," the receptionist said, obviously trying to find some positive in the situation.

"Oh, my husband is a godsend. Really he is. He goes to all of their sporting events, handles everything with their schools, and takes them everywhere. Most of the time they go on vacations without me. They know mom is out there making the money so they can do all of that," she said with a laugh. Her cell phone started to ring and she glanced at the display. "Oh, duty calls again. Talk to you later."

The receptionist and Shannon watched as she walked down the hallway to her office talking to whoever had called. Shannon caught the receptionist's shocked gaze and they both looked at each other for a moment as if to say, "Can you believe that?"

That was probably the saddest thing Shannon had ever heard. The woman had no time in her life for her kids or husband, and they went on with their lives without her. She provided monetary support and nothing else. She didn't cheer them on as they played their favorite sport or have fun with them on the weekend. She didn't help them work through their troubles, their schoolwork, or even offer a shoulder to cry on. She was a fleeting figure that rushed in and out of the picture, and Shannon wondered how they felt about that. Were they okay with it, understood that it was mom's job supporting their lifestyle? Or were they resentful and wished mom was more involved in their lives?

But that wasn't what bothered Shannon the most, however. The exchange hit her hard because that was her down the road. If she ever got married and had kids, she wouldn't be a part of their lives if she continued on this path. Hell, if she continued down this path, she might not ever meet anyone and have kids.

She pulled out her phone and studied the photo of Jerry and Zach again. She wanted that. She wanted that so badly. Why was she doing this to herself?

She missed Matt, so much so that everything ached. The pain of his rejection hurt so much, but she didn't blame him for turning away from her. She would have done the same thing. He'd stood up for their relationship in the truest sense of the word by literally using his body as a shield, while she cowered in the background, letting herself be pushed away from Matt and toward the life she didn't want, afraid to oppose, unwilling to stand up for herself. What the fuck was wrong with her?

Since when had she become such a pushover? Since when did she let someone else dictate things? She didn't, except when it came to her father. It was way past time for her to start standing up for herself. Shannon needed to put her foot down and she needed to do it now. She needed to tell him to let her live her life the way she wanted. To let her follow *her* dreams, her *real* dreams. Not the ones he wanted for her. She shouldn't feel guilty about not wanting to be the big-time lawyer with fame, prestige and money like he wanted. It wasn't who she was.

It didn't meant she didn't want to be a lawyer; it wasn't that. She did enjoy law, but she wanted to support the little guy who didn't have anyone to stand up for him. She didn't want to represent the big corporations or the executives who took advantage of their employees or misused their funds out of greed for wealth and power, and felt horrible for having done so. She wanted to be the advocate for those who had no voice, not those who should be silenced. But most of all, she refused to let her job control her life, be her life.

She shoved the phone back in her purse and grabbed her briefcase. She walked over to the receptionist's desk and gave her a smile. "I'm sorry, but something has come up and I need to leave. Please give Mr. Walters my apologies."

"Oh," the girl said, clearly surprised. "Would you like to reschedule?"

Shannon shook her head. "No, that won't be necessary. Thank you."

She turned and walked out of the office, away from the life she didn't want and toward the one she did.

CHAPTER 23

Shannon stormed into her father's office, causing his secretary to glance up in surprise. "Shannon? Is everything okay?"

"Hi, Carol. Is he available? I need to talk with him."

She reviewed his schedule. "It appears he does have a few minutes free before his next meeting. One second."

Shannon shook her head. "Don't bother calling him. He talking to me now whether he wants to or not."

Carol's mouth dropped open and she stood as she said, "But…"

Shannon ignored her as she went straight to the door of her father's office and opened it. She had to do this now before she chickened out again.

He sat at his desk and glanced up in surprise at the intrusion. "Shannon?"

"I need to talk to you." She stepped in and closed the door behind her. She leaned her back against the hard wood and took a deep breath. "I don't want to work in a large firm."

He tossed down his pen and frowned. "What?"

She pushed off and walked further into the room. "I don't want to work in a big firm. I don't want to work my ass off to become a partner. I don't want only work to be my life."

He leaned back in his chair and pressed his fingers into a steeple. "This is all quite a drastic change."

"I know, but…I'm not happy, Dad. Isn't that what you said you wanted?"

"Of course I want you to be happy. I don't understand how working toward your dreams has made you unhappy, however."

"Because..." she started, but then broke off, struggling to shore up her nerves. She couldn't back out now. She'd burst if she kept everything inside her much longer. She had to lay it all out there and deal with his reaction. "Because I've realized I want other things."

"Such as?"

"Such as a boyfriend, a family, a...a life. I'm so tired of work being my life and having no time for anything else. I haven't had time for myself since college and I'm done. I don't want that life. I thought I was willing to make those sacrifices, but the truth is I'm not."

He stared at her in silence and anger hardened the lines of his face. He didn't say anything for another moment before he finally sniffed a quick breath through his nose and cleared his throat. "Him. Is that what you're saying? You don't want all of this because of *him*?"

"Please stop," Shannon begged. "Stop talking about him that way. In fact, you should be thanking him."

He scoffed. "Thanking him? What on earth would I have to thank him for? Intentionally putting my daughter in danger? Oh, yes, please let me thank him for that."

"He didn't intentionally do anything. He was taken by surprise by this just as I was."

"Bullshit," her father swore, a rarity for him, unless his anger got the best of him. "He knew she was dangerous. Why else would he file a restraining order?"

"He knew she was stalking him and she wouldn't leave him alone, yes," Shannon said, refusing to back down this time. She wouldn't let him continue to drag Matt's name through the mud. "But no, he didn't know she was dangerous. He filed the order because he wanted her out of his hair."

He waved her off. "Excuses. Still nothing to thank him for."

Shannon leaned over the desk. "What he did," she said as she punctuated each word with a finger against the top, "was save me. If it wasn't for him, I may not be here."

Her father's shrewd eyes assessed her. "And exactly how did he convince you of that?"

She bit her tongue, ignoring his intimation. "When she pulled out the gun, she aimed at me. Not him. Me! He threw himself between me and her, and took the bullet clearly meant for *me*." She poked her chest as she tried to get her dad to feel some emotion other than anger. "Me, Dad. Not him. Me."

"Why haven't I heard this before? I don't recall reading this in any of the witness reports."

"I don't know. Everything happened so fast that maybe they didn't recall exactly how it all went down. You and I both know eyewitness reports are not always completely accurate. I certainly didn't remember it."

"I don't believe it. This is what he wants you to believe."

"No, Dad," she insisted. "He didn't tell me this. He hasn't said anything to me about it. Karen mentioned it, and after she told me, I remembered."

He chuckled. "Karen? Oh, now we're going to take the Queen of Drama's word on things?"

"Listen to me for once, please!"

He stopped laughing and stood. "Don't raise your voice at me, young lady. I always hear you."

"No, you don't! You don't ever hear me! You only hear what you want to hear."

"Well, what is it that you want me to hear so damn much? Say what you want to say."

"I'm not going to any more job interviews. I don't want that job."

"Don't be ridiculous. That's exactly what you want and what you've always wanted—"

"Stop!" Shannon cried and his mouth closed in shock. "Stop telling me what I want. It's not what I want. I just wanted you to be proud of me, proud I was your daughter, and so I went along with it."

"Well." He cleared his throat and shoved his hands into the pockets of his gray slacks. "This is all very surprising. I had no idea you felt this way." He shifted uncomfortably and toyed with a paperweight on his desk. "What is it that you want to do then?"

"I don't know," she said with a shrug. "I've been tossing around the idea of opening a private practice. Or maybe working for a small firm, one that would allow me to do some pro bono work on the side."

"Pro bono work?" he asked, not able to hide his distaste.

She hesitated, waiting to drop the biggest bomb of them all. The one that would be the deciding factor in where things stood between them after all this. "In fact, I'm going to study for the July bar in Arizona."

"Arizona? Why Arizona?" he asked, but he soon caught on. He sighed and narrowed his eyes at her. "Matt. You seriously are going to forgive him? After everything? Shannon, even you can see how foolish that is."

"There's nothing to forgive, Dad. He was stupid not to tell me about Natalie in the beginning, but that's all it was—stupidity derived from his own insecurities about the situation. He had no other reasons to hide it from me, and I believe him."

"You're going down there to be with him? You're moving to Arizona?"

Shannon nodded. "Yes. I love him and I want to be with him."

He sighed. "I don't know what to say…"

"How about nothing changes between us?" she suggested as she sniffed. "That you understand and only want my happiness? No matter what?"

His back stiffened, a clear indication she'd asked for too much. "I…I can't help you with any of this…I don't agree and I certainly don't approve, especially when it comes to him." He raised his gaze to her, his eyes hard and cold. "I'm done."

Shannon tried to swallow past the rock lodged in her throat. This was exactly what she'd been trying to avoid. He took this as a personal insult and didn't have the trust in her to accept, only reject. There was nothing more for her to say. To give in was to give up on herself and she refused to do that ever again. She could only hope with time he'd come around. And if he did, she would be waiting. But even if he didn't, she wouldn't put her life on hold because of his stubbornness.

She took a stuttering breath with a shaky nod of her head. "I understand. I'm sorry it has to be this way."

Walking over to the door to his office, with her hand on the knob, she glanced back. He refused to make eye contact with her.

"I love you, Dad," she said and walked out.

* * *

A warm late July afternoon, Matt sat in the conference room as they waited for everyone to pile in. This was it. Today he'd either be cleared to get back on the field or his comeback would be shelved, forcing him to remain on the disabled list for the remainder of the season. The team was doing well, but he could provide the extra oomph needed to get them over the hill in order to cruise into the playoffs.

When Coach Brooklyn finally walked through the door, the last of the group to arrive, the meeting started.

"All right," he said as he sat in the high-back black leather chair. "What's the story on our catcher, Mr. Buck?"

One of the therapists cleared his throat. "He's been doing really well with all of the exercises we've been running him through, and we've seen great improvements in his speed and mobility. Matt assures us there is no pain or stiffness in the leg."

All eyes shot to him as Coach Brooklyn asked, "Is that true?"

Matt nodded. "Yep."

"Nothing at all? You're back to one hundred percent?"

"No," Matt admitted to his coach, not bothering to lie as all players did since they'd see right through it. "I'm not one hundred percent, but I feel good. I just need to build up my strength more before I'm back to one hundred percent and can catch again."

"Ah, so no catching?" the General Manager asked Matt's doctor.

"We would advise against it this year. We need to ensure we don't put the newly healed bone through too much stress too soon. It's healed, there's no question about that, but we should exercise caution for the next few months."

"O'Shea's been filling in nicely," the GM said.

While everyone at the table murmured their agreement, Matt's coach eyed him.

"I'm going to assume your vote is to not sit out the rest of the season," he said to Matt.

"Yep. I want back in," Matt responded.

"And what should we do with you?"

"A bat off the bench or designated hitter. I can also fill in at first, if needed," Matt said. "I think we all agree I would be a huge bat to bring in late in a game."

"No doubt about that," the GM agreed before looking between the trainer and the doctor. "Any concerns with that?"

The doctor shook his head. "No. I don't think Matt would be taxing the leg any harder than he does working out every day."

Coach Brooklyn puffed up his cheeks and blew out a breath as he sat back in his chair studying Matt. Matt held his, waiting, the fate of his season depending on agreement from everyone in this group. Only one person had to express doubt and they'd shut him down for the rest of the year, which would be torment.

Coach finally turned to the General Manager. "We'll send him down to Dayton, get him in some games, and then bring him back up. We're going to have to figure out who we want to send down in order to make room on the roster until expansion in September."

Matt broke out into a huge grin as relief flowed through him. He needed this. He needed baseball and he needed to get back with the team. Slowly but surely, his life was coming back together. It wasn't there yet, but he was definitely in a better place than where he'd been only a few months ago.

Not only had he fully recovered, but also the legal interruptions from Natalie's case were starting to lessen for the time being. They'd charged her with first-degree attempted murder, and soon afterward her attorney declared doubt about her mental competency. Pending the results of her competency trial, which hadn't been scheduled yet, they'd go from there. Matt would do his job and testify as needed, but that was all he would do.

He needed to get back in the game and he needed to get his life back in order, which also meant moving on from Shannon. Disappointment remained and he wished things had turned out differently between them, but it was what it was. He didn't understand her compliance with her father's every wish when it led to her unhappiness. He was lucky his parents stood behind him no matter what he did.

As much as he might not want to, he had to keep his focus on the road in front of him. Baseball was finally back and that made almost everything right in his world.

* * *

Shannon walked out of the building and turned her face up to the hot July sun, closing her eyes at its brightness. She still couldn't get over how cheerful it was all the time, such a startling presence against the cloudless bright blue sky, but soon the oppressive heat that marked desert living was too much and she jumped into her rental car, immediately cranking up the air conditioning. Matt loved living in Arizona, but that was probably because he was never around during the scorching summer months.

Pulling out of the parking lot, she turned her car in the direction of her appointment as dictated by the GPS. Assuming she passed the bar, she was reaching out to local legal aid organizations, gathering information since she planned to volunteer her time once she was allowed to practice. She'd spent a lot of time soul searching, and this was what she wanted. She was going to open her own practice while at the same time volunteer her services to those organizations who handed out free legal advice. Any case she felt strongly about, her services would be available at a low rate or even free. She was finally following her heart and combining her love of the law with fighting for those without a voice, and it felt wonderful, freeing. A lot of work remained ahead of her, but she was ready and excited to get started.

There were some nerves, especially since she was doing all of this without knowing if Matt would even take her back, but she remained optimistic. This felt so right that she couldn't believe it was the wrong decision, that he wouldn't be happy with all she'd done. Despite all the changes in her life, everything felt for the better.

She hadn't spoken with her father since she stormed out of his office. His rejection hurt, she wasn't going to lie, but until he came around and stopping taking this change as a personal affront, then this was how it had to be. She couldn't live her life for him anymore. She'd done that for too long and had missed so much.

She refused to lose anything more. One day her dad would come around, she was fairly confident in that. But if not, then it was his loss and his choice, and she had to remember that.

Turning into the driveway, she parked her car before lowering the visor to check her reflection in the mirror. This was the last thing she had to do before she could head back to Michigan and back to Matt. This visit was going to be stressful, but she hoped that by the end, she'd be able to get the help she needed. If things went as she desired, then she'd have her office space. If not, then she'd keep looking.

She climbed out of her car and placed her briefcase strap on her shoulder. She opened the front door, stepping into a bright waiting area with an Indian-patterned area rug of greens, peaches and burnt reds. Tan chairs sat around a petrified wood table, and multiple photographs hung on the walls, all displaying the majestic mountains and magnificent desert. Shannon didn't need to look closely to know who had taken them.

The receptionist smiled at her. "Can I help you?"

"Yes," Shannon said. "Shannon Morrison to see Michael Buck, please."

CHAPTER 24

Matt sat on the bench in the dugout. The Rockets were at home, playing against the Cleveland Buffaloes on a warm and muggy August night. Tied four to four at the bottom of the eighth inning, both teams had run their starting pitcher for as long as possible, but had finally needed to make calls to their respective bullpens. A duel going go down to the wire, reminiscent of the season before. Tied for first place in the division, it was the final series between the two teams. Whichever team won the series would leap ahead in the standings and, barring an absolute meltdown, win the division.

The Rockets had won the first two of the four-game series and now the third game was in their grasp. If they won this game, then the series was theirs, even if the Buffaloes managed to win the last game. The Rockets needed to be in charge of their own destiny. They couldn't count on anything else to help them secure their place in the standings, so they had to pull this out.

Coach had yet to use him in a game since he'd come back. Matt understood Coach was worried he would hurt his leg, and the only reason he'd made room for him on the roster was as a confidence booster for his teammates, which was fine with Matt. He'd be the cheerleader in the dugout and help with defensive play-calling when needed. Sure, he itched to grab a bat and take a swing at the plate, but he had to wait until they called his number. Until then, all he could do was sit, watch, and wait some more.

Jason plopped down on the bench next to him. "This game needs to end next inning."

"Yes, it does," Matt agreed. "You need to get on base."

Being one of the fastest runners on the team, if Jason succeeded with getting on base, then his speed worked to their advantage and the play call would be to have him take second on a steal. Assuming he stole successfully, putting him in scoring position, they had a better chance of getting him home and winning the game.

"That's the plan," Jason said with a nod.

"If the call is for you to bunt, make sure you get it down the third base line. They'll never be able to get you if you place it perfect."

Jason smirked. "Thanks, Coach."

"I'm just saying…"

"I know, I know." Jason grabbed a handful of sunflower seeds and tossed them into his mouth. "It's killing you to sit, so I'll overlook you telling me like I don't know what I'm doing."

Matt chuckled. "Sorry. If I don't do something soon, I'm going to go out of my mind."

"You'll get your turn. Coach knows what you bring and he'll use you in the perfect moment."

Matt sighed as he removed his cap and rubbed his head. "Yeah, well, we need to get into the race if that time is going to come."

"We will." Jason stood when their teammate struck out. He grabbed his hat and glove, hitting Matt's knee with them before trotting up the stairs out of the dugout. "We will."

"Stay sharp, Kirb," Matt yelled as he paced down the length of the dugout to encourage the rest of his teammates taking the field.

They had to stay strong defensively and not let the Buffaloes get on the board, ensuring they went into the bottom of the ninth still tied. If they succeeded, then they had to bring out the offensive guns in order to prevent going into extra innings. The more chances they gave Cleveland, the higher the risk of it blowing up in their faces. They had to keep the momentum in order for him to play, if not now, then in the playoffs. It tried at his nerves to sit on the bench and do nothing, but that was what he had to do.

And, while he did nothing, he had to fight his mind from wandering to those things he shouldn't be dwelling on. One in particular was a girl named Shannon, who he absolutely couldn't move on from, no matter how hard he tried. Frustration and remorse gnawed at him, believing he'd given up too soon, but he could do nothing about it, wasn't even sure there was anything he *wanted* to do about it. The ball was in her court as far as he was concerned, and since he hadn't heard anything from her, he had his answer.

Despite understanding they were over, he had no interest in dating anyone else, he had no interest in meeting anyone else, and he had no interest in shutting the door on him and Shannon. Simply put, he was stuck. He and Shannon were not meant to be and his brain accepted this truth, but his heart was taking its sweet ole time in catching up.

Maybe if he put himself out there and somehow forced himself to move on, if he actually tried to meet someone else, doing so would be easier. Sure, being back with the team and back in the game he loved helped, but he wasn't *doing* anything. He showed up at the park, went through training drills and batting practice, and then sat in the dugout during the game. Go home and repeat. He needed a diversion. He needed to do something. He needed to play again.

Standing up, trying to ward off the wave of aggravation building, he climbed up to take a seat on the benches sitting at field-level of the dugout. He watched as his teammates defended the field, working hard not to make the smallest mistake. They had to close the door on any scoring opportunities before they appeared and shut the Buffaloes down one, two, three.

Turning around in his seat, he gaze roamed over the stands. No matter how many games he played in Rockets stadium, the sheer number of fans packing the place game after game always blew him away. Warm or cold, rain or snow, nothing stopped them. They came out in droves to cheer on their home team. The Rockets appreciated the loyalty and the constant support behind them. The dedication pushed them and reinforced why they did what they did for one hundred sixty-two games a year.

Just as he twisted around toward the field, a cap of blond hair caught his eye. A stroke of familiarity passed through him and he turned back, his jaw dropping. Shannon sat in the stands a few rows behind the dugout next to Karen and Maddie. Her attention was on him, not the game, and when he spotted her, she gave him a small smile. She appeared timid and unsure, but happy nonetheless. He was shocked to see her there, although he wasn't sure why. Her brother-in-law was the Ace of the team.

His heart skipped a beat, missing her with a fresh wave of pain, and longing weighed him down. His shoulders ached, his body tired and his heart heavy from the unfinished business still hanging in the air between them. But he wouldn't let her see his heartache. She'd moved on and probably had a new job in some big fancy law firm, working hard to make a name for herself. There was no reason to wear his emotions on his sleeve because he didn't want her guilt. He wanted her to be doing what was right for her, happily following her dreams, which, unfortunately, didn't include him. Therefore, he resisted launching himself over the top of dugout in order to rush to her side, tell her he missed her and still loved her, begging for another chance. He simply lifted his hand in a small wave with a smile, before returning toward the field and turning his back to her.

* * *

"I love you, Bucky," a shrill voice screamed behind her, causing Shannon to cringe. She spun around and spotted the teenage girl almost hyperventilating, believing Matt had smiled and waved at her.

Shannon started to feel sorry for the young girl, since Matt had been smiling and waving at her, but suddenly she was worried that perhaps she was wrong. Maybe he hadn't seen her and *had* been eyeing the girl behind her. That would suck.

Shannon slouched back in her seat and let out a heavy sigh. The entire game she'd kept her eye on the dugout, hoping at one point she'd spot him and be able to let him know she was here rather than approaching him after the game out of the blue, taking him by complete surprise. She'd also wanted to gauge his reaction at seeing her to determine if she should even try to contact him when the game ended. And, truth be told, even after doing as much, uncertainty remained. He'd definitely seemed surprised and happy to see her, but then just as quick, his face turned neutrally pleasant. His smile wasn't that big and his eyes weren't that bright. He'd reacted as if he'd come across an old, casual acquaintance, and she supposed that was exactly how he thought of her now.

So much had changed since the last time she'd talked with him. They hadn't left things on a good note, and she took some blame for that. But she'd come so far since then, needing the space to clear her head and sift through the confusion and guilt constantly weighing on her, and in doing so, she'd finally found herself.

Now the time had come to tell Matt everything, lay her heart on the line, and pray he didn't laugh at her and walk away. She had to believe he still cared for her as she did him, he still loved her as she did him, and they were meant to be together, otherwise she'd be lost. If they weren't, why did she still ache for him? Why did she miss the sound of his voice, the feel of his arms around her? Why couldn't she go one minute without thinking about him?

She had to try. If he turned her down, then he turned her down, but she'd prove to him she was serious about him, about them, and would do whatever to make them work. Not only that, but she was her own person making these decisions, no other influences drove them—not him, not her father—and she was doing what she wanted, not what anybody else wanted her to do.

She had to go after her happiness, and her level of happiness relied on the big hunk of a man sitting a few rows down in front of her with *Buck* splayed across his broad shoulders. He leaned his arms against the railing, resting his chin on his hand, taking in the game in front of him. From the telling slouch of his back, she could tell it was killing him to be watching rather than playing, especially since Jerry had said Matt was getting back into his old form.

Given the tied score lit up in bright lights on the scoreboard, his comeback most likely wouldn't be in this game. Shannon eyed his wide back and sighed. On one hand, she wanted him to play in order to reestablish himself in the game he loved that had almost been taken away from him, but on the other, she wanted the game and the season to be over so she could spend time with him.

Karen reached out and squeezed her hand. "It's going to be okay, sis."

"I know. I feel so bad watching him sit there like someone's stolen his favorite toy."

Karen smiled as she turned her attention back to the game. "It's hard to be on this side of things. It always drives me crazy watching Jerry, especially when he's struggling. I want to run out there, grab him off the mound and flip off everyone who's booing him."

Shannon laughed as the Rockets' left fielder caught the pop fly for the final out of the inning. "It's probably better that Matt isn't playing. If he was in this game, I'd be so nervous for him."

"You're nervous either way," Karen told her.

"You're right. I hope they can pull it out. Maybe if they make it into the play-offs, then he'll have a chance to play."

Shannon glanced down toward Matt and disappointment tugged at her seeing he'd left his perch to disappear back into the dugout. She took a deep breath and waited for the Rockets to come up to bat. She struggled with patience and hoped someone would get a run right away, because she wanted the game to end. She was done with waiting. She wanted Matt and nothing else mattered at this point.

* * *

Matt sat down on the bench as Jason walked up to the plate, causing the crowd to cheer loudly. In his first year with the club, Jason had won them over with his quick, flashy play either in the field or with his bat. He didn't have a lot of power in his swing, but he consistently got the ball in play. Once on base, he wowed everyone with his speed and now led the team with stolen bases, something the Rockets had lacked in recent years. He brought excitement into the game with him, which the fans appreciated. It also didn't hurt that all of the women adored him. Matt never understood it, but the ladies loved Jason's curly hair, worn just long enough to peek out from under his cap, brushing at the back of his neck. Matt's personal opinion was that it was too long and having his hair that length would drive him nuts.

As expected, Jason got the signal to bunt and placed down a beauty toward the third base line, slowly rolling through the grass toeing the foul line. Jason tore down the base path, stretching out to touch the bag before the ball hit the seat of the first baseman's outstretched glove. When the umpire called him safe, the en tire stadium erupted, including his teammates. Everyone was pumped and ready to put this game in the books with a win.

The next batter hit a grounder to first, which allowed Jason to get to second. With one out, the next Rockets' hitter battled hard, fouling off one pitch after another, wearing the pitcher down, but he eventually went down with a strikeout. The Rockets were down to their last chance to win the game without the need for extra innings. The dugout stirred restlessly, not wanting to lose the chance to score since they had a runner in scoring position, but unless someone hit to bring him home, the game would move into the tenth.

Before the next Rockets' hitter standing in the on-deck circle removed the doughnut from his bat and headed toward the plate, Coach Brooklyn called him back into the dugout.

"Buck, you're up," Coach yelled.

Matt jolted in surprise, and stood unmoving, momentarily frozen with shock.

"Is there a problem?" Coach asked when Matt hadn't moved toward the cubby where they kept their batting helmets.

"No, not at all," Matt said, coming out of his stupor as he rushed over to grab his gear.

His heart threatened to pound out of his chest as he pulled on his gloves and walked up the stairs out of the dugout. While he warmed up, Coach Brooklyn went over the lineup change with the umps. The crowd, quickly realizing who the new batter was, yelled and screamed. Out of practice, Matt struggled to ignore the frenzy, internal and external, and empty his head of all thoughts other than putting the ball in play in order to get Jason in for the run to win the game.

What a situation to put him in. He hadn't played a game all year, this being his first one, and the game, the season potentially, was on the line. This was what he wanted, but damn, he would have liked to have been a bit more prepared for it.

Taking a deep breath, he tried to work the stress out of his shoulders, determined to be calm and relaxed when he went up to the plate. Anything else, he would surely get a fly out or a strikeout. He'd faced this pitcher before, and the guy's play would be to pitch him low and away, not giving him anything to take out of the park. But Matt would be patient and when he had the pitcher in a hole, when he had to throw down the heart of the plate in order to get the out, Matt would take him deep. Either that or he would take a walk, but he hoped it didn't come to that. One thing he knew for sure, there'd be no repeat of last year. This time, he refused to go down.

* * *

Standing up, Shannon grabbed Karen's arm. Her nerves had shot through the roof once she'd seen Matt stroll out of the dugout with his bat in his hands and his helmet on his head. He appeared calm and collected, but he had to have some butterflies beating around in his stomach. She had no idea how he handled the pressure—she was dying from it and she wasn't even in the game.

"I can't believe they're putting him in," Shannon said.

"He's one of their best bats. They want him to end it for them," Karen told her.

"But what if he gets out?"

"Then he gets out," Karen replied, unconcerned. "They go into the tenth inning."

"But what if he has to run?" Shannon asked, still unconvinced he should even be in the game.

"Shannon, they wouldn't have put him in if he wasn't ready for it. He's fine," Karen promised.

As Matt slowly walked to the plate, his attention on nothing but the pitcher, Shannon closed her eyes and turned away. "I can't watch."

"Stop it, yes, you can," Karen said with a laugh. "You need to watch your hot man do his thing. Come on," she said as she turned Shannon back around.

Matt stepped up to the plate and raised his bat, waiting for the throw. The pitch came in hot, straight down the middle, and he swung hard, hitting nothing but air. A collective gasp emanated from the crowd. Shannon clenched her fists, watching for any signs of discomfort as he untwisted his body from his huge swing. He didn't seem to be favoring anything as he stepped back, tightening his grip on his bat. Palpable relief flitted throughout the stands when it was apparent he was okay.

He readied himself again and this time the pitch came in low and away. Matt let it go and took the ball. The pitcher did the same thing for the next two pitches, but Matt refused to chase and the count sat in Matt's favor with three balls and one strike.

"This is torture," Shannon complained.

"He's right where he wants to be," Karen murmured. "Johnson has to throw something right down the plate. Matt knows it and so all he has to do is connect with it. Jason will be running with the pitch, so hopefully he can get around third and home if Matt gets something over the head of the second baseman and into the outfield."

"I don't know how you can be all cool and assessing with this," Shannon said as she tried to calm herself down, a hopeless cause since her anxiety was so high she couldn't even take a deep breath.

She wanted Matt to succeed and she wanted it so badly. He deserved so much after all he'd been through. Until he had baseball back completely, he would feel incomplete.

Matt stepped back up to the plate, waiting for the pitch, and Jason took a healthy lead off second. Johnson, the Buffaloes pitcher, eyed Jason for a second, contemplating a throw over to the bag in order to shorten Jason's lead, but then decided against it and turned his back on him. Johnson threw, right down Broadway, just as everyone had anticipated, but Matt stood ready and swung with everything he had. A resounding crack filled the stadium and everyone, already on their feet, watched the ball sail through the air over everyone's head. The centerfielder backtracked all the way deep into center field and stopped at the wall as the ball crested over the top at the deepest part of the ballpark.

Everyone erupted at once, screaming their heads off as Matt trotted around the bases, cementing the Rockets' win with a walk-off home run. The entire team gathered at home plate. Matt rounded third base, the grin on his face growing bigger at the sight of his teammates waiting for him to come home. He tossed his batting helmet to the ground toward the dugout and jogged the remaining ninety feet. Once his foot touched the plate, the team surrounded him in celebration.

Shannon and Karen hugged as they bounced up and down in their seats, their eyes filled with tears of joy. The crowd was so loud they couldn't have heard each other despite standing next to one another, but nothing needed to be said as they both were thinking the same thing.

Matt was back.

CHAPTER 25

The celebration continued in the locker room. Showers of champagne drenched Matt, and someone handed him a cigar along with a bottle of beer. With the win, the Rockets had clinched the division, putting themselves ahead in the standings and out of reach from Cleveland since not enough games remained in the season for them to make up the points. Because of that, it was official and, as soon as they'd made their way off the field, the PR staff handed everyone black T-shirts proclaiming their conference win.

Matt had his shirt on as well as his uniform pants and everything was soaked, but he didn't care. The champagne stung his eyes and hurt like hell, but he didn't notice because they'd won and they'd won because he'd hit one out of the park. The sweetest home run he could remember hitting. Not only because the run cemented their place in the playoffs and was against the same team he'd failed to beat the year before, but mostly because he'd connected in the best way possible his first game back. He hadn't been sure he had it in him, sometimes finding his timing was still off, but once he'd seen the ball coming straight at him, instinct had kicked in. He'd put as much strength behind his swing he could muster and watched as the ball soared majestically through the air. It was a thing of beauty.

Jason came over to him looking like a drowned rat, but a huge grin split his face from ear to ear. He pulled Matt into a one-armed hug. "Amazing night, my friend. Amazing. I knew you had it in you."

Matt smiled. "You didn't know I was going to get in."

"I had a feeling that was exactly the situation Coach was waiting for. He knew you would be perfect."

"I don't know about that, but I'm glad I pulled it off." Matt puffed on his cigar.

"Feels good, doesn't it?" Jason took a hit of his stogie. "You're back, man."

Matt nodded and couldn't stop grinning. "Not all the way, but I'm getting there. Once I'm catching again, then I'll be solid, but this is pretty damn good, that's for sure."

Jerry walked over to them and put his arms around both of them with a big smile on his face. "Here they are! The two heroes!"

"It's about time some of us minions got the spotlight," Matt said to him. "You're always hogging it because you throw a ball faster than one hundred miles an hour."

Jerry hooted. "Glad to share the limelight, especially with that beast of a home run you hit. I don't think I've ever seen one go that deep in this park. That was a helluva long way!"

"Matt's good at that, always had been," Jason said. "Why do you think he's consistently in talks for being the Home Run Champ or a possible Triple Crown contender?"

Matt gave a small shrug as his smile fell slightly. "Not this year…"

Jerry squeezed his shoulder. "You're back, Buck. That's all that matters. You'll get it back and next year you'll be right back in those talks."

Matt nodded and took a sip of his beer not wanting to experience anything but elation at the moment, but some anger and frustration remained at all he'd missed this year. He would get past it, eventually. Time could only help.

Jerry tilted his head. "Come here, I want to show you something."

"What?" Matt asked.

"Come on, I'll show you."

Matt didn't miss the look that passed between Jerry and Jason, and he stopped. "What are you guys cooking up?"

"Just go," Jason said with a grin. "It's worth it, trust me."

Matt frowned at Jason as he followed behind Jerry. His teammates patted his back, pouring more drinks over his head as they included him in their celebrations when he passed. He rubbed his eyes trying to keep the champagne out of them and stepped into a hallway behind Jerry.

"Where are you…," Matt started to ask, squinting past the burn in his eyes, but then stopped when he stood face-to-face with Shannon. She was stunning and beautiful as always, but since this was only a friendly visit, her coming to congratulate him most likely, he kept his reaction neutral.

"Hi," Matt said as Jerry patted his back with a smile and returned to the party inside the locker room.

"Hi." Her gaze passed over him from head to toe. "Did you shower with your clothes on?"

"Champagne, beer…and whatever else, I guess," he said with a grin as he tried to find a dry spot on his T-shirt to rub his eyes with. "My eyes sting like hell."

"They are red."

"Worth the pain."

"Congratulations, Matt. That was amazing. I'm so happy for you."

"Thanks. Just doing my job," he said, a bit shy from her praise.

"You did more than that. I don't think I've ever seen a ball hit that hard before. Another one for your shelf?"

"Maybe," he said with a chuckle. "If they can find the fan who caught it and bribe them."

Shannon smiled and after an uncomfortable pause, she cleared her throat. "Um, I was wondering if we could talk."

"Oh…sure," he said. "Uh, right now?"

She glanced over his shoulder as if she could see the celebration through the closed door, and disappointment fell over her face. "Well, I guess not. I mean, you probably want to get back in there…"

"Yeah, I probably should." Part of him wanted to hear what she had to say, but part of him didn't. If she was going to tell him sorry again or that she'd taken a job in New York or some other state, and only wanted to say good-bye one last time, he didn't want to hear it.

"Okay, well, I'll give you a call, then?" she asked, but Matt could tell she didn't want to.

"Yeah, that'll work."

"Okay. I'll talk to you later then," Shannon said, wooden and formal, the awkwardness between them palpable.

"Okay, sounds good." He turned to the door when she started to walk away and, just as he opened it, she called his name, stopping him.

"Matt, wait," she said.

He let the door close behind him. With determined strides, Shannon walked over to him and pulled his head down to hers. Her lips smothered his as she plastered herself to him, not caring that her T-shirt and shorts were getting wet. Matt dropped the beer bottle and cigar to wrap his arms around her. He pushed her against the wall and leaned into her as their tongues tangled. He'd missed her so much and she felt so good in his arms that he didn't care she would soon walk away from him again. He was going to enjoy the moment before he lost it forever.

She squirmed against him and broke off the kiss, her breaths coming out in huffs. "God, I've missed you so much."

He continued to kiss down her neck and along her jawline. "Me too."

"I didn't take the job," Shannon stammered out in between kisses.

"What job?" he asked, with his lips against hers.

"The job, in the firm," she said.

In order to understand what she was trying to tell him, he needed to stop kissing her and give her some air. Matt leaned back a bit, but still kept her pinned against the wall underneath him. Her eyes opened and her blues eyes were dark with lust.

"What job are you talking about?"

She took in a deep breath. "Any of them. I haven't taken any of them. I don't want any of them."

He frowned, not sure where she was going with this. "Okay…"

She took another breath. "I need to start from the beginning."

"I think that would be best." Matt finally stepped away from her and took her hand, leading her down the hallway to a quieter spot. "Okay, what are you talking about?"

"Well, let's see. I was at this interview and overhead another attorney basically say she had no life with her kids or her husband and I realized that's exactly where

I would be headed. So, I had a fight with my dad and told him he needed to butt out, that I didn't want a job like that, no matter what he tried to say, and he had to let me live my own life."

Matt's eyebrows shot up. "How did he take it?"

"He's upset. He's not talking to me and things are tense, but hopefully he'll get it one day."

"And that's it? He's just backing down now?" Matt asked, not quite believing her father would give up so easily.

"I mean, he's not happy, but he told me he's done helping me, basically stepped out of my life." She waved her hand at him. "But that's not what's important."

"It's not?"

"No, even if he tries to tell me what to do again," Shannon said, her eyes strong on his, "it doesn't matter because I know now what I want and who I am. Before I was so confused since I didn't want to believe my wants could be as simple as being a wife and a mother, that I had to be part of something bigger or more important to matter. But now I know that's not what matters."

"What matters?" Matt asked her, still trying to catch up.

"What makes me happy, that's what matters."

"And what makes you happy?"

Shannon smiled at him. "You."

Matt still wasn't quite sure what she was telling him. "I'm not sure what I'm supposed to be thinking here."

"I guess," she said with some hesitation, "I'm wondering if you still want to try…with us…"

"Shannon," he said. "I never didn't want to try, but it didn't seem like it could work. Not including things with your dad, we both want two very different things."

"I've worked that out."

"What do you mean, 'worked that out'?"

"Well," she said as she cleared her throat. "That's where I've been for the past few months. I've been studying for the bar among other things."

"You already took the bar," he told her, confused again.

"Yes, in Michigan and Illinois, but not in…Arizona."

That stopped him. "You took the bar in Arizona?"

"Yes."

He studied her for a moment. He finally asked, "Why?"

"Because it's what I want. To be where you are." She hesitated. "That is, if you want me. Your dad is letting me rent office space for my own practice, and I've already reached out to local legal aid organizations in Tucson where I can volunteer my time and services. All that's left is your decision. If you want me down there with you."

Matt shook his head, unable to comprehend what he was hearing. "You've told your father to back off, turned down all the jobs around here, taken the bar in Arizona and worked out rent with my father for your own practice, all because you want to be with me, without even knowing if I still wanted to be with you?" he said, ticking each off on his fingers.

She nodded. "So, what do you think?"

He gave her a big grin. "I think you're amazing, that's what I think." He pulled her into his arms and took her mouth with his. "I can't believe you did all that."

"It took me a while to get my head straight, I'm sorry," she said.

"Just as long as you got here."

She kissed him before pulling back. "Are you sure you want to do this again?"

"I've never been surer of anything in my life. I've finally caught the girl of my dreams."

Shannon smiled and let him sweep her off her feet. He kissed her again and held her tight against him.

"I love you," she whispered in his ear.

"I love you too."

"I was so worried I'd lost my chance."

"You'd never lose your chances with me."

"I don't deserve it, but I'm going to take it."

Matt grinned and pulled her in for another kiss before setting her down and holding out his elbow to her. "Shall we?"

Winding her arm through his, she smiled up at him with eyes filled with love. "Absolutely," she told him and finally, everything in Matt's life was right.

* * * * *

OTHER TITLES BY RHONDA SHAW

Thank you so much for reading *Caught!* I hope you enjoyed it. If you loved Matt, don't miss meeting the other Men of the Show!

In book one, *The Changeup*, fall in love with sweet and sexy pitching phenom, Chase Patton.

Get to know the hunky prankster, the Ace of the team, Jerry Smutton, in book two, *The Ace*.

Intrigued by Jason Kirby? His story is book four in the Men of the Show. Make sure to sign up for my newsletter on my website at *www.rhondashaw.com* to receive updates and the latest release information. You won't want to miss it!

ABOUT THE AUTHOR

Rhonda owes her love of reading to her mother who would read to her each night before bed and sometimes give into her pleads for more than one chapter. These days, if Rhonda doesn't have a book in her hands, it feels like something is missing. While romance is her true passion, Rhonda enjoys reading multiple genres.

Born in California, but transplanted to the Midwest, Rhonda is warm weather girl to the bone (even years later, winter and her are not on speaking terms) and loves nothing more than a balmy, summer evening. She and her husband are diehard fans of pretty much all sports, but especially for their hometown Detroit teams. Rhonda received a bachelor's in Human Resources Development and continued onto a master's in Marriage and Family Counseling before making a drastic career switch into computer technology. She started out as a website developer and made her way up into management where she now spends most of her days in meetings. Rhonda was a life-long dancer before her body told her she needed to come down off her toes and wrap it up. She also loves all animals--especially moose. She is a proud member of Romance Writers of America.

Rhonda loves to hear from readers, so please visit her website at www.rhondashaw. com. You can also find her on Facebook at Rhonda Shaw, Author and Twitter at @AuthorRShaw. Make sure to sign up for her newsletter on her website to receive updates about upcoming titles and their release dates.